Smoky Mountain Rising

The Day That Changed Everything

By William Clark

WESTBOW
P R E S S®
A DIVISION OF THOMAS NELSON
& ZONDERVAN

WestBow Press books may be ordered through booksellers or by contacting:

WestBow Press
A Division of Thomas Nelson & Zondervan
1663 Liberty Drive
Bloomington, IN 47403
www.westbowpress.com
844-714-3454

ISBN: 978-1-6642-5619-4 (sc)
ISBN: 978-1-6642-5618-7 (e)

Print information available on the last page.

WestBow Press rev. date: 02/17/2022

Dedicated to those who have and will accept the wedding invitations to the wedding of the Lamb. The bride (of Christ) is making herself ready.

"As it was in the days of Noah, so it will be
at the coming of the Son of man.
For in the days before the flood, people were
eating and drinking, marrying,
and giving in marriage, up to the day Noah entered the ark."

- Matthew 24: 37-38 NIV

CONTENTS

Contents

INTRODUCTION

"What would your plan of action be, if you knew without a doubt that the world, as you know it, is coming to an end?" In my first novel of the trilogy, "A Light on the Path", Anderson had divine direction in warning loved ones about what lies ahead in the near future. The second novel, "Seeing Beyond the Shadows" goes back in time. It begins in the late 1940's, when Anderson's cousin, Andy is five years old and Anderson is ten years old.

Andy has special gifts in the Lord and is also a gifted athlete. Most of the story takes place in the early 1960's, when Andy is a young college student. After his freshman year, he becomes a special agent with the State Department. Andy heroically helps end a divided nation and a Southern Border War.

The current and last novel of the trilogy, "Smoky Mountain Rising", also stands on its own. Andy, Lydia and their friends, Larry and Melissa, take the lead in helping their fragmented country. As their world becomes more chaotic, Andy, a former Secretary of State, and his friends get stronger in their convictions and commitment. They become leaders, who help many others prepare for the imminent future.

If someone yells "fire" would you run and hide or would you take action and help? Andy and his friends share Anderson's story; the gospel message and proclaim that the time of the "silent" majority is over. They take a stand and call people to action and commitment. More and more of Andy's friends and contacts answer the call and follow him to the mountain tops.

My best wishes for being prepared,
William Clark
bill.clark@inumc.org
Facebook: Books by William Clark of Jefferson City, Tennessee

1

SMOKY MOUNTAIN SURVIVAL

After a hot summer, the cooler October burst into colors of orange, red, yellow and rust. The drive from east of Cosby to Gatlinburg is heaven on earth. Davina, Andy and Lydia's daughter, says, "I never get tired of this drive in the fall. I feel like I want to reach out and touch all of nature!"

Andy laughs and says, "You can; one leaf at a time!"

Lydia says, "I love this time of the year." In just a couple of months, the Smokies from their view will be snow-capped mountains with wavy bands between the bare trees that portray a myriad of natural ski runs.

Andy says, "Yes, it's beautiful throughout the year. Each season has its own mystique."

As the McGraig family gets close to busy Gatlinburg, the allure and tranquility of the Great Smoky Mountains is just a couple miles away. Lydia says, "It's hard to believe the expansive wilderness of the Smokies is right next to Gatlinburg."

Andy replies, "Every time we leave the hustle and bustle of Gatlinburg and drive into the Great Smoky Mountain National Park, I immediately sense the endless time of the mountains and breathe in a peace I can't describe."

Lydia reflects a moment and says, "I love the nature and the park." She hesitates a second and says, "Are you shopping with us this morning?"

As they park near the outfitter's store, Andy replies, "I think I will leisurely walk around. We had an early, light breakfast and by 11:30 or 12, I'm going to be ready for a hardy breakfast at my favorite breakfast restaurant."

Lydia replies, "Davina and I will be glad to shop the rest of the morning. We could meet you by noon at the restaurant. Order your meal, when you get there."

They get out of their Jeep Grand Cherokee, and Andy waves at his lovely wife and daughter. He says, "See you soon!"

Andy keeps an eye on his family until they go in the outfitter's store. Across the street is an intriguing rock shop that Andy enjoys. Just as he steps

1

on the sidewalk, he hears a booming voice calling out, "Andy McGraig!" Andy looks to his right and sees his old college teammate and friend, Larry Quarles.

Andy walks toward him. They shake hands and grasp each other's arm and Andy says, "Larry, it's been so long. It's so good to see you! I recognized you right away."

Larry says, "How could anyone miss a seven foot black man!" Andy laughs and Larry continues, "Avalanche Andy! Man. oh man, did we have a good team. Andy, you're still built like a Mac Truck!"

Andy says, "And you, my friend, look as fit as a fiddle."

Larry says, "At my age, I'm fortunate that I've only put on twenty pounds."

Andy says, "Me too, I've been 260 to 265 for thirty years."

Larry says, "Andy, that's great. I remember that you got up to 240 or more while we played round ball for the Boilermakers."

Andy replies, "I did. What are you doing for the next couple of hours?"

Larry says, "Just wandering the streets and window shopping while my wife shops."

Andy says, "What about that! My wife and daughter are doing the same thing.

They're going to meet me at the breakfast restaurant at noon. Why don't we head there, and we can catch up."

Larry says, "I would love to. I'll call my wife now and tell her to meet us there at noon."

Andy says, "While you call her, let's go into this rock shop for a few minutes."

As they walk toward the rock shop, Andy's tall, wide frame and Larry's height make them look like a formidable, senior A Team.

After Andy looks at the variety of shapes and colors of a few of the gems and rocks, Larry says, "On the way to the restaurant, let's stop at the general store. I want to get a newspaper."

Andy says, "Let's go."

After Larry gets his paper, they walk about two city blocks to the restaurant. Larry says, "Actually I thought I would see you before now. I coached at Carson Newman in Jefferson City for fifteen seasons before I retired."

Andy replies, "Several years ago, I read that your team made the final four in Division Two of men's basketball."

Larry says, "We did. It was a year before I retired. I actually coached three years longer, than I had planned."

Andy asks, "Weren't you the assistant coach at Duke?"

Larry replies, "Yes, I was there a long time and before that, I played eight years with New York and Atlanta. Before Duke, I was an assistant at UT for five years.

Everyone knows you became Secretary of State. What have you done since then?"

They walk up to the restaurant and Andy says, "Let's get a table and some coffee, and I will fill you in."

They wait for a couple in front of them, then the young, slender hostess looks up at them and says, "Good morning. Two for breakfast?'

Andy smiles and says, "Yes, two for a lot of coffee now, and my wife and daughter and his wife are joining us later."

She says, "I will go ahead and get a big table for you now." As she leads the way, many of the patrons stare at the gentle giants. One patron in his sixties immediately recognizes them. As soon as they're seated, he grabs a Gatlinburg brochure and hurries to their table.

He says, "I can't believe that I'm talking with the two greatest showmen who who played together in college. When I was a kid, I watched your games on our Zenith; Avalanche Andy and Larry Quarles and a national championship!"

Larry says, "We're glad you still know us!" Andy and Larry sign their autographs and order coffee. Larry says to Andy, "It's nice to still have fans.

By the way, I became a fan of yours, when it came out on the news that you were awarded the Presidential Medal of Freedom for your role in the Seven Day Southern Border War."

Andy says, "Thank you. For about ten years I was an undercover advisor to the Secretary of State, and the award was classified for ten years until I became a Deputy Secretary."

Larry says, "When you came back to Purdue to get your degree, weren't you already a security agent for the State Department?"

Andy replies, "Yes, and I was thrilled that we got to play together again. you, Damber and I and the others really tore up the floor."

Larry exclaims, "Man, oh man, did we have a great team. You mowed everyone down, like Karl Malone did later in the NBA. So, what have you been doing, since you left the State Department?"

Andy replies, "When I came back to Purdue, do you remember me saying that I bought two hundred acres of wooded land near the Smokies?"

Larry nods his head. "About twenty-five years ago, in the mid 1990's, I sold sixty acres of it to my cousin, Anderson McCollister. He retired early from Del Mar, in Delaware County, near Muncie, Indiana. He was V-P of international marketing for them. He and his wife had a house built on the land, as soon as he purchased it. I want to tell you about him before our families join us."

Andy continues, "First, I will answer your question. I officially retired from the State Department in 1993; after serving thirty years. My wife and I wanted to build a house on our land here soon after that, but the State Department kept me on their payroll as an advisor. Finally, in 2004, we had a house built, but we stayed so busy with family and the government that we only came down on vacations and for part of the winter. We didn't sell our house outside D.C. until two years ago. It took us about a year to get settled in our Tennessee home and here we are!"

Larry says, "God has blessed you with a wonderful life. I'm almost stunned that we retired in the same area. I'm roughly an hour from you. Before I retired from Carson-Newman, we built a house by Cherokee Lake, just outside Jefferson City. My assistant coach, Aaron Michaels, took my place. He played four years for UT and got into coaching. He became head coach for a big high school in Lexington, Kentucky. For a long time, he was assistant coach at the University of Georgia. Three years before I retired, he came to Carson-Newman with the promise that he would replace me, when I retired. He played power forward for UT. He's like a smaller version of you and Charles Barkley."

Andy says, "I would like to meet him. Speaking of Charles Barkley and Karl Malone, didn't they play college ball about twenty years after we did?"

Larry says, "I think you're right. They were probably born around the time we won the national championship."

Their waitress brings them a third cup of coffee and Andy says, "It's about 11:15, and I'm famished!"

Larry says, "You first. I remember in college we would usually order the same thing. We can drink coffee while our wives and your daughter have their meal."

Andy looks at the friendly waitress and says, "Okay, young lady, I would like three eggs over easy with two orders of wheat toast and apple butter and sausage."

Larry says, "Spot on! I want the same breakfast."

Andy laughs and says, "At home we cook turkey sausage and turkey bacon."

4

Larry says, "We do as well! Man, it's so good to get together."

Andy smiles and says, "I feel the same way. I think I have enough time to tell you about my cousin Anderson. I think you'll find his story captivating."

Larry says, "Shoot; no pun intended."

Andy begins, "My cousin turned eighty soon after he lost his wife. He was a hiker. He made a lot of trails in his woods; that included another sixty acres that he bought from a neighbor. His sister, Ann, Lydia Ann, had recently moved to his house, so he could help her financially. One day he had his hiking gear ready, including his walking stick and emergency gear. He normally took his cell phone, but forgot it. This hike took place less than a year ago. It also took place soon after the high rate of inflation and civil disturbance and increase in crime hit our country."

Larry says, "I remember too well, and it has gotten worse instead of better."

Their food is served, and Andy says, "I'll get back to the story."

Larry says, "Go ahead; I'm all ears."

Andy says, "I will try to be brief and give you the highlights. To make a long story shorter, Anderson didn't come back from his hike. His sister and his friend, Kenny, from Maggie Valley looked for him. They organized a search team and all they found was his walking stick."

Larry says, "Man, oh man, Andy; what a story. I'm totally captivated."

Andy continues, "They had his funeral without a body. It turned out to be a miraculous event. Anderson was concerned about his friend, Kenny from Maggie Valley, and his sister, because their faith was borderline. He was more concerned about his daughter, Angela, a psychology professor, because her faith in God wasn't even borderline. Larry, because our families will be here soon, I'm going right to the last part of the story. Anderson appeared to his sister, then to his friend and then to his daughter in Indiana."

Larry says, "I believe you, because I believe. About six months ago, I heard of reports throughout the world, like your brother's visitations."

Andy says, "With the little time we have left now, I will still be brief. Anderson told all three of them that he had passed on and that he couldn't stay. He said that everything is true that the Bible teaches. He wanted each of them to commit to Christ and to follow Him. He said there was not much time left before the rapture of the church and the tribulation. He wanted them to share the gospel and his story as much as possible."

"My aunt, cousin and Anderson's friend met together and stayed in touch as much as possible. They have shared the message in churches; on Christian radio and on the Christian TV network near Charlotte. They're doing what they can to get the word out. We made our permanent move here about a year and a half before this happened. The past five to six months, I've been helping them get the word out. Many people believe, but humanists, like the Pharisees, think we're out of our mind."

Larry says, "I want to help. My wife will be thrilled to hear the story. For years, she's been closer to God than I have. Do your wife and daughter believe the story?"

As Andy says, "Absolutely", Larry's wife walks up to the table. They both get up. Larry kisses her on the check and says, "Melissa, you remember, Andy, from college?"

Melissa says joyfully, "Of course, I do! Who could forget Andy McGraig."

Andy greets her and says, "Thanks, Melissa. It's wonderful to see you again." Just as they sit down, Lydia and Davina walk up to the table.

Andy and Larry get up again, and Andy says, "The gang is all here!" They all greet each other, and the waitress comes to take their drink order.

After they order, Andy and Melissa have their hand sanitizer out and Andy says, "Can you believe the China virus and other viruses are still around? We have high inflation, civil disturbance, high crime, pestilence and what's next?"

Lydia chimes in and says, "The rapture!"

They all laugh and agree. Melissa says a loud, "Amen!"

Andy says, "It makes me wonder how long we can still go to places like Gatlinburg in relative peace."

As soon as Andy makes his remark, they hear a loud explosion.

They're all shaken and several in unison say, "What's that?"

Davina says, "It's not some kind of show or fireworks is it?"

Larry gets up with Andy and Andy says, "No, I've heard sounds like that in the D.C. area during the southern border war."

Andy looks at Larry and says, "Wait here for a minute, I'm going to find the manager, and I will be right back."

Andy locates the manager and says, "I'm Andy McGraig from the State Department."

The manager says, "Yes, I know who you are."

Andy says, "My first work was in federal security. My friend and I are going to investigate the explosion. We're leaving our families here. Round up all the security you can and find out who here is armed. Have them at the exits and have them shield your patrons. Use your discretion, if you feel you should lock the front door. Have someone make sure any other doors are locked. Shield your employees with tables and anything you have. Have everyone wait here until we get back."

The manager begins following Andy's instructions and telling people that the safety procedures are coming directly from federal authority.

Andy gets Larry and tells their families to stay and wait until they return.

On their way out, Andy tells Larry that he's armed and with the traffic, they need to improvise the way they'll get to the explosion site.

Andy and Larry start asking people, if they know the location of the explosion. Through the chaos, Larry shouts, "Andy, a guy just told me that he heard a bomb went off at a church."

Andy yells back, "Let's get a ride." A second later he yells, "There's an officer at 11:00. Let's hurry over there." They dodge a mass of people to get to the police officer. Andy stops abruptly and says, "Officer, I'm Andy McGraig from the State Department," and he shows him his State Department I.D.

The middle-aged officer looks at the I.D. and says, "Yes, Mr. McGraig, I've seen you on the news. How can I help you?"

"My friend and I need to get to the explosion location."

The officer says, "I'll flag down a car or truck with a siren." As he looks for their ride, he continues to direct people to the north and east. He says to Andy, "There's a black and white coming from the north." He flags down the city police car that has its blue lights on. The officer says, "Take Mr. McGraig and his friend to the emergency site. Mr. McGraig is with the State Department."

When they get in the car, Andy asks, "Officer, what details did dispatch give about the site of the explosion?"

As they make slow progress through the crowd of people and traffic, the officer says, "A bomb was exploded at the Evangelical Church and Day Care on 321; less than two miles west from the next turn. Our problem is getting through this congestion." He hits his siren, but there is little maneuver room for the traffic ahead. The officer continues, "There are several witnesses that saw three men get in an older grey SUV. They sped west on 321 toward Townsend and Maryville."

While the officer edges his way to 321, Andy gets on his cell phone and selects the direct line to homeland security. He gives them the location and tells them to notify the FBI. After ten minutes, they get on 321, and they are able to speed to the crime scene. When they arrive, there are over a dozen police cars, ambulances and fire trucks. Immediately Andy can see a church wall that has been blown away. The officer who drove them says, "I will take you to the Lieutenant in charge."

When he finds the Lieutenant, he introduces Andy and Larry and says, "Lieutenant Conard, Mr. McGraig notified Homeland Security and the FBI about ten minutes ago."

The lieutenant says, "Good. Mr. McGraig, how can I help you?"

Andy asks, "Do you know how many people were in harm's way in the explosion?"

He replies, "So far, we know that the pastor and secretary were in the church building, and they were both injured; the pastor is in serious condition. Their adjoining Day Care was still in session, and the blast occurred between the church and the Day Care annex. The church secretary thinks there were four adults and twenty-one children under the age of five in the annex. We have taken a count and came up with the same total of twenty-seven, including the pastor and secretary."

The lieutenant hesitates a second and bows his head. He continues, "So far, we know that four children have died and two of the Day Care staff. It appears that both staff members shielded the children."

As Andy talks with the lieutenant, Larry begins to shed tears over the tragedy.

Lieutenant Conard says, "We know that twelve of the children have minor injuries, and the other five have serious injuries. The surviving staff members also have serious injuries. Mr. McGriag, I remember you, when you served as Secretary of State. We know that most every major city in America has been hit by terrorism, as well as many tourist areas. I have to be honest and say that I thought Gatlinburg would be hit before now."

Andy says, "I understand, lieutenant. Here is my number, so you can give me an update later today or tomorrow. Have you already swept the area?"

The lieutenant replies, "We're finishing now. Once we're done, we will have a squad car to take you back."

Andy says, "Larry and I know first aid. He was a college coach for many years. Can we help you with that or anything else?"

The lieutenant says, "Thank you. We are fortunate to have enough EMTs to take care of the injured. The coroner is also helping us with the deceased. Keep helping the community and nation with security and advice, Mr. McGraig. You've always been a big help to our nation."

"Thank you, Lieutenant Conard. Until a squad car is free, I think we will stay here, in case something does come up."

About twenty minutes later, the Lieutenant's officers report that they have finished their sweep and the area is clear. The Lieutenant takes another call and says hold on, officer. The lieutenant looks at Andy and says, "By any chance, Mr. McGraig, do you have any family waiting for you in Gatlinburg?"

Andy replies, "Yes, my wife and daughter. Larry's wife is also there."

The lieutenant says, "One of our female officers is with a mother of one of the children, who survived with minor injuries. She arrived at the time of the blast and is one of the witnesses of the suspects who sped away. She and her daughter are very shaken, and the mother can't drive home. They live in Cosby."

Andy replies, "If they need a ride, we would be glad to take them home. We live near Cosby; off Rocky Flats Road."

The lieutenant gets back on his mobile and says, "Officer Walling, bring them over to my station."

In a few minutes, Officer Walling arrives with a young mother and the cutest, little blonde headed girl. The three year old has a small cut above her eye; a minor cut on her cheek and scrapped up knees. The officer says, "This is Gladis Restrepo and her daughter, Tracy."

Lieutenant Conard says, "Officer Walling, Miss Restrepo and Tracy, this is our former Secretary of State, Andy McGraig and his friend, Larry Quarles."

Andy touches Tracy's chin and looks at her mother, "Don't worry. We're leaving now, and my wife, daughter and I are taking you home. In a few minutes, we'll pick up my wife and daughter in Gatlinburg."

Andy and Larry shake the lieutenant's hand and thank him. They get in Officer Walling's squad car. Andy says, "My wife, daughter and Larry's wife are waiting on us at the breakfast restaurant on the main road in Gatlinburg."

The officer pulls away from the scene of terror and says, "Yes, I know where it is. Thank you for helping us. When I was in school, I remember seeing you on TV."

Andy replies, "Thank you for your service. We are still praying that things will improve in our country. If your department doesn't mind, my wife and I will contact you in the near future. We have a story to share, that we think you will want to know."

The officer says, "Yes, that would be nice. Talking with our former Secretary of State, tells me it's a small world."

Andy replies, "Yes it is, and unfortunately a troubled world."

On the way back, Larry says, "The traffic flow is much better. It looks like the city police have dispersed a lot of the crowd."

Andy says, "Let's put each other's number in our cell phone contacts, Larry. I know we will be in touch soon about the conversation we had in the restaurant."

Larry says, "Absolutely."

With her blue lights on, Officer Walling comes to a stop in front of the restaurant and gives Andy her number. She says, "All of you take care and be careful." She waits until they open the restaurant door, then she leaves for her station.

When they get inside, Lydia hugs Andy and he says, "Lydia, this is Gladis Restrepo and her daughter, Tracy. They have been through a lot today, and we're taking them home."

Melissa also greets Gladis and Tracy, and Larry says, "Brother, I will call you soon. I'm looking forward to being part of your outreach. I will share it with Melissa on the way home." Andy shakes his friend's hand.

Andy walks over and thanks the manager. He says, "Things went well. It calmed down after 1:00, and our customers started leaving. My last employee left just a few minutes ago."

Andy says, "Thank you so much. Did my wife pay for the meals?"

He says, "It's all taken care of." Andy gives him $20.00 for his help.

Andy shakes his hand and the five of them walk to the car. Davina carries Tracy, and Lydia talks with Gladis.

Gladis says, "My parents will take me to my car tomorrow. It was just horrible, and I couldn't drive. My husband was killed in Afghanistan, and this was too much for me. Lydia puts her arm around her and says, "Things will be better in the morning."

Andy takes Tracy, and says, "Let me give you a rest, Davina."

On the way to Gladis' home in Cosby, they let her talk and Davina talks with Tracy. When they get close to Cosby, Gladis directs Andy to her house.

A few minutes before they get there, Lydia says to Gladis, "Do you know that my husband was the former Secretary of State?"

Gladis says, "Yes, the officer was talking about it earlier."

Lydia says, "Andy had a cousin who had a very unique experience about six months ago. I would like to call you and tell you the story."

Gladis says, "That would be nice. Here is my phone number."

They pull in front of the small, neatly kept house, and Andy and Lydia walk Gladis and Tracy to the front door. Her parents come to the door and hug Gladis and Tracy. Her mom says, "We're so thankful you're alright." Her father shakes Andy's hand and he says, "Thank you, and I hope we'll see you again."

After they get back on the road for home, Andy looks at Lydia and says, "That is one more family that will hear Anderson's story."

The old country church on Rocky Flats Rd.

2

A DIVIDED NATION

They stop at Subway in Cosby for carry-out. After a long day, they decide to rest for the evening. Andy drives a few miles north of Cosby to their home in the country. Davina decides to wait until morning to drive back to her home in Crossville, Tennessee. She says, "Ron has to be at work by 8 a.m. and Tiann and Trent are both on campus." Davina retired just a year ago, after teaching for thirty years. Her husband works for an engineering firm in Farragut, west of Knoxville, and plans to work until he's sixty-five.

Everyone retires early in the evening. Andy is up early and fixes breakfast for the three of them. They finish with breakfast by 8:00, when Andy calls Homeland Security. When he gets off the phone, he goes back to Lydia and Davina in the kitchen. Andy says, "Homeland Security said the state police picked up the three men in Lenoir City about the time we got back to the restaurant yesterday. They haven't released any details yet, since their people and the FBI are still interrogating them. It looks like all three are illegal aliens. My contact said the report indicated they were going to take I75 to Atlanta."

Lydia says, "I'm so glad they caught them."

Davina says, "It is horrible that the New Age Socialist party has allowed so many undocumented illegal aliens into the country."

Andy says, "I'm greatly disappointed that their party caved into their faction of hard line socialists. After we won the Seven Day Southern Border War in 1962, I was very grateful that the party dropped their socialist name and returned to being constitutionalists. I can't express how sad I felt, when they reinstituted their old socialist name over ten years ago. It took them eight years of lying and infiltrating the media to win back the presidency and congress. Our country was doing well for decades until this root of evil took hold."

Lydia says, "I know, honey. You fought for our country a long time and did a great job. We know Biblical prophecy is being fulfilled. I'm thankful that we have an important mission to get Anderson's story and God's Word to as many people as possible."

Davina says, "I'm going to take a shower. I need to leave soon, so I can stop for gas and pick up groceries for supper. I want to fix Ron pork stir fry and a salad."

Andy says, "Give me your keys, sweet pea, and I'll check your tire pressure, oil and fill up the windshield washer tank."

In an hour, Lydia and Andy walk outside with their daughter. Andy kisses her on the cheek, and Davina hugs her mom and dad. As she's ready to get in her car, Andy starts to say "Be sure to….."

Davina smiles and says, "I know, dad. Take a hard look around me. I love you."

As she pulls out of the drive, Lydia says, "I can never get use to our daughter leaving."

As Andy waves, he replies, "Me too." Andy puts his big arm around his wife, and they walk back in the house."

Lydia asks, "What are your plans today?"

Andy says, "Let's sit down at the table with a second cup of coffee and make a list. I want to call Gladis and Officer Walling, who brought us back to the restaurant yesterday. We can find out today, when we can share Anderson's story."

Lydia replies, "Absolutely. I'm looking forward to going with you, if we can meet with them in person. It would be nice to meet with Gladis and her parents."

Andy says, "When is the next conference call with Kenny, Angela and Ann?"

Lydia says, "We can set it up by this weekend. We need to plan when the five of us can meet in person again."

Andy replies, "Yes, and we need to go over what churches and media we can contact next." After they finish their coffee, Andy calls Officer Walling, and Lydia calls Gladis and her parents.

Andy goes back in the kitchen right before Lydia and almost in unison, they say to each other, "I've got good news!" They both laugh and Andy says, "Go ahead, honey."

Lydia says, "I talked with Gladis. Her parents took her to get her car this morning, and they returned less than an hour ago. She invited us for supper this evening at 6:00."

Andy exclaims, "Excellent! I talked with Officer Walling, and she wants us to call Monday to set a time for lunch in Gatlinburg next week."

Lydia says, "We're striking a hundred today!"

They go in the great room to watch the 12:00 news. The station out of Knoxville first reports on the terrorism at the Evangelical Church and

Day Care. They are already reporting that the three men are illegal aliens. One is from Venezuela and the other two are from Somalia. Intelligence found that they entered the United States through the southern border.

Lydia spends part of the afternoon cleaning the house, and Andy works in his office, including straightening up the clutter. They each take a shower between 4 and 5, and they leave for Cosby a little after 5:30. They get in their Grand Cherokee and head for Cosby.

On their drive to Cosby, a creek runs along Rocky Flats Road. The trees are losing some color, but the firs and pines hold fast to their enduring green. The McGraigs enjoy the prominent view of the Smokies during their brief trip.

They arrive at the Rivera's fifteen minutes early. Mr. Rivera greets them at the door. He opens the door for them, and says, "Welcome, Gracie and Gladis are in the kitchen finishing supper. Have a seat in the living room." They walk into the small living room, which adjoins a dining area just big enough for a table and six chairs. Mr. Rivera says, "I'm Gus. Yesterday we were so thankful to see Gladis, when you brought her home that I forgot to introduce myself. We can't thank you enough for helping Gladis."

Andy says, "We were blessed to meet her and her Tracy. I'm Andy and this is my wife, Lydia."

Gus looks at Andy with a sparkle in his eye and says, "I know who you are. I'll be right back." He brings them a scrap book, and Gus says, "My parents lived in Berea, Kentucky, when you and Purdue played against Ohio State in the Final Four. In 1962 we saw you play in the first round, when we went to see Kentucky play UT. I was only ten. My dad and I enjoyed watching you play, so we went back to Louisville for the Final Four. You were the best player of the tournament. Look at these two clippings. Here you are dunking against Jerry Lucas, and this one was taken of you and your team at the tournament."

Gus continues, "I showed them to Gladis last night and she recognized your teammate, Larry Quarles, from yesterday."

Lydia gets up and looks at the pictures. She says, "We met just a few months before the Final Four."

Gus continues, "Later my dad read that you turned down an offer to play for the Boston Celtics. Even at my young age, it intrigued me, so I followed your career. Here is a clipping of you as a special agent with the State Department standing by the Secretary of State in 1963. Here's a picture of you, when you first became Secretary of State. You can tell I'm a fan."

Andy says, "I'm flattered by your support and having these pictures."

Mrs. Rivera comes in the room and announces supper. Gus introduces her and Gracie says, "Gladis wants to serve the food, so let's have a seat at the table."

Gladis walks in the room, so they can pray. Gus says, "If you don't mind, I would like to say a prayer of thanksgiving and pray for both of you."

Andy smiles and says, "Please do."

They bow in prayer and Gus says. "Our Father, we thank you for this time and your many blessings. Bless Andy and Lydia. Watch over them during these perilous times. We thank you for this food and home that your provide; in Jesus' name, Amen."

Lydia says, "Thank you, Gus, for that lovely prayer." After Gladis serves the food, she seats Tracy by her and Lydia and Andy greet Tracy. Lydia asks, "How is Tracy feeling today?"

Gladis says, "She appears to be fine, but more quiet than usual. She has been clinging to me all day."

They all dig into a delicious southern meal of fried chicken, sweet potato casserole and green beans with bacon. After they have a few satisfying bites, Andy asks, "When did you move to Cosby?"

Gus says, "Gracie and I met in Berea and married in 1974. I worked in construction all my life, and I was laid off in 1980. I heard about a big company hiring in Gatlinburg. It was booming there, and we moved to Gatlinburg. We found this house in 1989, and Gladis was born a year later."

Lydia says, "We're glad you're hear. Do you have a church home here?"

Gracie replies, "We were both raised Catholic. After we moved we only went to mass off and on. About twenty-five years ago, Gus was working with a man, who invited us to a little country church. We went and loved the people. We joined the church about a year later, and we're still there."

Lydia says, "That's wonderful. We have a true story, and I want Andy to share it. The story is mainly about his cousin and some of his cousin's family."

Andy says, "I'm glad that you love the Lord and follow Him. I'm also thankful that you have a good church home. Do you remember about six to seven months ago, when the media was reporting that some people in this country and in other countries were being visited by those who had passed on?"

Gladis, Gracie and Gus all nod their heads and say, "Yes."

Andy continues, "My second cousin, Angela; my cousin, Ann, Lydia Ann, and my cousin Anderson's friend, Kenny, were all visited by someone who we thought had passed on. My cousin, Anderson, lived a quarter mile from us. Many years ago, we bought wooded land just a few miles from Cosby. We bought it to use mostly as a nature reserve. My cousin, Anderson, was an avid hiker, and he made a lot of trails in his woods."

Gracie says, "Excuse me, Andy. I don't want to miss any of the story. Gladis and I want to serve coffee and apple pie. Does everyone want both? Everyone answers in the affirmative. Gracie says, "We will bring it in a couple minutes."

While Andy, Lydia and Gus talk about the Cosby area, Gracie and Gladis serve the pie and coffee. In a minute they come back from the kitchen and take their seats.

Andy wipes his mouth after a bite of the apple pie and says, "Thank you, Gladis and Gracie for the pie and coffee."

Gracie says, "Please continue. We're curious about your story."

Andy says, "I've known Anderson all my life. When we were growing up, we were with him and his family every week. They lived in Hartford City, Indiana; just thirty minutes from us. He and his family were our closest relatives. Anderson was also a close friend, and he loved the Lord. He earned his business degree from Purdue. He became V-P of international marketing for a big company near my hometown, Muncie, Indiana. He lost his wife, Ruth, last December.

Anderson always wanted the best for everyone. He was dedicated first to the Lord and then to family. We talked many times about the things of God. I knew he was concerned spiritually for his sister, Ann; his daughter, Angela and his close friend, Kenny, from Maggie Valley. Kenny is from Cherokee. He's a marine vet and a retired state trooper."

Andy stops and takes a sip of coffee. He says, "Gracie, before I get into the heart of the story, could I get a little more coffee?" Gladis gets up and pours more coffee for her dad, Andy and Lydia. When she comes back to the dining table, everyone thanks her. Andy takes his last bite of apple pie and another sip of coffee. He says, "Before I finish the story, I just want to say that I could talk all evening with this kind of pie and coffee." Everyone laughs, and Gus says, "Take your time sharing the story. We're enjoying it."

Andy continues, "Most of the details came from Anderson's sister, Ann. She sold her house in Crossville and moved to Anderson's house, so she would be secure financially. One early spring day, Anderson started his hike in his woods by noon. He was due back between 1:00 and 1:30. Ann started getting worried after 1:30. She found his cell phone, which he forgot to take. Later in the afternoon, Kenny came with two friends to search for him. Kenny was familiar with some of the trails. By evening, several officers came and helped with the search. They didn't find him.

He never showed up, and his memorial service was held without a body. About three weeks after he disappeared, later one evening he shows up at his house after Ann went to bed." (Gracie and Gladis make gasping sounds) Andy stops and asks, "Ladies, are you alright?"

They say, "Yes, go ahead."

Andy says, "I will go right to the three visitations, or it will take all evening to tell the story. Anderson also visits his friend, Kenny, at this home in Maggie Valley and his daughter, Angela, at her home in Greenfield, Indiana. He shares the same message with all three. He tells them to commit to Christ and to share the gospel and his story with everyone they can. He said the rapture of the church is soon. No one except the Father knows the day and hour. He said I can tell you that it can be any time and possibly in less than two years. He mentioned that the great tribulation will happen after the rapture. He wants us to share his message with as many people as possible. We are working with groups of people to also reach churches and media."

Andy can see that Gus is shaken, when Gus says, "I knew it; I knew the Lord would come soon for the church. Tell us what to do. The only thing we're limited on is the amount of gas we can buy for travel. After the world bankers and trade people dropped the dollar as the standard trade currency, gas has gotten so high that we can't budget the $9.00 per gallon for many trips beyond Gatlinburg."

Andy replies, "I totally understand. We have a much smaller car that gets 30 miles per gallon. We can work it, so you can cover the Gatlinburg area. Areas between Newport and Townsend would help also help."

Gracie says, "I know we can do that."

Lydia replies, "Some weeks you could stay in the Cosby and Gatlinburg area.

I don't think many trips with the car would be needed. We need help also with email and phone work."

Gladis says, "I can help some in Gatlinburg, since I work there. I can also help with email and phone calls here at home."

Andy says, "Thank you so much for your hospitality; wonderful meal, and your willingness to be part of our gospel outreach group. Lydia and I look forward to working with our new friends. We love to share the gospel and Anderson' story.

Did you hear the news report about the three men who bombed the church and day care?"

Gus replies, "Yes. We heard they're illegal aliens. The report said two are from Somalia and one is from Venezuela."

Lydia says, "We share in your joy that Tracy didn't have serious injuries."

Andy gets more serious as he lowers his voice and asks, "Gus, have you and your family been safe in your neighborhood?"

Gus replies, "Thanks for asking. We thought with all the disturbance in the country, we might have more problems where we live. The neighbors I know are traditional Americans, and they are good neighbors. About a block down, two men broke into a house. They stole some valuables, but they were caught and arrested. Each of us have a gun, and if someone breaks in, they will get shot at from three directions!"

Andy laughs and says, "Good! Let me know, if you have any concerns. My early work with the State Department was security."

Gus says, "That's good to know. Has your area been safe so far?"

Andy replies, "Yes. It's fairly remote, even though it's only a few miles from here. We pass some areas that have more houses along the road. In our area, some of the neighbors are a quarter mile apart. We're a quarter of a mile from Anderson's house, where my cousin Ann lives. She has a good neighbor and friend, who lives fairly close to her. Just less than a year ago, while Anderson was visiting his daughter in Indiana, there was a car load of young men, who tried to rob him. It was late at night, and the neighbor scared them off with his gun."

Gus says, "Everyone should have a gun or more for protection. It's absurd that the New Age Socialist Party is trying to take our guns away, while there are so many problems in our society."

Andy says, "Absolutely. Many neighborhoods still have neighborhood watch groups. Before Anderson disappeared, some of his neighbors formed an all day and all night watch group. They still have it. One evening, they had to run off a car that had several young men in it." Gus replies, "A neighborhood about three blocks from us has a 24/7 watch group. Because of all the problems in our society, I thought our neighborhood would need an around the clock watch group before now."

Andy says, "We'll be in touch. Call anytime."

When Andy and Lydia leave it's almost dark. Lydia says, "In a couple weeks it will be dark by this time."

As they head back home, Andy says, "I know. I use to dislike the coming of winter. Now I like it, and I dislike the heat of summer!"

Lydia smiles and says, "I understand. I think it's one of those senior experiences."

Andy smirks and says, "Oh, yeah. I have several years before I hit 80!"

They're half way home and Lydia says, "Well don't hit the shoulder, we're getting to the area, where there are steep drop offs."

Andy's long arm reaches over, and he touches Lydia's shoulder and says, "Like my uncle use to say, the sign says "soft shoulder".

Lydia laughs and says, "That's another senior experience, romance becomes more like shoulder to shoulder or should I say, tete-a-tete?"

Andy smiles and says, "Funny!"

Before they pull in their drive, Lydia gets silent for a moment. She says, "Before we left the Rivera's, I listened to your conversation with Gus. Do you think our country will come out of this mess?'

Andy pauses a few seconds before he answers. He parks the car in their drive, and he leaves the engine running. He says, "I'm a positive person, and I want the country to heal, but I don't think it will. As you know, I think we're close to the Great Tribulation. Like a lot of evangelicals, we believe the rapture of the church happens right before the beginning of the seven year tribulation. Even though I hope the country gets better, I believe that it won't, because we are so close to the rapture and Great Tribulation."

When they get out of their SUV, a bright flood light comes on above the garage, and as they walk to the front door, another bright flood light from the front porch comes on. Lydia walks into the entrance and Andy turns and locks the front doors. Lydia says, "I was also thinking about your conversation, when you said that Ann's neighbors still have a 24/7 neighborhood watch group. We're a quarter mile away from their neighborhood. Do you think we should have more security here?

Andy says, "I think we are fine for now. We have our cameras on the outside and a lot of security lights. We have all kinds of back up lights, and the doors and windows are secure. We also have Mr. Smith, Mr. Wesson and Mr. Ruger for protection."

Lydia replies, "I guess we're okay for now. Sometimes I think it would be nice to have a security person, but you were in specialized security and even though Ann has a neighborhood watch group, she lives by herself."

Andy smiles and puts his arm around his wife and says, "And you have ole' Andy Avalanche to look out for you."

Lydia says, "Okay, Mr. Bodyguard, you get the job. Do you want tea?"

Andy says, "That sounds good, honey. Give me Anderson's favorite, a cup of hot green tea."

Andy sits in his recliner in the great room, and Lydia brings him tea. Lydia says, "I'm going to take a shower."

Andy says, "I'm going to watch the business news. By the way, you've been doing the grocery shopping. What are some of the prices on common products now?"

Lydia says, "A 12 pack of soda is $15 to $16. A head of lettuce is usually $3.89. A dozen large eggs are $3.99. Depending on the brand, a loaf of bread is $5.99 to $6.99,"

Andy exclaims, "It's shocking. As a kid in the 1950's, mom would have me walk to the general store to buy bread on sale for two loaves for 29 cents. Imagine 15 cents compared to $6 now; that's an inflation increase of 4,000 per cent."

Lydia says, "A year ago, I was spending $100 per week for groceries. Now I'm spending over $300 per week. I don't see how people with kids at home and a modest income make it."

Andy sadly replies, "They struggle." Andy watches business news while Lydia gets ready for bed. He also decides to retire early for the evening. He sets his alarm for 5:30 a.m. Andy thinks about the problems in the country, but just before he falls asleep, he thanks God for the beautiful time of the year.

5:30 seems to come early, but Andy shakes it off and fixes some hot tea and starts the coffee maker, before he starts prayer and Bible study. After 6:30, he turns on the early morning news. He is stunned by what he sees. He turns up the volume, so he can hear the details. As the news story is reported, they show a downtown totally devastated by fire.

The reporter says, "The downtown area of Emeryville, California, was totally destroyed by fire. At this time, 106 people were killed; 38 have serious burn wounds and 45 others have been wounded. Two firefighters were killed while fighting the intense blaze. The buildings that were burned down included a Jewish Synagogue, a Presbyterian Church and Day Care Center, the police dispatch center, a 24 hour call center, a propane business, apartments in office buildings, the town hall, 14 other business buildings and six blocks of houses that bordered the downtown area. The police have not reported any suspects, but the chief of police made the comment that the area is full of anarchists and illegal aliens. The national guard have been called to Emeryville and nearby Oakland and San Francisco."

Lydia, half awake, comes out and asks, "Why is the TV louder than normal?"

While Andy is looking something up on his phone, he says, "Have a seat, honey. I'll get you some coffee. I'm looking up the population now of Emeryville, near San Fran. It says 16,056. The entire downtown was destroyed by fire."

Lydia exclaims, "Oh, Lord."

Andy says. "I'll get your coffee now." When Andy comes back in the room, Lydia says, "They just updated the death toll to 110 people. Look at that downtown area. It's completely burnt down."

Andy sits down and the reporter starts interviewing a police officer. He is livid and says, "We will get, whoever is responsible. It's too bad that this state doesn't have the death penalty".

The reporter asks, "Officer, do you know what started the fire?"

The officer replies, "The chief has to give the official report, but it looks like they set bombs at several building, including the propane building."

The reporter breaks for commercials.

Lydia sees the sadness on Andy's face. She says, "Do you want to have breakfast in the kitchen?"

Andy says, "Sure. I think I'll have some grapefruit and cereal; what about you?"

Lydia replies, "That sounds good." Andy puts the grapefruit, cereal and milk on the table, while Lydia gets the table settings.

They sit down and Andy gives a prayer before breakfast.

They're both silent for over a minute, then Andy says, "In 1962, we both remember the Seven Day Border War. We had only been married for a few months. Not long after you were in D.C. I had to spend most of two weeks at the State Department."

Lydia says, "I remember well. It was a stressful time."

Andy continues, "Our parents and their generation hoped World War II was the war to end wars. I have to admit that I thought our victories with the border war and the government would end our country's major problems. America did well for more than a decade, but then things gradually got worse. Now the country is worse than just before the Border War."

Lydia says, "I remember. We both hoped the major problems in our country were behind us."

In another minute Andy snaps out of his melancholy. He asks, "On the lighter but pricey side, tell me how much the milk, Cheerios and grapefruit are selling for."

Lydia says, "The milk is $5.99 a gallon; the Cheerios were about $5.00 and the one grapefruit was $4.00."

Andy replies, "Wow, $15.00 for just milk, cereal and a grapefruit."

Lydia says, "I'm calling Ann in a few minutes. If she wants to walk the trails this morning, do you want to go with us about 9 or 9:30?"

Andy says, "Sure thing. I'm ready to breathe in that refreshing, October air."

3

WORD OF TRUTH

Andy pulls into Anderson's old driveway. When he and Lydia get out of the car, Patches comes down the hill to greet them. Andy leans over and pets her as she rubs against his leg. Andy says, "You miss Anderson too, don't you Patches?"

As Lydia pets her, Ann yells from the door and says, "Are you ready to walk into God's country?"

Andy replies, "Let's get at it!"

Lydia follows Ann into the house and gives her a hug. Lydia says, "It's a beautiful day. Thanks for having us over."

Andy walks into the kitchen and hugs his cousin. He says, "It looks like you're ready for the hike."

Ann says, "I'm glad we can walk two miles or more this morning. After Lydia and I talked on the phone, I turned to the weather channel. They were reporting about a huge hurricane that is headed toward southern Florida and the Gulf. They think it might hit Miami and New Orleans. In a few days, we might get a lot of rain."

Andy says, "We'll enjoy the walk and hope the storm doesn't get too severe."

As they walk off the trailhead onto the main eastern trail, Andy says, "It looks like our grandson, did a good job on the trails before he went back to school."

Ann replies, "He did a great job; all the main trails look real good."

Ann, Lydia and Andy take in the sites of the tall pines and stately oaks. When they get on the back trail and start walking west, Andy says, "I remember Anderson talking about the age of the old oaks along this trail. He said some of these old oak trees look like they go back to the Civil War days."

While they walk along the horse pasture, Ann says, "While you're here, we should probably do an evaluation of how we're doing the last couple of months on getting out Anderson's story."

Andy says, "Absolutely. We have two new families that want to help and possibly a Gatlinburg police officer. We should also look at a tentative plan for the next two or three months."

As they walk near the edge of the back woods, all three friends love watching the black capped chickadees, the tufted titmice and the robins flying through the trees. As the trail turns northwest, they are about half done. When they walk down the trailhead into Ann's backyard and by Anderson's old fire pit, Ann says, "We walked a little over an hour."

Lydia says, "It feels like we walked well over two miles."

Ann says, "Let's go inside; take off our jackets and I'll fix some hot tea and coffee."

Andy replies, "What a great way to start our meeting today. I should have brought some sugar free cookies or something."

Ann says, "I have some!"

Andy and Lydia have a seat at the dining room table in the great room. As Ann walks toward the kitchen, she says, "I loved sitting at Anderson's long table with him, our family and friends."

Lydia says, "Me too. Sitting here with Anderson and family were special times."

Andy says, "And they're still special. I miss Anderson a lot, and I appreciate every moment we have together."

While Ann waits on the tea and coffee to brew, she gives everyone a water bottle and places the sugar free cookies in front of Andy. Before they start the outreach meeting, they enjoy coffee, tea, cookies and laughter.

Andy says, "Time is precious. If we had more of it, we could fulfill more goals, and share more with each other."

Ann says, "What a good thought. Our time together is precious."

They discuss their accomplishments and shortcomings in getting out Anderson's story the last two months. They talk about what they want to accomplish the next two months. They decide to call the Charlotte TV station to attempt a second appointment and interview. They all agree that they should try to schedule an interview on one or two Knoxville stations. They also discuss what radio stations, churches and newspapers they could contact to set appointments with their team members.

Andy says, "I will call Kenny to see what he can do the next two months."

Ann says, "I will call Angela about the same thing."

Lydia says, "I will check with the new team members and see where they want to fill the upcoming appointments."

They visit with Ann until early afternoon, and then Andy and Lydia go home to rest awhile.

About 3:00, Andy's phone rings. He talks over fifteen minutes with an official from the State Department. Before they hang up, Andy says, "I will think about it and call you Monday."

Lydia asks, "Who was it, honey?"

Andy says, "The State Department. They're meeting with the Chinese and Russian ambassadors next Thursday and Friday. They want me to attend the meetings and fly down Wednesday and fly back Saturday. They offered me $15,000 and all expenses paid."

Lydia says, "They want to use your gift for discerning the truth."

Andy says, "We could use the money to help get Anderson's story to the public."

Lydia replies, "That's true and a lot of people, who don't have enough to eat, need help."

Andy says, "I can get a direct flight from Knoxville to D.C. A deputy secretary said that he could get me on a flight Wednesday that leaves Knoxville at 11:20 a.m."

Lydia says, "Hurricane Samson is forecasted to hit Florida by Saturday or Sunday. By Wednesday morning, most of the rain should be past us."

Andy says, "I will probably go. I will call back by 9 a.m. Monday."

The next day Lydia and Andy make calls to Kenny, the Rivera's, the Gatlinburg officer and Larry. The also call several radio stations, churches and a TV station.

At supper, Andy says, "We had some good responses to getting God's Word out."

Lydia replies, "I'm excited. I love to share the gospel and Anderson's story." After they clean up the kitchen, they sit down and watch the news and the weather. The weather report says that Hurricane Samson is expected to hit Miami Saturday and New Orleans on Sunday. The reporter says, "Hurricane Samson was upgraded from a category 3 hurricane to a category 4, and it's still gaining strength."

Andy says, "It doesn't sound good."

When they turn on the news Saturday morning, they find out that Hurricane Samson became a category 5 before it hit Miami. The reporter says that the storm is so large that 165 mile winds hit Miami from midnight until after 7 a.m. He says, "Throughout the night there were many times that sea water surged to over fifteen feet It appears that Miami is mostly covered with water and has become three islands. We are saddened to announce that the Keys are completely covered with water and thousands of lives have been lost."

Andy says, "Let's turn off the TV and pray for the victims and their families. It looks like the death toll and property damage will be the worst in our history."

After they pray, Andy says, "A pastor in Knoxville recently told me to come and share our story anytime. He said that I can take all the time I want. He also said that he doesn't have to preach each service, and that I could call him on short notice. I think I will call him about tomorrow."

Lydia says, "I think I would considering all the things that are happening to our country."

Andy replies, "I'm having the same thoughts."

Andy calls the pastor acquaintance, and he schedules Andy tomorrow for the 11:00 worship service. After he hangs up he says, "Lydia, I want to do what I can now, because the D.C. trip next week will take Wednesday through Saturday.

Lydia replies, "I totally agree. People don't have much time left. When the rapture happens, the world will be thrown into havoc, then the Great Tribulation will begin."

In the afternoon Andy prepares his notes for tomorrow, and they both do some odd jobs inside and outside the house. After supper they sit down to watch the evening news; mainly to get an update on Miami and the hurricane.

They find out that the death toll in the Keys and the Miami area is up to 18,000. Property damage is already close to $300 billion, and over 10,000 people are missing. The weather reporter says that Hurricane Samson will probably hit New Orleans by early morning.

Lydia says, "So much is happening that I'm glad you scheduled with the Knoxville church for tomorrow."

In the morning, they drive to Kingston Pike in Knoxville and pull into the lot of a mid-sized, independent church. They arrive fifteen minutes early to talk with the pastor and a few church members. By 11:00, it looks like they have about two hundred people in attendance. About 11:20, the pastor says, "Some of you already know about Andy McGraig, our former Secretary of State and Presidential Medal of Freedom recipient. For you basketball fans, he was an outstanding player at Purdue and in the NCAA. Today he has a true story and serious message for you. We welcome Andy and his wife Lydia."

The congregation applauds, and big Andy walks to the pulpit. Andy talks a minute about the beauty of the area and the Smokies. He talks about the violence in America; the recent bombing in Gatlinburg and the terrible tragedy of Hurricane Samson. He also talks about the high inflation and the appearance of China, Russia and Iran itching for a confrontation with America.

Just before he shares Anderson's story, he describes the great increase in famine and pestilence worldwide. He says, "The only thing that hasn't hit us hard lately is a disastrous earthquake."

After Andy tells Anderson's story, about twenty people come to the altar to make commitments to follow Christ. The congregation weeps and praises God until 12:30. After the service the pastor says, "Andy, we haven't had a revival meeting here for six years. We haven't seen a service like this for over ten years." The pastor and his wife have tears in their eyes, when they say goodbye to Andy."

When they get in their SUV, Andy says, "I have more fulfillment from this service, than I will from my work in D.C. this week."

Lydia says, "I would too. It was a wonderful service. It is always a great feeling, when people respond to God's Word."

Monday morning, they find out that the devastation in New Orleans is almost as bad as Miami's. They also learn that Ft. Myers has been hit with a lot of damage and death. Andy calls the State Department at 9 a.m. and gets his flight number and other travel details.

Off and on the rest of the day and Tuesday, Andy prepares for his D.C. trip. In eastern Tennessee, lawns still have to be mowed in October and November, so Andy gets out his lawn mower. When he finishes, he calls Larry.

Larry answers the phone and Andy says, "Hey, Brother Boilermaker, I have to go to D.C. this week. Can we postpone our plans to next week?"

Larry says, "No problem. My wife is looking forward to working with us and and getting Anderson's story out. She's actually excited. I told Aaron Michaels, the coach who took my place, about Anderson's story. He's a believer, but is wife isn't even borderline yet. He wants to talk to us about how he can share Anderson's story."

Andy replies, "That's excellent. When you and I meet, let's find out, if he can join us."

Larry says, "He would like that. Hey, bro, not to change the subject, but have you heard the current death toll and destruction left from the hurricane?"

Andy says, "Not the current stats."

Larry continues, "The total death count so far, is 36,000 with 21,000 missing. The total destruction so far, is over $700 billion. I believe the totals include Miami, Ft. Myers and New Orleans."

Andy says, "It's so sad. I heard there was another church bombing yesterday."

Larry says, "Yes. I think it was in Texas."

Andy says, "It doesn't look good, but it also looks like the Lord is coming real soon."

Andy says, "I just mowed the lawn, so I'm going to sign off in a couple of minutes."

Larry says, "I hope you have a good and safe trip. I will be praying for you."

Andy says, "Thank you. Keep Lookin' Up!"

Larry replies, "I will and back at ya!"

They sign off and Andy jumps in the shower and enjoys the hot water on his seventy-six year old muscles."

Andy stays busy until suppertime on Tuesday, and he takes the evening off to enjoy it with Lydia. They watch the movie "The Book of Eli" and talk about the great promises in God's Word. Before bed they pray together for the time they're apart and for Andy's trip. They pray for the country; for the people making commitments to Christ and for the people who haven't.

Lydia drives Andy to the McGhee-Tyson Airport in Knoxville. Andy checks in one bag for cargo, then he and Lydia walk pass the big nature display of rocks, trees and a creek to the security line. Andy gives Lydia a kiss and a hug and says, "You should be going with me."

Lydia says, "You know I would like to, but you also know that this time of year at home is so pleasant."

Andy replies, "I agree. I would rather stay home."

Lydia waits on Andy until he checks in with the first officer in security, then heads back to the Smoky Mountain foothills.

Andy's flight leaves at 11:20, and he lands at the Ronald Reagan National Airport in D.C. at 12:28. Two special agents meet him at the airport.

One agent says, "Mr. Secretary, I'm Agent Lopez and this is Agent Dockery."

Andy says, "Good to meet you."

Agent Dockery says, "Follow us, Mr. Secretary, and we'll take you to your hotel."

As they drive to the hotel, Agent Lopez says, "Secretary Logner has meetings today, but your hotel has a five star restaurant, and he says to order whatever you would like."

Andy says, "Thank the Secretary for me."

Agent Dockery says, "We've heard, Mr. Secretary, that you use to be a talented special agent for the State Department."

Andy says, "I was the body guard for the Secretary of State at that time."

Agent Lopez asks, "When was that, Sir?"

Andy laughs and says, "I started in 1962."

Agent Dockery also laughs and says, "Just a few years ago!"

When they arrive at Tabard Inn, Agent Lopez shakes Andy's hand and says, "Mr. Secretary, it has been a pleasure; thank you for your service. Agent Dockery will carry your luggage and take a sweep of your room."

After Andy's room is checked, Agent Dockery shakes his hand and says, "I will pick you up at 7:30 in the morning. Secretary Logner would like to meet you in the cafeteria for breakfast at 8:00 a.m., then he wants to meet with you at 9:00 to discuss the meeting with the Russian ambassador which is set for 11:00 a.m."

Andy says, "Thank you, Agent Dockery. I will be ready."

When Agent Dockery gets back in the State Department car, Agent Lopez says, "I think that is the biggest and strongest hand that I have shaken."

Agent Dockery says, "You're telling me! I wouldn't want to have a run in with him; back then or now."

After lunch, Andy takes a nap then spends an hour in the fitness room running on the tread mill and lifting weights. He can still bench four hundred pounds."

He decides to have a real nice and nutritious dinner at 5:30. He goes to their elegant dining room and orders fruit for an appetizer, salmon and shrimp, new potatoes and broccoli. For dessert, he orders strawberries and blueberries with yogurt. When he gets back to his room, he calls Lydia about his day and the delicious dinner.

Andy is up by 5:30. He shaves and showers. He listens to the early morning news to get an update on the weather and the report on the hurricane destruction. He dresses in a suit and tie. He takes a brief case to the dining room at 7:00 and orders water, coffee and a bowl of Cheerios.

Agent Dockery walks in right at 7:30, and by 8:00 Andy greets Secretary Logner in the State Department cafeteria. The Secretary says, "Andy, you have a great reputation in the State Department and in D.C. I appreciate you coming to help us."

Andy says, "My pleasure, Mr. Secretary."

The Secretary says, "Please call me, Rob."

After they enjoy a traditional breakfast of eggs, bacon, hash browns and toast, Andy meets with the Secretary in his office. Secretary Logner says, "Andy, the meeting with the Russian Ambassador is today at 11:00, and the meeting with the Chinese Ambassador is tomorrow at 11:00. The Vice President wants to meet us for lunch at 12:30 tomorrow. I thought if you wanted to fly home tomorrow afternoon, there is a flight leaving for Knoxville at 4:50 and arriving in Knoxville at 6:00."

Andy says, "That would be great."

The Secretary says, "Good. I will give you your check after the luncheon engagement tomorrow. All of your expenses are paid, so order at the hotel anything you want. Our luncheon engagement tomorrow is at the White House, since they have a private dining room. Of course, our meetings with the ambassadors and with the Vice-President are classified. Agents Dockery and Lopez will get you to your hotel tomorrow around 2:30. We've made arrangements with the hotel manager to check you out late. You will have plenty of time to freshen up and to go through security at the airport."

Andy says, "I appreciate everything."

The Secretary says, "We're looking forward to your feedback on the ambassador meetings. Tomorrow, Agent Lopez doesn't have to pick you up until 9:00. We can meet in my office tomorrow at 9:30."

Andy says, "That's fine. I'll have breakfast at the hotel and catch up on the news."

The Secretary says, "I have to admit that I have wondered, if you've been a consultant for corporations after you retired."

Andy says, "I did a little with corporations off and on, but as time passes I've done more and more church work than anything else."

The Secretary simply replies, "Very good."

They talk about some classified information on Russian-American relations, then take a short coffee break before they go downstairs for the meeting in their international conference room.

The Secretary greets the Russian Ambassador. Both the Secretary and the Ambassador have their entourage of assistants and agents. They have a fairly formal meeting for about forty-five minutes. After the Secretary says his good byes to the Russian Ambassador and his party, Secretary Logner walks over to Andy and says, "I'm looking forward to hearing what you have to say.

We need to meet in private. Do you want to have lunch in the cafeteria and then meet in my office?"

Andy says, "That's a good plan."

After they sit down with their meal in the cafeteria. The Secretary says, "For dinner I've made reservations for us and three others."

Andy smiles and says, "Okay, lay it on me."

The Secretary says, "The Senate Minority Leader, your friend, Gordon O'Neal, wants to see you, and because of your celebrity status, my wife and his wife want to join us for dinner."

Andy says, "That's great. Where are we going for dinner?"

The Secretary says, "I've heard you like the Old Ebbitt Grill."

Andy says, "An excellent choice! Thank you."

They finish lunch and go upstairs to the Secretary's office.

They both have a seat, and Secretary Logner says, "Do you want anything before we start?"

Andy replies, "A bottle of water would be good."

The Secretary says, "I have that in this little frig." He takes out two bottles, then takes out a pen and notepad. He says, "Go ahead, Andy, then I will ask questions, if I have any."

Andy says, "It appears that the main purpose of the meeting was to see if the Russians are planning any type of military aggression against our country. It also appears that the other main purpose was to see if Russia would support China over being our ally or remain neutral."

The Secretary says, "Yes, Andy, those were the two main reasons for the meeting."

Andy says, "The Russian ambassador was telling the truth about Russia not planning their own military aggression toward our county. He was lying when he said that their first desire is to remain neutral, if China attacked the United States. He was also lying, when he said that if they had to choose an ally, they would choose our country over China."

The Secretary ponders Andy's discernment for a minute, then asks, "Andy, do you believe your insight on all three points is 100%?"

Andy confidently replies, "Yes, sir."

Secretary Logner says, "My notes are not rocket science, but this is so important to national security that I just want to confirm my notes with you."

Andy says, "Take your time. I know it's very important."

The Secretary looks at his notes, then looks at Andy and says, "There are three main points that our security heads need to know. Confirm that

I have recorded your feedback correctly. First of all, it's true that Russia is not planning its own act of aggression. Secondly, it's a lie that Russia would remain neutral in case of China's aggression against the United States. Thirdly, it's a lie that Russia would choose us over China in case of China's aggression. In other words, Russia would be an ally of China's instead of having an alliance with our country."

Andy replies, "That's right, Mr. Secretary."

The Secretary looks down; shakes his head and says quietly, "How disappointing."

Andy says, "Yes it is, sir; very disappointing."

Secretary Logner looks back up at Andy and says, "Mr. Secretary, you've been a big help to our nation for many years. Thank you for being here."

Andy says, "I'm glad I can help."

The Secretary looks at his watch and says, "It's about 2:30. We won't leave for the restaurant until 5:45. Agents Lopez and Dockery are taking us, and they're both working security during our dinner engagement. What would you like to do until we leave?"

Andy asks, "Does the department still provide workout clothes and a bath towel?"

The Secretary smiles and says, "Yes, we do."

Andy says, "I have plenty of time to lift weights and do some target practicing."

The Secretary says, "Excellent. I will have someone take you to the facilities in the basement."

Andy runs a little on the tread mill, then lifts weights. Word gets around to the agents working out that the former Secretary of State and special agent is headed to the firing range after his workout. When Andy opens the door to the firing range, a line of over ten agents start applauding, then they call out, "Welcome, Mr. Secretary!"

A broad smile comes over Andy's face, and he says in a booming voice, "Thank you! It's a pleasure being here with talented agents." Andy walks along the line and shakes everyone's hand. Three agents ask for his autograph, then he walks over to the equipment clerk.

The clerk says, "What can I get for you, Mr. Secretary?"

Andy says, "I have some extra time. I know I need to check out the weapons one at a time. It has been a long time, since I fired a .45 caliber and a M16. I also want to practice with an AR15, and I need ammo for my .38." Andy starts with the .45 and practices with all four guns."

Andy finishes by 4:45, so he can take a shower and go back upstairs.

While the Secretary finishes some calls, Andy waits in the reception room for a few minutes. The Secretary greets Andy about twenty minutes before it's time to leave. He says, "Andy, let's take a walk on the main floor, then Agents Lopez and Dockery will take us to the restaurant."

When they enter the classic restaurant, it's humming with a crowd of customers. Andy and Secretary Logner are seated at a large table and five minutes later the remaining party of five join them. Everyone is real cheerful and happy to see Andy. The ladies give him a hug. Andy's old friend, Gordon O'Neal, says, "Okay ladies, let's have a seat. You're making your husbands jealous."

The party of political leaders enjoy good food, conversation and laughter. At the table, only Andy and the Secretary have a burden on their minds after the day's events. Before Agents Dockery and Lopez take Andy back to the Tabard Inn, Gordon's wife inquires about Lydia. She says, "Andy, it's been so long since we have seen Lydia. How is she doing?"

Andy says, "She's as beautiful and joyful as ever."

Tippi says, "Give her my best. I always admired her."

Andy says, "I sure will. You and Gordon take care and keep following Christ."

Gordon shakes his hand and says, "We sure will."

While Agent Dockery drives Andy back to the hotel, Andy asks, "Did you men get something to eat tonight?

Dockery says, "I ate first and had a great BBQ sandwich."

Lopez says, "When Dockery came off break, I ordered a huge, grilled shrimp appetizer and a chef salad."

Andy says, "It sounds like you got your fill. Going back to the Old Ebbitt Grill was a treat for me."

Before Andy goes to bed, he calls Lydia about being with Gordon and Tippi at their favorite restaurant in D.C.

Lydia says, "Wow, you don't know how much I would have enjoyed being with them at the Grill. I can't complain though, the weather and God's country have been perfect here."

Andy says, "I got good news today. I can take the 4:50 flight to Knoxville tomorrow and be there at 6:00."

Lydia exclaims, "That is good news! Ann and I have plans to go out for supper. It would be nice, if I could bring her with me, and on the way home there are a lot of nice restaurants between Strawberry Plains and Sevierville."

Andy says, "It will be nice to be with both of you for supper. It's on me; wherever you want to go."

Lydia says, "Looking forward to seeing you, big boy."

Andy replies, "Sleep tight; love you."

Lydia smiles and says, "I love you."

Andy leans back on the bed and searches for a news channel. He gets sleepy before 9:00 and gets ready for bed.

He sleeps soundly for eight hours and gets up and makes coffee. He does devotions, and then he turns on the television. He doesn't shower until 7:30, since Agent Lopez is picking him up at 9:00. He dresses and takes his brief case to the Inn's restaurant at 8:15. He orders a full breakfast, since he is meeting the Secretary at 9:30 in his office.

One of Anderson's old trails that they walk with Ann

Signs

Secretary Logner's receptionist announces Andy's arrival. Andy walks in the Secretary's office at 9:25. The Secretary greets Andy and says, "I just ordered some coffee for us. We'll meet here until 10:30, then we'll go downstairs to the conference room. Do you want anything with the coffee?"

Andy says, "No thanks. I had a big breakfast."

The Secretary says, "The Vice-President called about 9:00. He said he's looking forward to meeting with you over lunch."

Andy says, "I'm looking forward to it as well. It will be enjoyable being at the White House again."

The Secretary says, "I will be frank about China's disposition now, which I expect to be reflected in their ambassador today. They keep demanding that we accept more of their exports, and their import volume with us has grown next to none. You probably know from the news that they're expanding in their part of the world. They have Japan greatly worried."

Andy says, "Mr. Secretary, the former President was making strides toward correcting those things. No offense, but your party fought him all the way."

The Secretary says, "I know, Andy. Some of us are having regrets already, but other party leaders are standing their ground."

Andy says, "No disrespect, but they're standing on shaky ground."

Secretary Logner says, "I hate to admit it, Andy, but just between you and me, their ideology is beyond reason."

Andy replies, "It's a sad time."

The Secretary continues, "I'm guessing that we'll be confronting a pushy ambassador. We're searching for answers to the same inquiries presented to the Russian ambassador."

Andy says, "I understand, Mr. Secretary."

The Secretary adds, "The nation has always counted on you, Andy, regardless of politics."

Andy replies, "I know. You can count on me. I love God and America."

A staff member knocks and brings in two coffee mugs and a pot of coffee. As the staff member leaves the office, Secretary Logner says, "Andy, let's drink the coffee in silence for a few minutes. I know you're a man of prayer."

Andy says, "Thank you, sir. Being still will be helpful at this time. As Andy drinks his coffee, he prays quietly and communes with God."

About fifteen minutes later, the Secretary breaks the silences and asks, "Do you want any more coffee before we go downstairs?"

Andy says, "I'm good." He stands up and grabs his briefcase. The two Secretaries walk to the elevator to face the Chinese delegation.

When they get off the elevator, they meet with their own entourage. As they walk into the large lobby, the Chinese delegation is a few minutes early and walk just ahead of their U.S. counterparts.

Even though it doesn't follow decorum, the Chinese enter the State Department conference room just before the Americans.

They greet each other very formally and take their seats to begin precisely at 11:00 a.m. The Deputy Secretary of State introduces Secretary Logner. The Secretary welcomes the Chinese delegation and shares a brief general message of good will. He invites the ambassador to the podium.

Before he begins to speak he appears angry. He tells of his president's disappointment in America refusing some of their trade proposals. As he continues, the interpreter clears his throat more often. As the Chinese ambassador gets louder and more forceful, the interpreter hesitates a second then says, "If America doesn't become more cooperative, we have a secret weapon that we will use on your country."

At that point, the American delegation stands up and begins booing the ambassador. Two special agents of the State Department open the double doors, and motion to several agents outside. As those agents enter the conference room, the ambassador storms out and his entourage quickly follows him.

Andy is standing with the rest of the American delegation, and he makes sure that the Secretary is safe. The Secretary looks up at Andy and says, "I have never seen such disrespect and belligerence from an ambassador before. Andy, we have a car that we use for mobile conferences. Agents Dockery and Lopez can sit in front, while we can meet privately on the way to the White House."

When they get in the car, Secretary Logner gets out his notepad and as they pull out, the Secretary says, "Andy, you know my questions. Go ahead when you're ready."

Andy says, "To answer your question about the possibility of China attacking America, the Chinese Ambassador is not bluffing. They are ready and willing to attack our country. By the way, it is true that they have some kind of secret weapon. They will not be neutral toward America. They would ally with Russia or another country against the United State."

The Secretary looks down at his notepad and shakes his head as he says, "I was afraid of that."

Andy says, "I know that it is tough to meet with the Vice President at a White House luncheon right now, but we have had difficult assignments before."

"Yes, Andy. You're totally right. We will make the most of the luncheon."

Agent Dockery pulls the car to a stop in front of the White House. Agent Lopez opens the door for the Secretaries.

A White House receptionist leads Andy and the Secretary to the private dining room. She shows them to their seats, as two staff members complete the table setting. In five minutes, the Vice President and his wife and several members of the President's staff come in the room. The Vice President walks over to Andy and shakes his hand. He says, "Andy, it's good to see you again."

Andy replies to his political opponent, "Thank you for inviting me, Charles."

Andy is seated by the Vice President. During the lunch, the Vice President asks Andy several questions about the two ambassador meetings. When they finish, the Vice President stands up and shakes Andy's hand again and thanks him for coming. He goes over to the Secretary and whispers something and hands him a white envelope.

When they get back in the car, the Secretary says, "Agents Dockery and Lopez will drop me off, then take you to your hotel, so you can pack for your trip back home. They know you will have an extra two hours, so they are looking forward to relaxing in the hotel lobby and restaurant while they wait for you."

Andy says, "Thank you again for everything. After I get ready, I'll join them in the hotel restaurant."

Secretary Logner says, "Here's your check for helping us." He pulls a white envelope out of his coat pocket and says, "The Vice President said that the President wants you to have this. He said the President wants to give you and your wife a tax free bonus for helping the country and for her supporting you these many years."

Andy looks at the bonus check; it's for $2,000. He says, "Please thank the President. I hope our thank you card will reach him."

"If your name is on the return address, I'm sure he will get it."

They drop off the Secretary, and the agents take Andy to the historic D.C. hotel.

Agent Dockery has a seat in the hotel lobby, while Agent Lopez goes with Andy to sweep his room. When Agent Lopez finishes, he says, "Take your time, Mr. Secretary. We have about ninety minutes before we need to leave for the airport."

Andy says, "I'll join you in the hotel restaurant before it's time to leave." Agent Lopez shuts the door. Andy takes off his shoes and coat, and takes a short nap. When he wakes up, he grabs the remote and looks for the news network. He freshens up; packs and joins Agents Lopez and Dockery in the fashionable restaurant.

All three of them enjoy their conversation about being special agents. They share the way things are now in their work, and Andy shares memories about his days as a special agent.

They park in the airport lot at 3:30. Agent Dockery says, "We'll be with you until your flight leaves. One of us will sweep the plane before you board." After Andy checks his luggage and goes through security, Agent Lopez sweeps the plane while Agent Dockery watches Andy's fellow passengers.

At 4:25 the airline attendant directs the passengers to board. Andy shakes the agents' hands and thanks them. Agent Dockery says, "It was an honor to be with you, Mr. Secretary. I'm sure you were one of our best special agents as well."

The agents watch the passengers as they board, and they don't leave until the plane takes off.

Andy's plane lands in Knoxville exactly at 6 p.m. After he goes through security, he sees Lydia and Ann. He gives Ann a hug and hugs and kisses Lydia and says, "I have the loveliest woman in the world waiting on me."

They pull off at the Strawberry Plains exit and have supper at Puleo's Grill. After supper, they only have a forty minute drive to reach home. They drop off Ann, and Andy walks her to the door. After Lydia and Andy get settled at home, Andy says, "I had lunch with the Vice President at the White House yesterday. He gave the Secretary an envelope from the

President. For my service to the country and my recent work in D.C. and for your lifetime loyalty to me, he gave us a tax free bonus of $2,000!"

Lydia excitedly says, "We can give it to those who don't have enough food!"

Andy says, "Yes, I've had similar thoughts. Out of the $15.000, I'm giving a large donation to the local food pantry; to the Gatlinburg food pantry and to the church. What do you think about asking the Rivera's, if they need anything? You might have to prod them. They may want food to store or money for their power, but guess what?"

Lydia smiles and asks, "What big boy?"

"After you talk with them, they might expect a hundred or two, but we'll surprise them with a check for $2,000!"

Lydia says, "I love it! That's so nice of you, Andy."

Andy says, "We've been blessed a lot, and I know we like blessing others. Also, I know they're sincere people, and they want to share the gospel and Anderson's story."

Lydia replies, "Absolutely. They plan to share the story at their church in Cosby this Sunday. The pastor is giving them his sermon time to share the gospel and Anderson's story."

Andy says, "That's great! Let's call them now. Since I'm tired from the trip, ask them if we could visit their worship service Sunday. Tell them we want to take them out to eat after church. You can go ahead and ask them tonight what they need. Before they leave the restaurant Sunday, we'll surprise them with the $2,000 check."

Lydia says, "Good idea. I will call them now."

After Lydia hangs up, she comes back in the great room and says, "I talked with Gracie, and I did have to prod her with suggestions like storing up food. She admitted that they didn't have enough money weekly to buy the groceries that they're use to. She also said that they haven't been able to store much except a few canned goods. I have a feeling that she thinks I'm going to bring her food or give her money for food. I love the surprise we have for them."

Andy says, "Very good. While I was gone, I was busy with the business at hand, but the hurricane devastation kept crossing my mind. I got to hear some news a couple of times, but I didn't get the update on all the losses."

Lydia says, "I listened to the morning news and got the update then. The reporter said the devastation in Miami, Ft. Myers and New Orleans was so bad that they only have an estimate of the property destruction and casualties in those areas. $900 billion in property has been destroyed, and there are over 45,000 casualties. They're reporting that over 30,000 people are missing. Only 30% of the land is left in Miami."

Andy is silent a few seconds. He quietly says, "Lydia, how sad. I have no doubt that the Lord is coming soon for the church. We know the Great Tribulation will be much worse, but this tragedy is so hard for the families and the nation. It reminds me that we need to get the group together soon. I don't know if Anderson's daughter can come from Greenfield, Indiana, but Kenny could probably come from Maggie Valley."

Lydia says, "We know that Ann can come and probably Davina. Why don't we invite them to come on a mid-afternoon, and we can have food out for them, and they can eat during and after the meeting? Davina and Angela could share a room, and we would have a room for Ann and another one for Kenny."

Andy replies, "Good idea. For that meeting, we'll invite Davina, Kenny, Ann and Angela and invite them to spend the night. While everyone is still here the next day, probably a Saturday, we could invite Larry and his wife, the Rivera's and possibly Officer Walling."

Lydia says, "Alright. I will have time to get brunch ready and serve it at 10:30 and then we could have our second meeting and finalize our plans for the next two or three months."

Andy says, "Perfect. Our first group will be here from mid-afternoon Friday to mid-afternoon Saturday, and our second group will be here from roughly 10 a.m. to mid-afternoon Saturday."

Lydia says, "Tomorrow I could call Angela first and give her a choice between next Friday and Saturday or the following Friday and Saturday. Then I will call Davina, Ann and Kenny with the dates, right after I talk with Angela."

Anderson says, "Good plan. I may go to bed by 9:30 tonight; maybe it's jet lag."

Lydia says, "You've had a busy three days."

They turn out the lights, and they both hit the sack by 9:30.

Andy gets up before 6:00 and has devotions. An hour later he's fixing scrambled eggs, turkey bacon and toast for Lydia and him. By 7:30 they turn on the news and in five minutes Andy remarks, "Can you believe this. Look at the earthquakes that have hit in the last twenty-four hours!" The news reports that an estimated 89,000 have been killed by an earthquake in Western Iran. In Mexico City and the surrounding area, they believe 140,000 people have been killed. In Southwest China about 800,000 people were killed by an 8.8 magnitude earthquake. Over 500,000 of the dead were killed in Chengdu. Andy says, "Lydia, let's see if Angela can come this next Friday and Saturday. It looks like we don't have much time left."

Lydia says, "I will. This is terrible. It's hard to imagine how bad the Great Tribulation will be. I'll do a quick clean-up of the kitchen, then I'll call her."

Lydia picks up her cell phone and thinks that she might get voicemail, but Angela answers right away. Angela says, "How are you doing? I'm surprised you're calling this early."

Lydia says, "I'm fine. You might say this is an urgent call. Have you heard that in the last twenty-four hours, over one million people have been killed by three earthquakes?"

Angela replies, "Oh, no. Where did this happen?"

Lydia says, "In China, Iran and Mexico City. Andy and I feel that we need to meet as soon as possible. We've been active with getting your dad's story to the public. We both feel there is not much time left. Can you be here Friday afternoon and stay through Saturday afternoon?"

Angela says, "I have a class Friday morning, but I can cancel an appointment I have in the afternoon. I will call the Indianapolis airport and see when their flight leaves. I know I will have to transfer in Charlotte, so I can get to Knoxville. I'll call you right back."

In the meantime, Lydia calls Ann and Davina to make sure they can come. She just finishes talking with Davina, when Angela's call comes in. Angela says, "Lydia, I can catch a flight out of Indianapolis at 11:55 and be at the Knoxville Airport at 4:00."

Lydia replies, "That's great. Ann and Davina will be here. Davina lives in Crossville, so she will be coming through Knoxville. I will probably ask her to pick you up. Ann and Kenny may be here by 3:30, but we'll wait on you. When is the return flight?"

Angela replies, "It leaves Knoxville at 3:42 Saturday, and I get back to Indianapolis about 7:45."

Lydia says, "That will work. Andy could take you to the airport. Some of the guests will be here a little longer, but you can have brunch with us at 10:30 and have time to spare."

Angela says, "Sounds good. I will be in touch with you this week. I'm looking forward to seeing everyone."

Lydia says, "I'm so happy you can come. I will be looking forward to your call. Love you."

Angela says, "Thank you for calling me. Love you."

Andy is sitting in the same room, and says, "I got the gist of the call. I'm sure Davina can pick her up at the airport. I'm going to call Larry now to see if he and his wife can be here by 10:30 Saturday for the brunch."

Andy grabs his cell phone and dials Larry, "Hi, Larry, this is Andy. Have you heard the news about the devastating earthquakes?"

Larry replies, "Yes, it's a terrible catastrophe."

Andy says, "We feel an urgency about having a meeting. My daughter in Crossville and my second cousin from Indiana are coming in Friday. We are also calling Anderson's good friend, Kenny. Can and you and Melissa come to our house this Saturday by 10:30 for brunch?"

Larry says, "Melissa is right here; I'll ask her." In a few seconds Larry says, "We can be there."

Andy says, "Great! After brunch we're having a meeting that I'm going to ask Lydia and my cousin to lead. I plan to take Angela, Anderson's daughter, to the Knoxville airport. We need to leave for the airport around 12:45. On the way there, I would like for you, Angela and I to have our own meeting."

Larry says, "No problem. We don't have any other plans Saturday."

Andy replies, "Good. We'll have plenty of food from Friday and early Saturday for a meal, when we return."

Larry says, "I talked with Aaron Michaels, the basketball coach at Carson Newman. He wants to help share your cousin's story. He has told me before that his wife is not a believer."

Andy replies, "After we leave the airport, we'll talk about getting with him. If you and I share the message at a church in Jefferson City, do you think he could get his wife to go with him?"

Larry says, "I will ask him that before Saturday."

"Good. We could probably schedule a date at one of the churches within a month."

Larry says, "I will get Aaron's input. First Baptist is on the campus."

Andy says, "We're looking forward to seeing you Saturday. I think Lydia plans to sit down for the brunch by 10:30. Don't bring anything except a pad and pen for notes."

Larry says, "Will do. Lord willing, we will see you then, brother."

Just as Andy hangs up, Lydia's phone rings.

Lydia answers and Gladis says, "Lydia, I just told Dad that Andy and you are coming to service Sunday. He asked me to call you. He said our pastor's messages usually last twenty-five to thirty minutes. Dad and I were planning to share the time Sunday, but Dad would like for Andy to speak the last eight to ten minutes."

Lydia replies, "Hold on, Gladis. Maybe Andy can give us an answer now."

Lydia looks at Andy and repeats Gladis' inquiry. Andy says, "Tell her I will be glad to."

When Lydia gives Gladis Andy's message, she says, "Oh, thank you! I know that Dad and the church will be glad to hear from Andy Sunday."

Lydia says, "Thanks for calling, Gladis. We look forward to being there and having dinner with you and your family after church."

When Lydia hangs up, Andy says, "How would you like to spend a quiet day at home?"

Lydia says, "I would love to. I know you need to rest, and I would enjoy not having to go anywhere today."

The Lord's Day in Cosby, Tennessee

Andy has recovered from his trip to D.C. by Sunday morning. He has his notes ready by 8 a.m. He has breakfast with Lydia and takes a shower. They have a cool but pleasant October drive. It takes them about fifteen minutes to get to the Cosby church. It's on the outskirts of Cosby. It's a small and modest, country church with a prominent white steeple. An usher greets them, and Gladis and her dad are waiting on Andy near the front door. The usher seats Lydia near the front by Gladis and Tracy.

Gus says, "Andy, the pastor wants to meet with you, Gladis and me for a few minutes before the service. They walk in the pastor's office. The very friendly and energetic pastor says, "Welcome, friends, I'm Mike Pike, the pastor." Gus introduces them and the pastor says, "Have a seat. It looks like we're going to have a full house today. The people are excited to have a former Secretary of State and NCAA champion, Mr. McGriag."

Andy replies, "Please call me Andy and if you would introduce me as Andy McGraig. It's an honor being here today."

Pastor Pike says, "Andy, Gladis or Gus probably told you that we have asked Gus, Gladis and you to share between eight and ten minutes each. As an honored guest, we want you to feel free to take longer."

Gus says, "Pastor, Gladis and I agreed to take only seven to eight minutes each, so Andy would have at least fifteen minutes to share what is on his heart."

The pastor says, "Very good. Andy, feel free to lead us in an altar call. Just call on me after your message, if you need anything.'

Andy says, "I'm looking forward to the service."

They get up and the pastor says, "After I introduce the three of you before your messages, please have a seat on stage and you can stay there through the rest of the service."

They have several minutes to greet people, as they make their way to the front of the church.

It's already a full house and the ushers start putting out a few folding chairs. Andy guesses that a little over a hundred people have filled the sanctuary.

By 11:00 Andy sits by Lydia, and Gladis and Gus sit by Gracie and Tracy. The pastor opens the service; prays and the Sunday School Superintendent gives the church announcements. The congregation sings "Wonderful Words of Life" and the ushers take the offering. The worship leader and congregation sing "Victory in Jesus", then a young family comes to the stage and sings "Sheltered in the Arms of God". The pastor steps up to the pulpit and says, "Gus Rivera, his daughter, Gladis Restrepo and Andy McGraig are going to share God's message today. Gus and Gladis are members of our church family and Andy lives near Cosby. He is active speaking at churches and on public media. As most of you know, Andy McGraig is the former Secretary of State and the leading member of the 1965 NCAA basketball championship team. Gus Rivera will begin the three messages on this Lord's day."

Gus thanks everyone for coming and shares how much the Lord, his church family and his new friends, the McGraigs, mean to him. As Gus finishes, he says, "I want Andy to tell the story about his first cousin, who he grew up with. Gladis will share now how God intervened in her life and Tracy's during the recent tragedy in Gatlinburg."

Gladis describes the afternoon, when the bomb exploded at her daughter's daycare. She said, "It was like a war zone. I immediately thought of Tracy's well-being, and then I saw the terrorists racing to their car and taking off. I thank God that Tracy only had minor injuries. The officer took us to the police command site on the grounds. There I saw the biggest man and the tallest man I had ever seen. (The congregation laughs.) It was Andy and his former teammate, Larry Quarles. Andy and Lydia drove us home to safety, and we have continued to be blessed by Andy and Lydia's friendship. Andy has something very important to share with you."

Big Andy stands up and walks to the pulpit. The congregation spontaneously applauds for him for over a minute. Andy thanks everyone for coming out and thanks Gus and Gladis for their messages. Andy begins by telling Anderson's story and how after his disappearance, he returned to his sister; to his close friend in Maggie Valley and to his daughter in Indiana. He tells the people what God has in store for those who follow Jesus Christ and do His will. He stresses the urgency of being prepared for Christ's soon coming for the church, The Rapture.

Andy concludes by briefly sharing the state of the world and American society. Andy says,

"We know from Biblical prophecy that in the last days the love of many will wax cold, and there will be a great falling away. We are in that time. Evil has infected the whole world with communism, humanism, materialism, famine, pestilence and natural disasters in many places. America has been ensnared by humanism, socialism and pathological liars in government and in the media. The victims of the worst of America's trespasses are crying out for God's judgment on legalized abortion. Those who follow Christ ask for justice, and God demands judgment. It has been fifty years that the followers of Christ, the church, have not been able to stop the horrific human rights violation of legalized abortion. God is judging this country for the seventy million babies that abortionists and their supporters have murdered. The lives and blood of these babies are on the hands of millions of Americans."

Andy is then silent and just looks out on the congregation. Applause erupts and shouts of, "Amen, brother and That's Right, brother!"

Andy says, "I ask that everyone who believes my words and pledges to follow Christ to the end, please come forward." Everyone in the building gets out of their seat and comes forward. People are in tears, including Gladis, Gracie, Lydia and many of the men and women in the church. The pianist begins playing, "Just As I Am". The pastor and church leaders talk with a large number of people for close to half an hour. People are still crying and praising God as well.

The pastor closes the service as everyone sings, "Amazing Grace".

Lydia, Andy, Gus, Gracie, Gladis and Tracy don't leave the church building until 1:00. Gus says, "That was the best service I have ever been in."

Andy says, "Thank you, Gus and Gladis, for making it possible. How about you lead the way to our dinner location! It's on me, and I want you to pick the best restaurant in Cosby."

Gus drives down a scenic road to his favorite restaurant and gift shop in town. When Andy and Lydia park beside him, Gus gets out and says to Andy, "They have the best food and pie here in East Tennessee." Andy laughs and says, "We'll take your word for it."

Andy walks in with Gus and Lydia accompanies Gracie, Gladis and Tracy. As they get inside, Lydia says, "Look out how cute the country décor is."

Gladis replies, "And it's just as nice at the tables."

A young waitress in a red and white checkered dress says, "How many?" Both Andy and Gus say, "Six."

The waitress says, "I'm Charlotte. I will be your waitress today. Our hostess was busy for a a couple minutes." When she takes their drink order, Andy says, "Put all the meals on my check."

After the waitress is finished with the drink order, Gracie says, "I will remember our service for the rest of our life. We have never seen such a packed house and response, as we did today."

Gus says, "Yes, it was exceptional! Andy, once again you're a winner."

Andy smiles and says, "Thank you, but our Lord gets all the credit today."

Gladis says, "Amen!"

Lydia feeling a little mischievous says, "Gracie, have you wondered what Andy and I have brought you today?"

Gracie is a little embarrassed and says, "I'm trying not to think about it. You and Andy are so good to us."

Lydia replies, "That's fine, dear. I didn't mean to put you on the spot. We'll have dinner first, then Andy and I will unload the things for you."

Andy gives Lydia a slight bump with the elbow for teasing Gracie.

During the meal order, everyone orders a side of sweet potato casserole. The entries ordered vary from fried chicken, pork chops and pulled pork. Gladis orders Tracy a chicken leg, sweet potato casserole and green beans with milk."

Lydia asks, "Tracy, is that your favorite meal here?"

Tracy's eyes light up and she says, "Yes, Ma'am!"

After the meal, Andy tells everyone that they must order pie. He says, "If you don't have room for it, take it home."

All of the pie orders are apple and pecan.

After the waitress serves everyone their pie and makes sure that everyone has coffee or water, Andy says, "After we eat our pie, Lydia and I have something for you."

Everyone digs into their pie. In a couple of minutes, Gracie assumes they brought them canned goods and says, "You didn't have to bring us anything. You have already done a lot for us."

Andy smiles and asks Gracie, "What are the things you need?"

Gracie says, "Since everything is so expensive, we haven't been able to store up staples like baked beans and tuna. A can of baked beans and a can of tuna cost over $4.00."

Andy takes a minute to finish his pie and does some quick figuring in his head. He nonchalantly wipes his face and asks, 'Is everyone finished with their pie?"

The reply is unanimous and Andy with a straight face looks at Gracie and says, "Do you have room for a thousand cans of beans or tuna?"

Gracie says, "What? What do you mean?"

Andy just smiles at her and reaches into his sport coat pocket and pulls out a check, which he hands to Gus."

Gus looks at the check and says, "Thank you, Lord!" He gets tears in his eyes.

Surprised, Gracie asks, "What is it, honey?" Gus hands her the check.

Gracie cries out, "Oh, Lord!" She starts crying and Gladis peers over to look at the check.

After Gracie starts wiping her eyes, Andy says, "Lydia and I want you to use it for whatever you need. We especially want you to buy the food you're use to and to store up food and water." Gracie gets up and hugs Lydia and Andy.

Gus says, "You don't realize how much the both of you mean to us. You are like close family."

Lydia says, "You have been a joy to us. We are so happy to be with each of you."

When they go out to the restaurant parking lot, Gus, Gracie, Gladis and Tracy hug Andy and Lydia."

Lydia says, "We will see you at our house at 10:30 Saturday morning."

Gus says, "Yes, Gladis and I will be there, and Gracie is going to spend some quality time with Tracy at home."

After they get in their SUV, Andy looks over at Lydia before he pulls out of the parking lot and asks, "Are those tears I see in your eyes?"

Lydia laughs and says, "I can't help it. Thanks for helping them."

Andy says, "I thank the Lord for being able to."

When they get home, Lydia says, "That was a lot of food for dinner."

Andy replies, "And an excellent restaurant. It was a good day in Cosby.'

Lydia says, "Yes, I like their church and the restaurant."

Before they take a Sunday afternoon nap, Andy says, "After I do devotions in the morning, I can have breakfast ready for us by 7:30, and we can go over our activities for the week."

Lydia replies, "Good idea, we can have our own at home meeting."

Andy gets up at 5:30 Monday morning and has devotions. About 7:00 he starts the coffee maker. By 7:30 he has breakfast ready, and Lydia and Andy sit down at the dining table and pray. After they start eating breakfast,

Andy says, "For our own meeting after breakfast I would like for us to talk about what media we could reach out to in the next couple months. I also would like to list the people who are coming in Friday and our discussion topics and then the same thing for Saturday."

Lydia says, "Good planning. We do need to go over those things."

Andy asks, "Do you want to watch the 8:00 news before we start our meeting?"

Lydia replies, "Sure. I will clear the table after breakfast, and we'll turn on the TV."

Lydia comes in the great room right before 8:00, and Andy turns on the television. A commercial runs before the news, then Andy and Lydia are rattled about what they hear. The news commentator says, "Between 3 a.m. and 5a.m. Pacific Time, six earthquakes have hit areas between San Francisco and Palm Springs. They were all between 5 and 6 magnitudes. The strongest one was a magnitude 6 that hit Hollywood at 4:40 this morning."

Lydia says, "I'm overwhelmed!"

A shaken Andy says, "The nation and the world are going through terrible times. Maybe we should start our meeting, then turn on the news channel for an update."

They go back to the table and get out their notes. They spend almost an hour talking about media in different locations and the discussion topics for the meetings on Friday and Saturday. Andy says, "Do you want to take a coffee break before we turn the TV on?"

Lydia says, "Yes, I'm apprehensive about what I might hear. Do you want some of the small, sugar free cookies that we have been using for snacks?"

Andy says, "Yes, they will be perfect with coffee." He makes some fresh coffee. They enjoy the coffee and the cookies in the great room before they turn the TV on, It's almost 9:30, when the announcer comes back on with the California updates; it's not good.

He says, "Since 5 a.m. Pacific Time, there have been more earthquakes at a greater magnitude. At 5:45 San Francisco had a 6.7 magnitude earthquake and San Bernardino had a 6.5 magnitude earthquake. Scientists are worried since the earthquakes have continued with increasing magnitudes."

Andy turns off the TV and says, "Why don't we pray before we get into our routine for the day?"

6

Smoky Mountain Calm
before the Storm

After supper, Lydia turns on the 6:00 news. Andy goes outside to tend to their bird garden.

He fills up the bird baths and puts out seed. In the last two weeks, he notices the black-capped chickadees, the tufted titmice and the Carolina wrens are still with them for the upcoming winter months. When he walks into the great room, Lydia says, "They just gave the update on the California earthquakes. They died down instead of escalating."

Andy says, "Wow, that's good news. They got through that by the skin of their teeth."

Lydia says, "They know about six deaths and less than two million in property damage has been reported from San Francisco to Palm Springs."

Andy says, "It's possible that what we heard this morning could be a final warning for that area."

Lydia asks, "How would you like to take a peaceful break on Wednesday?

Andy replies, "What do you have in mind?"

Lydia says, "I checked the forecast for Wednesday. We should have clear skies. I thought we could go to the Smokies and do some bonding with Ann, Larry, Melissa, and possibly Davina. If you like the idea, we could ask them to meet us here about 9:30. We could stop at Sugarland and then go to Clingmans Dome or Alum Cave Bluff."

Andy says, "Good idea; that will be fun. We should probably go to Clingmans Dome after we leave the Sugarland Visitors Center. The walk to the Dome is uphill but moderate. Both ways, I think the walk is much less than a mile, and it's good for bird watching. On the way back we could stop at Alum Cave Bluff, if everyone wants to."

Lydia says, "Great! I will make the calls this evening, and let them know that you will be doing some bird watching on the walk to the Dome."

While Lydia talks with their friends, Andy catches up on some reading. Before they get ready for bed, Lydia says, "Everyone can make it, except

Davina; she has to sub. She said she's looking forward to being here Friday and Saturday. Larry said that he likes bird watching too. He said he would join you and bring his binoculars."

Andy says excitedly, "We'll have a good time! I'm looking forward to it."

Off and on Monday night and Tuesday, Lydia and Andy plan for their meetings on Friday and Saturday. Tuesday goes by quickly and before they know it, they are up on Wednesday morning getting ready for the trip to the Smokies.

A little before 9:30, Larry and Melissa arrive. In a few minutes, Ann arrives. Larry says, "We appreciate going with you on this outing."

Melissa says, "Absolutely, we don't take enough time to go to the Smokies and other beautiful places like the Blue Ridge Parkway".

The five friends get in Lydia and Andy's SUV. After they pull out Andy says, "I need to stop at the Sugarland Visitors Center to get a new Life List for my bird watching."

Larry replies, "That's a good idea. I want to write down what we see today."

In very little time, they drive through the edge of Gatlinburg and arrive at the Visitors Center in the Smoky Mountains. Everyone goes into the visitor's center. Three of them get bottled water, and Andy and Larry get their Life Lists.

When they park at Clingmans Dome, Andy says, "Larry and I will be lagging behind. At one point we will get off the walk to see more birds along the edge of the woods and the clearing, We might get to the Dome about thirty minutes later than you."

Lydia says, "That's fine. Is everyone okay with the steep walk to the Dome?"

Ann says, "We're old, but not that old!" Everyone laughs.

They grab their water bottles, and Andy puts a pair of binoculars around his neck. Everyone wears caps to keep the sun out of their eyes. Larry also sports his binoculars.

Melissa says, "This is great. It's cooler here. How high are we?"

Andy says, "Ove 6,000 feet."

Ann, Melissa and Lydia walk ahead of Larry and Andy.

After walking uphill for over five minutes, Larry and Andy get off the walk to sight more birds. They hear the lady's conversation and laughter getting fainter, as they walk closer to the woods. About ten yards from the woods, they see several black-capped chickadees flying in and out of the tree line. When they get close to the trees, they spot a red breasted nut hatch climbing on a tree trunk about fifteen feet off the ground. They learned years ago to stand still, so the birds don't fly off. In a few minutes, they see one of the cutest birds in the park, the little, winter wren. Andy says, "We have about fifteen minutes before we get back on the walk to join our gang."

Larry says, "It will be a good bird outing, if we could just spot another species."

Before they get back on the walk to the Dome, they see a Canada Warbler and a Dark Eyed Junco at the tree line. Larry says, "A great session! I remember the five types, but I haven't written them down."

Andy says, "I abbreviated the sequence. At the Dome, we can enter them in our Life Lists."

Before Andy and Larry arrive at the Dome, the three ladies are enjoying the views with and without the Park's binoculars. Melissa says, "All of these panoramic views are breathtaking!"

Lydia says, "We're looking at the states of Tennessee, North Carolina, Georgia, South Carolina, Alabama, Virginia and Kentucky!"

Melissa says, "It's almost unbelievable."

Ann is just finishing looking through the binoculars near the walkway. Andy and Larry quietly come up the walk. Ann's back is to them, so Andy sneaks up behind his cousin; touches her on the shoulder, and says with a loud voice, "Can I help you, Ma'am?"

She lets out a squeal, looks behind her and says, "Oh, Andy. You scared the living day lights out of me!"

Lydia hears the commotion and says, "I think they're back."

Larry and Andy with his arm around Ann's shoulder walk toward Lydia and Melissa, and Andy says, "Look who we found walking too close to the cliff."

Lydia laughs and says, "Maybe she needs a paddling". By this time, Ann is getting embarrassed and she says, "Oh, cut it out, guys."

Melissa asks, "How did you do with the bird watching?"

Larry says, "We found five species, and we need to write them in our Life Lists before we enjoy the views here."

They stay at the Dome for a while to take in the views. Melissa takes more pictures. She says, "It's almost like I can't get enough of the beauty from this vantage point."

Andy looks at his watch, he asks, "Do you want to do some hiking at Alum Cave?"

Lydia says, "Why don't we stop there, and maybe do a quarter or half mile into the trail then come back."

Ann says, "That sounds good. By the time we get to your house, it might be 2:30 or 3:00."

Andy says, "Okey-dokey. If you want hoagies for a late lunch, we can pull into the drive through at the hoagie shop, which is just inside Cosby."

Everyone says in unison, "Okey-dokey."

They walk downhill and enjoy the scenery to the parking lot. As they get to a lower elevation, Melissa says, "There's still a lot of color in the leaves. It's like heaven here."

Andy says, "It's hard to imagine, but heaven will have this beauty and more."

They find a parking space near Alum Cave Bluff Trail, and everyone takes their water bottles. Andy says, "The first part of the trail is a very gradual incline. No one brought their walking sticks, and we don't need them during the first half mile of the trail." At times they walk in pairs and most of the time they walk single file. Not long after they start out on the trailhead, they come to an alluring creek. It's wide and rocky and has rapid flowing water. Melissa stops to take a picture.

She says, "This is definitely God's country. The woods here are absolutely enchanting."

After they walk about ten minutes they get to a steeper incline. Andy says, "This might be a good place to turn around."

Larry says, "My stomach says that it is!"

When they return to the parking lot, everyone looks a little haggard. Andy says, "I think we're beginning to wear down a little. We're a little overdue for lunch."

It's about 2:00, when they pull into the hoagie shop drive through. Larry and Andy each order a foot long and Melissa, Ann and Lydia each order a six inch hoagie. Everyone decides on a medium drink. Before they get to the window, Andy says, "I'll get the food."

Larry replies, "Oh, no; it's on me. It's my turn; I insist."

Andy says, "Thanks, brother. You won't get an argument from me."

The cashier at the window says, "That will be $119.60."

Andy asks, "Are you sure the order is right?" She repeats the order.

Larry pays the tab and Andy says, "A couple of months ago, it would have been half that amount."

Larry says, "No problem; we can afford it."

Lydia says, "Thank you, Larry. It's sad that many people can't afford it."

On their way back to Lydia and Andy's home, Ann, Melissa and Larry express how much they enjoyed the day and how pleasant it was to be in the Smokies. Larry says, "We're looking forward to the meeting Saturday. Do you know when you could tell Anderson's story at First Baptist in Jefferson City?"

Andy replies, "Why don't you ask the pastor, if there is an opening one Sunday morning in the next two months. We will be talking about media contacts and dates Saturday. If you know then, we'll book it."

Larry says, "Excellent! I will talk with Aaron Michaels to make sure he can come. He's hoping his wife will come with him. With the church being on the Carson-Newman campus, I'm sure there will be standing room only."

They pull into their driveway. Larry and Melissa leave first. Before Ann gets in her car, she says, "I'm glad we can be here Friday evening with Davina and Kenny. As you know, Anderson was Kenny's best friend. Like the rest of us, Kenny misses Anderson a lot."

Andy says, "Yes, it's hard to take. I'm not use to him being gone either. When we moved here, we thought we would be near Anderson and Ruth."

Ann says, "Yes, I miss Ruth a lot too. It wasn't long after Ruth passed on that Anderson disappeared."

Lydia says, "I know." She gives Ann a big hug and walks with her to her car.

When Lydia comes in the house, Andy says, "It's sad yet joyful to remember Anderson."

Lydia says, "Yes, he was a light on the path."

Andy continues, "Even though we got melancholy after our outing, it was refreshing being with friends in the Smoky Mountains"

Lydia says, "No pun intended but going to the Smokies and Clingmans Dome was top of the world."

Andy says, "Having that kind of break was a great idea before our meetings Friday and Saturday."

Lydia replies, "Yes, we have a lot of important things to go over, but God wants us to have joy in what we do."

Andy smiles and says, "Why was I so fortunate in finding such a good wife?"

Lydia laughs and says, "You went to Purdue!"

Andy says, "Friday and Saturday are almost here. Are we ready to lead the meetings?"

Lydia replies, "I think we are. We've gone over media and church contacts."

Andy says, "Yes, and I think we have some good scriptures to share. I'm glad Larry reminded me about going to the church at Carson-Newman. I hope his friend, Aaron, can get his wife to come to that service."

Lydia says, "Yes, it's difficult, when one spouse follows the Lord and the other one doesn't."

Andy says, "I wouldn't want to be in that situation. Let's make it a whole day of enjoyment. We had a late lunch, so in a couple hours how about cheese and crackers and hot tea?'

Lydia says. "Sounds good. I might also make some popcorn."

Andy replies, "That would be great with a movie. I will surf the channels and go through some of our DVDs and VHS movies."

Lydia says, "A good comedy like "Grumpy Old Men" or "Ground Hog Day" would be nice."

Andy replies, "Good idea. I'll try to find "Grumpy Old Men" or "Grumpier Old Men".

Lydia says, "I think I will go ahead and make some tea. Do you want a cup now?"

Andy says, "Yes, black tea sounds good for a change."

After they have a light supper, Andy puts the "Grumpy Old Men" DVD in their player. They laugh and talk through the whole movie. Lydia says, "Lemmon and Matthau were perfect for these two characters"

The movie ends by 8:00. Andy gets up and says, "Wow, that movie is a barrel of laughs."

Lydia gets up and asks, "Do you want to get ready for bed early?"

Andy smiles at her and says, "I was thinking the same thing." He puts his arm around her and says, "This is like old times."

The next day flies by and the McGraigs spend the end of the day making sure they're ready for Friday's and Saturday's events.

On Friday, Kenny arrives at 3:30 and Ann arrives a couple of minutes later.

Lydia greets them, "Welcome! Good to see you, Kenny."

Kenny says, "It has been too long, since I've seen you and Andy."

Lydia replies, "I agree," as Ann comes walking in. She continues, "Well, look who is right behind you."

Ann says, "Kenny, it's great seeing you." She hugs Kenny and Lydia.

Lydia says, "We have a variety of pizza arriving by 5:00. Davina and Angela should be here by 5:15. Until then, we can visit and get settled at the dining table. We have strawberries and yogurt and chips and dip to snack on."

Ann says, "I love your long table. Does it seat eight?"

Lydia replies, "Yes. We'll have six here this evening and tomorrow we'll have eight."

Kenny asks, "Can I make coffee for us?"

Lydia says, "I use the Keurig. What kind do you want?"

Kenny replies, "Mild roast would be great!"

Andy comes in the back door, and as always brings a big presence with him. In a booming voice, he says, "Kenny, it's so good to see you!"

Kenny says, "Likewise, my friend." Andy shakes his hand.

Andy says, "I just finished taking care of the birds."

Kenny says, "Aww, Anderson loved birds. Many times on our hikes, we would stop and watch the birds. Based on his love of nature, he was like my Cherokee people."

Andy replies, "Yes, that was one of the things that Anderson and I have in common."

Lydia says, "Have a seat at the table. Andy and I also have sugar free cookies that we will add to our country menu this evening."

Andy, Kenny, Lydia and Ann have such a good time talking that when they hear a knock at the door, they don't realize that it is 5:00 already. Andy gets up to see if the pizza is here."

Lydia says, "Davina just sent me a message. She says Angela and she will be here in a few minutes."

Andy comes back in the room with three large pizza boxes. When he opens the lid, Kenny says, "You did get a good variety and my favorite, meat lovers."

The four friends sit down at the dining table, and Andy asks Kenny to pray.

Kenny prays, "Our Father, we thank you for all blessings. We thank you for our hosts and ask you to bless this home. Thank you for our good friends, and thank you for the food. Guide us in this meeting by your spirit. In Jesus' name. Amen."

Just as Lydia says, "Dig in", Davina and Angela walk in. Everyone hugs them, and the six friends sit down to enjoy the food and company.

After a few minutes, Lydia says, "We will start the meeting in a minute or two. Get any drinks you want. You are welcome to eat during the meeting."

After everyone gets settled, Lydia continues, "Andy asked me to chair the meetings tonight and tomorrow. We will be taking questions and having discussions at your request. We want your input about contacts you can make with churches, media and any other resource." Lydia looks at Andy; smiles and nods her head.

Andy says, "It's wonderful having every one of you here. Angela came from Indiana on short notice. Angela, as Anderson's daughter and closest relative, we look at you as our honored guest. Anderson also visited Kenny, his best friend, and Ann, his sister. It is a great privilege that the three of you are here. Angela, would you share something about your dad, his visitation, or anything that is on your mind."

Angela says, "I'm honored and humbled to be here. I was an unbeliever, but because of God's grace, dad and his visitation, I am now a follower of Christ. Like you, I know that the world, as we know it, is coming to an end. I also know the rapture and great tribulation are imminent. It's a blessing to be with you this evening and tomorrow."

Angela's words touch them. They applaud and say, "Amen".

Angela says, "I want to add that as a family member, Andy is very special to me; he grew up with my dad."

Andy says, "Thank you for those kind words. We love you. Lydia and I have discussed the importance of each of us using our professional and personal contacts to share Anderson's story. Of course, Ann, Kenny and Angela have great testimonies, since they were visited by Anderson. Angela also has her contacts at the University of Indianapolis and her other psychology contacts. Lydia has contacts in public education. Kenny is a Marine Veteran, a retired State Trooper and a member of the Eastern Band of the Cherokees. His contacts include many people in the Cherokee and Maggie Valley areas. Larry and Melissa will be here tomorrow. Larry and I have contacts at Purdue and in the NCAA. Larry also has NBA contacts and contacts from coaching in college.

We're in a critical time. We know the rapture will take place soon, then the world will fall into the Great Tribulation. When Larry and Melissa are here tomorrow, we will look at some scriptures that are about the rapture. From scripture and from Anderson's visits, we know that it is critical to reach as many people as possible as quickly as we can. Let's stop for any questions or comments you have."

Kenny says, "I'm confident that we all agree on the message and the urgency. I know that I need to focus more on my contacts. I'm sure that the first step is to start a contact list. I'm sure some of you have been much more active than I have in getting out the message. Asheville, Chattanooga and Charlotte are major media outlets in my general area. I'm sure that we can plan areas where I can call. One more thing; I would like to go with you to a couple of presentations. The experience will help me prepare."

Andy replies, "Excellent comments. Kenny, Larry may have a date tomorrow for one of Jefferson City's bigger churches. You can go with us, and with the pastor's permission, I would like for you to tell about Anderson's visitation. Your other comments pertain exactly to why we're meeting this weekend. We want everyone to be thinking about planning and doing what you just covered."

Almost everyone has comments and constructive input. Andy adds, "This week Lydia and I talked about how the mainstream media stations have become a propaganda machine for the New Age Socialist Party. Anything related to politics is fabricated in favor of the socialists and against the Traditional American Party. If a traditionalist politician is on the family farm milking a cow, the news media would report that the traditionalist is milking funds in favor the Traditional American Party. Even though the media is highly biased, we decided to get the word to their home offices that Andy, former Secretary of State, would like to tell his cousin's story; a story that has happened to others throughout the nation and throughout the world."

Angela says, "I think that is an excellent effort. The field of psychology has become very radical. I use to be one of them. You are inspiring me to take dad's story to functions in my own field."

Ann says, "I think we can all challenge ourselves. Like Davina and Lydia, I was in public education. We not only have comfortable contacts, but I imagine that every one of us has challenging contacts we could make."

Kenny says, "We can all take a stand. I can do more to share the gospel with Anderson's story. I can also do more to stand for freedom in America. Our country was not founded on socialism, and we did not fight for socialism."

Andy says, "This first part of our meeting has been very productive. It's after 7:00. Let's take a coffee break, then start again at 7:30. We will try to wrap up tonight's meeting before 9:00. If you want to clean-up before bed, we have two showers, two tubs and two and a half bathrooms."

Lydia says, "About 9:00, I will show Davina and Angela their room and Ann her room. Andy will show Kenny his room."

Just before 7:30 they sit back down with their drinks. Lydia says, "I hope everyone is enjoying our gathering so far. This is the last leg of our

Friday meeting. Our Saturday meeting starts after brunch in the morning. Larry and Melissa will be here by 10:30, and I will serve breakfast burritos at 10:30. If you are an early riser, you can use the Keurig to make coffee or heat water for tea in the microwave. If you get hungry early, there are cereal and granola bars in the pantry. Tea bags and the coffee are in the same area. You will find milk in the fridge. I believe Andy still has something to share. Before he begins, does anyone have a comment or question?"

Angela in an empathetic tone says, "First of all, Lydia, you and Andy have been wonderful and great hosts. I have a comment about Andy's decision to reach out to national media. We don't expect Andy and Larry to do most of the work, because they have been in the national eye. People remember Andy and Larry from the NCAA championship team. They also remember Larry from years in the NBA. Many people remember Andy as the former Secretary of State. Because of their status, they can reach the most people, but every one of us must do as much as we can. Personal, community and regional contacts are just as important, including local radio and TV stations. I would like to know, if everyone here believes they can reach out to local media, churches and other organizations."

Lydia says, "Thank you, Angela; excellent points. Before we hear from Andy, do you want to reply to Angela's comments?"

Ann says, "Yes, she is right that we need to reach everyone we can. If a group or organization has people, reach out to them. It could be Kiwanis, Rotary Club, BNI or any other group. I have helped the C.A.R.E. Animal Shelter for years. We have monthly meetings, and I need to share with them and with any person or any group."

Kenny says, "Amen to that. I need to reach my neighbors and friends. I'm active with the Eastern Band of Cherokees, and I need to speak with them as a group and individually. I need to act on my thoughts about certain radio and TV stations in my general area. I need to call more churches in my area."

Davina says, "So far, I've been the quiet one this evening, but just see me in action in the classroom!" Everyone laughs. Davina gets more serious and says, "I'm guilty of being captive to my own routine. I need to break out of my shell, because I also believe the Lord is coming soon. My convictions and response are the same as Ann's and Kenny's. I need to look for every potential person and group that will listen to Anderson's story."

Lydia says, "That's unanimous! Andy and I feel the same way. We are a core group. Each of us need to encourage others, who have like passions. What we have just shared, we need to pass it on to our larger group of workers. By doing this, we multiply our efforts. We should get back to Andy now."

Andy smiles and says, "What wonderful comments and convictions! Your input excites me and gives me that extra drive I need. We have plenty of time for discussion before the 9:00 hour rolls around. I don't have a lot more to share this evening. What I'm going to share now helps give us a solid foundation for our convictions. Many believers know we're in the end time, and many believers understand that the rapture of the church will occur immediately before the Great Tribulation. I think most of us fall short of a having a working knowledge of where these facts are in the scriptures.

After brunch tomorrow, I will open with the scriptures that we need to support the signs of the end time; the Rapture and the Great Tribulation. We should become familiar with these scriptures, and we should also realize the impact of witnesses like Anderson, who God has given to us. When I share the scriptures tomorrow, I will also share the gospel recording of other witnesses that God gave the world, when Christ was crucified."

Lydia opens the floor to comments and discussion. Every one appears to be satisfied with the outcome of the meeting. Lydia says, "It looks like we're beginning to quiet down, so if everyone is in agreement, we will adjourn our meeting until after brunch tomorrow."

Lydia closes the meeting. The six friends having plenty of time to get ready for bed. It's a few minutes after 8:30, when they get up from the table. Davina, Ann and Angela have their own pow wow, while Lydia and Andy visit with Kenny.

By 10:00 Lydia and Andy and their guests are in their own rooms and lights out.

Everyone is up by 8 a.m. They come out to the great room in a mixed bag of robes, sweaters and jackets. Andy starts laughing. He says, "Overlook my laughter. We're not use to it getting that cool at night in October. I'm going to start the gas fireplace now. It will feel even better than starting the furnace."

Lydia says, "We have two hours before I start brunch. Why don't I make a pot of coffee, then you can raid the kitchen for cereal, granola bars, fruit or anything else you want."

When everyone has a seat in the great room, they do look funny in their different warm clothes. Andy says, "After coffee or tea and any food you want, you're welcome to take a shower, if you didn't have one last night."

Lydia comes in the room and says, "The coffee is ready. If you want hot tea or food help yourself. I put out table service on the counter top."

No one takes a shower right away. They take their time visiting and catching up on each other's stories. In about an hour they go to their rooms and bathrooms to clean up and dress.

About thirty minutes before brunch time, Lydia sets the dining table and gets everything else ready, so she can take the homemade breakfast burritos out of the freezer one at a time.

Larry and Melissa arrive a few minutes early, and everyone gets seated around the long, oval meeting table. Lydia says, "Andy is going to serve you coffee or hot tea, while I take your breakfast burrito order one at a time. They don't take long to heat up, so we'll have everyone served soon. Let's go ahead and pray, and when you get your burrito, you can go ahead and eat." Lydia asks Andy to pray.

After prayer, Lydia announces that they have their choice of egg, egg and cheese, bacon and egg or ham and egg. Everyone is laughing and talking while Lydia and Andy serve them. Larry says, "Lydia, these are the best breakfast burritos I've had, and I'm not blowing smoke!"

Melissa adds, "They certainly are. You and Andy are great hosts. We want you to come over some time."

Lydia says, "Definitely. We will be getting together a lot in the near future. Wait until you hear what we have planned."

Melissa says, "We're anxious to find out."

Andy, Kenny and Larry take seconds on the burritos. After brunch Lydia asks Davina and Angela to help her clear the table. Andy makes sure everyone has a notebook and pen.

"While we get ready for our meeting, I'm going to ask Davina and Angela to get any refills you want on coffee or tea. Lydia is our chair person, so I'm going to ask her to start the meeting after the ladies bring the refills."

Lydia opens the meeting and asks Larry to pray.

Lydia welcomes everyone and thanks them for a productive meeting yesterday. She turns the meeting over to Andy.

Andy thanks Larry for a prayer of spiritual guidance during the meeting. Andy says, "By God's Spirit, we believe God will guide us to say the right things and to plan the right things. There is an urgent need for the gospel and Anderson's story in these troublesome times. Scriptures I'm going to share will give us added knowledge of the signs of the end time; the Rapture and the Great Tribulation. I will also share some scriptures that will give us confidence in communicating the gospel. Before we begin our study, I want to share two things. Larry and I will be leaving in about two hours to take Angela to the Knoxville Airport. On our way there, we will have our own meeting, and we will share our plans from yesterday with Larry. While we're gone, you will have plenty of time to share the same thing with Melissa. You also will have plenty of time for any discussion. You are welcome to stay and visit. It might be 4:00 or a little later before we return."

Lydia says, "Excuse me, Andy. I just want to mention that when we take a break about 1:00 and then adjourn around 3:00, we have plenty of leftover pizza and burritos. We also have soda and flavored water."

Andy says, "Thank you. Does everyone have a Bible?" Three raise their hands and say they don't have a Bible with them. Andy says, "No problem. We have several Bibles; they're King James and NIV." Lydia gets the Bibles and passes them out.

Andy continues, "It looks like we're all set to begin. How many have a King James?" Four hands go up. "Do the rest of you have a NIV?" Three answer in the affirmative and Andy says, "I also have a NIV, so that makes it four and four. We mainly want to write down the scripture and the topic. I will give you the book, chapter and verse. You can easily reference it."

"God's Word tells us to be prepared and to correctly handle the word of truth, which is found in 2 Timothy 2:15. Any quotes or paraphrases I take from the Bible today will be from the NIV. We will end the study with scriptures about how to communicate the gospel. The first part of our study will be scriptures about the signs of the end. The second part will be scriptures about the Rapture, and then we'll look at the Great Tribulation. Many books of the Bible address signs of the end time, including Daniel, Joel, Matthew, Luke, 2 Timothy and Revelation. Matthew 24 tells us there will be more wars, pestilence, famine and earthquakes. You can reference Matthew 24: 7 and Luke 21: 11. There are a lot of scriptures about the signs of the end, but let's look at one more from Revelation 6: 5-7. It indicates how bad famine and plagues get by the beginning of the Great Tribulation. In Revelation 6: 7, the pale horse and its rider bring famine and plague to the earth. The rider of the horse is named "Death".

Today over 800 million people go to bed hungry every night. It is getting worse by the day.

In our country, it is one problem and disaster after another; earthquakes, terrorism, high inflation, disregard for the Word of God and the church, arson, murder and general insurgency."

Kenny says, "I have a question. In Revelation does the Great Tribulation begin in chapter 6? Are you saying that pestilence and famine increase as we get closer to the great tribulation?"

Anderson replies, "Good questions, Kenny. The answer is "yes" to both questions. In Revelation, the Great Tribulation is covered between chapters 6 and 19. Famine and pestilence is much worse during the Great Tribulation, and it's getting worse now. We could spend several hours on signs of the end scriptures, but we don't have that much time. Also, note 2 Timothy 3: 1. It talks about the degrading attitude of mankind and society in the last days.

Let's move on to scriptures about the rapture, so we don't run out of time. We want time for discussion and for your questions. Are there any comments before we look at the rapture?

Everyone is quiet, so Andy continues with the Rapture.

Andy says, "The most recognized verses about the Rapture are 1 Thessalonians 4: 16 and 17. The two verses written by the Apostle Paul say that the Lord himself will come down from heaven. With a loud command, the dead in Christ will rise first. The followers of Christ, who are alive and remain, will also be caught up in the air to meet the Lord. We will be with the Lord forever.

Some believers think that Matthew 24: 40-41 is about the Rapture and some don't. The way The verse reads, it certainly sounds like the Rapture. Verse 40 simply says that two men will be in the field; one will be taken and the other will be left. Verse 41 is similar. It says that two women will be grinding at the mill; one will be taken and the other will be left. Are there any comments or questions?"

Ann says, "The "day of the Lord will come like a thief in the night." (1Thessalonians 5: 2 NIV) These scriptures sound like a surprise. I understand that Jesus said only the Father knows the day and the hour. Does that mean that we could know the year or that the Rapture is very close?"

Andy replies, "A very good comment." Your scriptural understanding is good. Yes, I think many believers feel the Rapture could happen within a year or a few years. To be fair, we also need to remember that the Apostle Peter wrote that to God a thousand years is like a day and that a day is like a thousand years. When it does happen, it will turn society and the global economy upside down.

Before we go on to tribulation scriptures, I want to share two scripture that take us immediately from the Rapture into the Great Tribulation. These are concrete scriptures that tell us the church will be spared the tribulation. The two pre-tribulation verses are in Revelation and 2 Peter. Let's start with Revelation 3: 10. Again, all of the scriptures I quote or paraphrase are from the NIV. God tells the Apostle John and the church (those following Christ), "Since you have kept my command to endure patiently, I will also keep you from the hour of trial that is going to come on the whole world to test the inhabitants of the earth."

Andy continues, "Before I take questions or comments, let me quote the other pre-tribulation scripture. It is from 2 Peter 2: 9, "the Lord knows how to rescue the godly from trials and to hold the unrighteous for punishment on the day of judgment." The church is not mentioned during the tribulation, which is more evidence of a pre-tribulation rapture. Well, we better move on and take any questions before we get into the tribulation references.

Angela says, "I was guilty, like many psychology professors, of not believing. Unfortunately, the university culture is caught up in humanism. I was blind and did not see how wrong pro-choice is. Now that I follow Christ, I am embarrassed to even say that I voted for politicians who supported abortion. I am very strong about pro-life now. Do you believe that our country is being judged for the millions of babies they have killed?"

Andy says, "I have no doubt that our country is being judged. The New Age Socialist Party is out of control. We are still not out of a pandemic, yet they allow illegal aliens to flow into the country. They don't believe in freedom of speech. They give you a pass, if you believe like them,

Their media allies do the same. We don't hear factual reporting from them. They want complete control. Most universities have also become intolerant to other views.

Hitler and his Nazis murdered six million Jews and murdered another eleven million people.

In the past fifty years, the New Age Socialist Party, their supporters and abortionists have murdered seventy million babies; over six times as many people that Hitler and his supporters murdered. It is easy to understand why followers of Christ, who believe God's Word, know that God is judging our country.

I would like to just mention something from Daniel 2. Historically, many Biblical teachers taught that the interpretation of Nebuchadnezzar's dream included the Greek Empire. My comment on this is not important to our mission, but I believe the Greek Empire is not part of the statue in his dream. Alexander the Great led a vast empire for a few years, then he was killed in his early thirties. His short-lived kingdom was divided among his four generals. Great Britain had the biggest worldwide empire in history. For centuries, they controlled many colonies and countries like America. I believe the iron legs of the statue represent Great Britain. There is one world power left in the statue; the feet mixed with iron and clay. From Great Britain, we have the English language and many other traits, including the structure of our government and economy. We are a mixture of Great Britain (iron) and everything else (clay). In Daniel 2, it says this country of iron and clay will never be united again. Let's not stop and spend our time with Daniel 2. I mention it, because I believe it helps answer why our country is splitting at the seams."

Kenny says, "I have not heard that explanation before, but it makes perfect sense to me. I know we have an important mission to fill, but there are times we need to share."

Andy replies, "Thank you, Kenny. I am not going to spend much time with the tribulation, since the church, the bride of Christ, will be with the Lord. Before I continue, are there any more comments or questions."

Melissa says, "I just want to say that this scriptural information is very helpful to what we are doing. I encourage everyone to review these scriptures. I believe we need a working knowledge, so we can be the most effective messengers possible."

Andy says, "Thank you, Melissa. You're absolutely right.

Right now we can't go into detail about the Great Tribulation. It is a time of God's judgment upon the earth. It is a terrible time of death and destruction. Again, if you want to know details about the tribulation, read Revelation 6-19. The tribulation lasts seven years, then Christ and His followers are victorious at the War of Armageddon. The Second Coming is when Jesus appears at Armageddon and defeats His enemies. The next thousand years is peace on earth, when Jesus Christ with His followers reign on earth. After the millennium, God judges the saved and unsaved. Christ called them the sheep and the goats. Satan, his demons and the unsaved are thrown into the Lake of Fire; not a pretty picture. At last, is the new heaven and the new earth. Revelation 21 and 22 are the most beautiful passages I have ever read.

If we don't stop now, we can finish by our 1:00 break. We will still have time to take your comments and questions after we look at the scriptures that help us communicate the gospel. These same scriptures will also help us share Anderson's story. Sometimes the good news, the message of God's love, includes confronting people about their problem. Jesus confronted the Pharisees. He even called them vipers and hypocrites. The Apostles Paul and Peter would confront people. Even though Christ, Paul, Peter and others would confront people, they would follow their statements with a message of God's love and grace. In 1 Peter 3: 15 the apostle tells us to always be ready to share the hope we have. Peter says to share the good news with kindness and respect.

In Matthew 10: 16 Jesus said, "I am sending you out like sheep among wolves. Therefore be as shrewd as snakes and as innocent as doves." Christ also tells us to not worry about what we are going to say, when we share the gospel. He promises that God's spirit will give us the right thing to say. I want to give us a chance to make comments and ask questions. To stay on schedule, let's start taking comments now."

Larry says, "This is very helpful instruction on how to share the gospel. The Bible also encourages us to be quick to listen and slow to speak. We definitely need to be in a spirit of prayer when we share the good news, including our testimonies and Anderson's story."

Andy smiles and says, "Thank you, Larry. Your comments have put icing on the cake. I'm confident that everyone here is ready to share Anderson's story and the coming of Christ for the church."

Kenny says, "I agree. Everyone needs to pray and study scriptures before any presentation. When our witness is impromptu, God will give us the right thing to say."

Andy says, "If there are no more comments or questions, I'm going to turn the meeting over to Lydia, since it's almost time for our break."

Lydia says, "What a productive meeting today! I appreciate all of you participating. Thank you, Andy, for leading us in this study. After this break, we will have roughly 90 minutes before we adjourn the meeting at 3:00. It you want to stay awhile after 3:00, make yourself at home. We will also have food and drinks available after 3:00.

They start visiting with each other before they find their way to the kitchen. Larry comes up to Andy and says, "We have thirty minutes on the third Sunday in November at First Baptist in Jefferson City on the Carson-Newman campus."

Andy says, "That's great! Let's go over and share the news with Kenny. He wants some experience with sharing Anderson's visit, and I think it would be wonderful to have his first hand account."

Larry says, "Before we tell him, what do you think about you taking fifteen minutes and Kenny and I splitting the other fifteen minutes. They already know me, so I think we should give Kenny ten minutes."

Andy replies, "I think that would be perfect; let's go tell him."

Larry and Andy give Kenny the information, and he's delighted. Andy says to Kenny, "We'll meet Larry and Melissa at the church. Could you be here about 9:15 that morning, and we'll leave for the church shortly after that?"

Kenny says, "No problem. I'm looking forward to it."

Larry says, "After church, Melissa and I want to take the three of you out to dinner."

Kenny says, "Anderson, Andy and you are such good friends. I'm a blessed man."

Andy pats Kenny on the back and says, "So am I, my friend."

In a few minutes, everyone says goodbye to Angela, so Andy and Larry can take her to the airport.

As they travel to the McGhee-Tyson Airport, Andy says to Angela and Larry, "There is an important point that Lydia is going to share in the meeting this afternoon. I also want to share it with you. People who know the story of Lazarus and the rich man may say that Abraham wouldn't send Lazarus back to warn the rich man's brothers about hell. You may remember when the graves were opened after Christ died on the cross. Matthew 27: 52-53 records that graves were opened and many saints arose. They went into Jerusalem and appeared to many people. We know this happened when a significant event took place for the Kingdom of God; Christ's death and resurrection. If someone reminded me of Abraham's response, I would share that Anderson and people like him appeared, because God is preparing us for the rapture; another significant event in God's Kingdom."

Larry replies, "Well said."

Angela adds, "Yes, that's a very good point."

After they arrive at the Knoxville airport, Larry and Andy walk with Angela to the security line.

Before Angela gets in line, she hugs Andy and says, "It was wonderful being with you and Lydia." Angela looks at Larry and says, "I enjoyed being with you and your wife and everyone there."

Andy says, "I hate to see you go, but all of us have our work to do."

Larry says, "Take care of yourself, and keep lookin' up!"

Andy and Larry wait near the security line until Angela disappears into the sea of passengers.

When they return to the parking lot, it's almost 3:00. Andy says, "I hope we still get to say good bye to most of our friends.

In less than an hour they walk into the house and everyone is straightening up the kitchen and getting ready to leave. Andy and Larry have some coffee, and Melissa says to Larry, "Angela packed some food for us and for Kenny."

Larry says to Andy and Lydia, "You are just too good!"

Everyone says their good byes. Andy says, "Kenny, I'm looking forward to seeing you soon. Have a safe trip and stay in touch."

Kenny says, "Thank you for everything, my friend."

Lydia and Andy walk outside with their guests and wave as they pull out of their driveway. As they walk back in their house, Andy says, "What a wonderful time and good meeting."

Lydia says, "Everything went well. It was enjoyable and peaceful."

Scenic view from Alum Cave Bluff

7

Chaos on the Homefront

Before church, Andy catches up on the weekend news with the Sunday morning newspaper. He just finished devotions and a cup of hot green tea, while Lydia is still sleeping. He starts to read some grim news, but he's not going to bother Lydia, since she's in bed. He sees that the inflation rate is much higher than it was in 2008. The article says the 2008 inflation rate was 4%. The average rate after 2008 was 2.44%. It says that after the New Age Socialist Party started running the country, the rate has continually increased and is now a whopping 7.66%. In the same article Andy reads the average price of gas in the country is $6.59 gallon. The independent journalist says that some media outlets and New Age supporters are having second thoughts about who was put in charge of the government. The journalist ends the article with the words, "I would think so!"

The next article really gets Andy up in arms. It says that a college and high school in Brownsville, Texas, were attacked by terrorists an hour before classes were let out on Friday. The terrorists detonated a bomb at each school and fired automatic weapons into crowded hallways and full classrooms. Investigators said that seven or eight terrorists were at each school, and it looks like all of them escaped into Mexico through the Rio Grande. So far, the college reports ninety-four killed and one hundred and thirty wounded. The high school has accounted for one hundred and fifteen killed and one hundred and forty-six wounded. From videos, one terrorist was identified as a convicted terrorist that was let out of prison by the New Age Socialist administration. Another terrorist was identified as an illegal alien on parole. The other terrorists are thought to be members of the Mexican Drug Cartel and illegal aliens. In 2021 the New Age Socialist President stopped the building of the border wall before contractors got to Brownsville.

Andy is so shook up and disheartened that he gets up and makes some coffee to try to get through the rest of the news section. In about three minutes he sits back down with the paper. He can't believe what he reads next. Over the weekend there were seven major earthquakes that measured from 5.5 to 7.6 on the Richter Scale. They were in Chile, Malaysia, Japan, Turkey, New Delhi, Buenos Aires and near St. Louis. The lowest reading occurred near St. Louis. The article says that over 1,800 hundred died from the seven earthquakes.

The next article says, "U.S. Pandemic Cases on the Rise". Andy reads that the southern border states have had over 100% increase in pandemic deaths, since the New Age Socialist Party has allowed illegal aliens to flow into the country. Nationwide the increase in deaths have gone from 21,000 pandemic deaths per month to 50,000 deaths per month. The report says that in the past month the Speaker of the House and six leading Hollywood actors and actresses have died from the pandemic.

Andy is thinking, "Is there any end to this madness?" He's glad that Lydia will be up soon, so he can lay the paper down. The next news article he reads is about the number of arsons and looting over the weekend. It says that the major cities hit by many arsonists and looters are run by New Age Socialists. Every major city that has incurred this devastation has cut funds for law enforcement. Many officers have retired or sought other employment. It reports that New York City, Chicago, Brooklyn, Los Angeles, Portland, Seattle and Minneapolis have had a combine loss of twenty-four billion dollars from property damage. The end of the article reports that less than ten per cent of the looters and arsonists were arrested, and most of those were released after their court dates were set.

Just as Andy finishes the article. A sleepy Lydia walks into the room and says, "Good morning, honey."

Andy puts the paper down and slowly says, "Good morning."

Lydia asks, "Is something wrong?"

Andy says, "Yes, all the dire news I read about from just this weekend."

Lydia says, "It sounds bad."

Andy replies, "It's unbelievably bad: the staggering increase in inflation; terrorism and many deaths at two schools in Texas; earthquakes throughout the world that killed almost two thousand people; a big increase in pandemic deaths and a huge loss of property in seven major U.S. cities."

Lydia says, "That is dreadful."

Andy says, "It was so upsetting that I was hoping you would walk into the room, so I could stop reading the bad news. First thing tomorrow I will start reaching out to national media. When I was Secretary of State, I got to know a freshman Congressman from Southern California, Jimmy Eastman. He's still in Congress. Even when he started out in Congress, it appeared that he had a lot of contacts. He might be my best source to find the right media contacts."

Lydia replies, "That would be just what we need, if he can put you in touch with the right people." Lydia's domestic instincts surface and she says, "Let's enjoy a good breakfast today. We have plenty of time to get ready for church."

Before and after church Lydia does her best to help keep the state of the nation off Andy's mind. After church, they have dinner at one of their favorite restaurants in Cosby. They go home and take an afternoon nap. Lydia is reading in the great room, when Andy gets up. He says, "I want to touch base with Larry, the Rivera's and Officer Walling. I think I will call Larry and the Rivera's this afternoon. When I call Officer Walling, why don't I tell her that you and I want to take her out for lunch or dinner in Gatlinburg. I will let her know that we want to share some of our plans with her."

Lydia says, "That's a good idea. Maybe we could do it this week."

Andy replies, "I hope so. I want to have lunch or supper with Larry and Aaron Michaels as soon as possible. Larry is going to invite Aaron and his wife to our service at First Baptist in Jefferson City. I think I will call Larry now."

Andy calls Larry and finds out that Larry will call Aaron right away. Larry says, "Since it's Sunday, he might be home. I'm on his quick dial, so he might pick up right away."

In about thirty minutes, Andy's cell phone rings. Larry says, "It's a go! Aaron said he only has classes in the morning on Tuesday. He said he could meet us for lunch at 1:00. He doesn't have basketball practice until 4:00 that day. I told him that Perkins by I40 and 92 in Dandridge might be good. It's closer than Jefferson City for you, and its close enough for us."

Andy says, "That will work. I'm writing it down now."

Larry says, "Aaron has been wanting to talk with you. He's a fan of your basketball and state department careers. He's very concerned about his wife not being a believer."

Andy says, "Let's spend some extra time praying for him and his wife before we meet him with him Tuesday."

Larry replies, "I will."

Andy says, "Tomorrow morning I will call an old friend in D.C. So far, he is the one person I can think of, who may have contacts with national media personnel."

Larry says, "I hope that works out. National media exposure will be a big help with what we're doing."

Andy says, "Your remember Office Walling in Gatlinburg who drove us back to the restaurant?"

Larry says, "Absolutely!"

Andy continues, "I'm calling her to see if she can meet Lydia and me for a meal in Gatlinburg. Of course, we'll tell her about our outreach plans. I also need to get in touch with the Riviera's. I will probably call them today."

Larry says, "I feel good about our plans and activities."

Andy says, "So do I. I'm looking forward to meeting with you and Aaron on Tuesday."

Larry replies, "I know that Aaron is excited about meeting you. I hope his wife comes to church with him, when we speak in Jefferson City."

Andy says, "I will be praying for them."

Larry says, "I appreciate our friendship. I'm glad we ran into each other in Gatlinburg."

Andy replies, "Me too. Like Jackie Gleason use to say, "How sweet is!"

Larry laughs and says, "Have a good night, brother."

Andy hangs up and tells Lydia about his luncheon meeting with Larry and Aaron Michaels on Tuesday. He calls the Rivera's and has a nice conversation with Gus. He updates him on some of their plans. Andy says, "I want to go over some strategies with you in the next couple weeks."

Gus says, "You set the time and place, and I'll be there."

They say good night and Andy stretches back on the recliner in the great room. Lydia brings him a cup of coffee with cream. He says, "How did you know I was wanting some coffee?"

Lydia smiles and says, "I can read your mind." She starts reading in one of her favorite books, and Andy dozes for a while.

They call Davina and have a restful evening.

After Andy reads his devotional and Bible early in the morning, he makes coffee and fixes turkey bacon and English muffins with apple butter for their breakfast. During breakfast he says, "I'm going to shower, then call my Congressman friend, Jimmy Eastman, about 9:00."

Lydia says, "I will clean up the kitchen, then do some grocery shopping in Cosby."

Andy gets up from the table and goes over to Lydia. He says, "What time are you coming back from grocery shopping? I don't want anyone nabbing my beautiful woman."

Lydia says, "About 11:00." Andy kisses her on the cheek.

Lydia leaves for Cosby right before Andy calls his friend. Andy still has his cell phone number and dials it. He's surprised that Jimmy answers. Andy says, "Congressman Eastman, this is the Secretary of State."

His friend hesitates then it dawns on him, "Is this the old war horse that use to be Secretary of State?"

Andy laughs and asks, "How are you doing, Jimmy?"

"Just fine, Andy. It's good to hear from you. Did you call for a political favor?"

Andy laughs and says, "Yes, a favor, but not a political favor. But first, how is the family?"

Jimmy says, "Natalie is doing well. Trudy got in the new space program and Daniel is teaching at M.I.T. What about your family?"

Andy replies, "They're good, but first of all, I'm not surprised to hear great things about Trudy and Daniel; they have a smart dad. Lydia is doing well, and Davina retired from teaching after twenty-five years. Her husband is a successful engineer, and they're doing well. Just over a week ago I was in D.C. two and a half days doing some State Department work. I would have called, but it was a full schedule."

Jimmy says, "That's great news; the country still needs you."

Andy gets serious, "I want to be open about why I'm asking you a favor. Do you remember about six months ago, when the media ran reports of people coming back from death or a disappearance, and they were warning people to be ready for the Lord?"

Jimmy says, "Yes, I do."

Andy says, "It happened to my first cousin, who was a very successful business man in international marketing. He came back and visited his best friend, his daughter, and his sister, who is a good friend of ours."

Jimmy exclaims, "Wow! I didn't know that had happened to your family."

Andy explains, "We have family and friends; quite a few people, who are getting the message out. The biggest need we have is to get the word out by national media."

Jimmy thinks a few seconds, then says, "I can help with that. Your need is much bigger than mine, but I keep forgetting to ask a small favor of you. As you know, I'm not only a fan of your work as Secretary of State, but I'm a basketball fan. You probably remember me saying that on TV I saw you and your team win the national championship, when I was only ten years old. For years I've meant to ask for your autograph on something from Purdue, like an old schedule or game night program. If you don't have something old, anything will do."

Andy says, "I can probably find something old from Purdue, but I will make sure that it is a Purdue item that I autograph. I will get your mailing address before we hang up."

Jimmy says, "Thank you. I can think of a couple people off hand that could help you. Give me two days, and I will send their information to you. I will call them first to give them a heads up. I will get your email address, when I give you my mailing address. One man is a national talent agent, who owes me a favor. I think he will come through for you."

Andy says, "Thank you, Jimmy. There are many others who will appreciate your help."

The old friends visit a few more minutes and exchange addresses. When Andy gets off the phone, he thanks God for opening doors.

He thinks, "I'm looking forward to telling Lydia the good news. I will wait until something is scheduled before I tell the others about it." He decides to read the morning paper while Lydia is shopping. He looks at current news and looks for an update on the recent destruction in the seven major U.S. cities. In current news, an article talks about a recent surge in the pandemic. It says, "Before the recent surge, the pandemic has caused almost two million deaths in the United States. This month the pandemic deaths have increased from 50,000 to 68,000 with a few days remaining in October." Andy finishes the article, then finds an update on the seven cities where mass arson and looting were committed. The news article says, "So many expensive buildings were burned that adjusters now estimate the destruction to be over thirty billion dollars."

Andy feels like he just dozed off, when he hears the front screen door slam. Lydia is bringing groceries in. Andy gets up and says, "I'll give you a hand." They both bring in one more load. As Andy helps her put the groceries up, he says, "Not to be a bearer of bad tidings, but I was just reading the news section of the paper. In the country, there are 18,000 more deaths from the pandemic this month than the average monthly rate. I found an update on the destruction in the seven major cities. The estimate is up to thirty billion dollars."

Lydia says, "How sad. How are insurance companies going to cover all of the destruction due to hurricanes, earthquakes, bombings, arson and looting?"

Andy says, "The cost will contribute to the high inflation rate. Insurance rates will probably increase soon."

Lydia replies, "I hate to tell you, but the price of gas here is now up to the national average, $6.59 a gallon."

Andy says, "More people will be affected and many won't be able to afford what they need." Andy looks through the kitchen window at the bird garden.

Lydia starts to put the groceries up and asks, "Do you see something, honey?"

Andy says, "Yes, look at the bird bath. The green female tanager and the red male scarlet tanager are together. We only see them two or three times a year, but it's more rare to see them together."

Lydia looks at the window and exclaims, "What a beautiful sight!" As she finishes with the groceries, she asks, "Did you talk with your congressman friend?"

Andy says, "Yes! He is going to talk with a good contact; someone who is a national talent agent. He will let me know by Wednesday."

Lydia smiles and says, "That sounds like real good news!"

Andy says, "I thanked God right away! Before lunch, I'm going to walk in the woods for about thirty minutes."

Lydia says, "I will join you. I'm not hungry right now."

They drink some water and grab their walking sticks. As they head up their trailhead, Lydia asks, "Do you think we will ever have as many trails as Anderson forged?"

Andy laughs and says, "I doubt it. I don't have the time or extra energy to clear that many trails. If the Lord tarries and Davina and her family take over the house, they might forge that many trails."

Lydia says, "That's true. The commute to Farragut would be as close or closer from here as the commute from Crossville."

Andy says, "I think the trails I cleared run about two miles, if you walk all of them."

Lydia says, "I sure like the woods better during this time of year. You can see farther; hardly no bugs, and we still have some autumn colors."

Andy replies, "Yes, it's beautiful. The weather is perfect. There is nothing like being comfortable with just a light weight jacket."

About eight to nine yards from Andy and Lydia, there is a loud rustling sound through the saplings.

Lydia jumps and says, "What is that?"

Andy laughs and says, "A wild turkey, they're fast and strong!"

In a few minutes, closer to the edge of the woods, they hear a fluttering sound through the tree limbs. Lydia, says, "I know what that is; I saw a couple of tufted titmice flying by."

Andy says, "That's a good observation. I'm ready to add to my life list of birds. The last new bird I identified was a Willow Flycatcher. It was on a dogwood limb in front of the house."

As they walk by one of the older, big oak trees, Lydia says, "Not to change the subject, but refresh my memory about what you, Larry and his friend are doing Tuesday and at the church in Jefferson City."

Andy replies, "We're meeting for lunch at Perkins in Dandridge tomorrow at 1:00. Larry's friend, Aaron Michaels, replaced Larry, when he retired as coach of the Carson-Newman men's basketball team. Aaron wants to talk with me about Anderson's experience, and Aaron is also a basketball fan. In three weeks, the third Sunday of November, we're going to First Baptist on the Carson-Newman campus. Larry, Kenny and I are giving the message that Sunday about Anderson's story. Larry, as the former head basketball coach, is basically introducing Kenny and me. Aaron plans to invite his wife to the service; she's an unbeliever. Kenny is going to meet us here that Sunday morning, so he can ride with us.'

Lydia says, "Thanks, I just needed to fit the pieces together. I remember now that Aaron is a believer. He's not only concerned about his wife being an unbeliever, but he also believes the Lord is coming for the church soon."

Andy says, "That's right. What's for lunch today?"

Lydia looks at him; smiles and says, "Grilled salmon and caviar."

Andy says, "Really? ... you must be kidding."

Lydia says, "How about raw carrots, chicken and noodle soup and P & J sandwiches?"

Andy nods and says, "That I will believe!"

After lunch, Andy and Lydia continue to make outreach plans for the next two months. They have a quiet evening together.

Andy is up early thinking about his meeting with Larry and Aaron today while he makes a pot of coffee and a cup of hot green tea. He usually prays after he reads his devotional and Bible, but he begins by saying a short prayer for their meeting and for Aaron and his wife. Just as he finishes breakfast, Lydia comes into the great room and says, "Honey, why don't you go ahead and shower, since you have a meeting today, and I'll have breakfast ready, when you get done."

About thirty minutes later, Andy sits down with Lydia for breakfast. She surprises him with grapefruit, oatmeal and an English muffin with honey. Andy says, "What a treat! Thank you."

They pray and enjoy the early morning hours. After they watch the morning news, Lydia says, "I haven't heard you say anything about Judy for a while."

Andy replies, "You're right. She use to spoil me by calling me two or three times a week, and I haven't heard from her for almost two months. I need to call her."

Lydia says, "I know it was a big adjustment for her after you lost your dad."

Andy reflectively says, "Yes, it was a big loss for me, but much harder on her. She took a long time selling dad's house. She and dad were real close after the illegal aliens killed mom. After she moved to Lafayette, she spent more time teaching math at Purdue. After her move, I haven't heard from her much. It's a shame, since we were close most of our lives."

Lydia says, "Maybe you can call her this evening. It would be nice, if she could stay with us during her Christmas break."

Andy says, "I will ask her this evening. I would love for her to stay here for a week or more in December. I will be back from my California trip by December 18th."

Lydia says, "I would love for her to be here for a week or more!"

Andy says, "I think I will go ahead and take a shower. If I leave by 12:00, I should get there a few minutes early."

As Andy gets ready, he thinks about all the things he wants to do in the next two month. Every time he feels anxious, he says, "Lord, I will do it by faith; in your time."

Before 12:00, he's ready to go and gives Lydia a kiss. She says, "Have a good meeting. I'm praying for Aaron and his wife."

Andy replies, "Thank you, dear. I am too."

When Andy leaves at noon, it's still cool. The temperature gauge in the car says 63 degrees. He thinks, "It's hard to believe that Halloween is Monday already." Andy goes through Cosby and Newport on Hwy 321. He turns on I40 West and exits at the Jefferson City exit on 92.

Perkins is by the interstate and he gets out of his car about fifteen minutes before Larry and Aaron are due to be there.

The hostess greets him right away, and Andy says, 'There will be three of us. You will see two tall men and one is real tall."

The hostess laughs and says, "I'll be looking up for them!"

Andy requests a semi-private table, and she takes him to a table in the back. Right after Andy orders a water and coffee, he sees Larry and his stocky friend.

Andy stands up and Larry introduces them, and Andy shakes Aaron's hand. As they sit down, Aaron says to Andy, "You don't know what it means to me to meet you and to have lunch with you."

Andy says, "It's a pleasure to meet you. Larry says that you're doing a good job with the team."

Aaron replies, "The practice and the early games are good. It looks like we'll have a winning season. Larry did a great job for the team. I think in the near future we can get back in the Division II playoffs."

The waitress returns for Larry's and Aaron's drink orders. She says, "I'll be back in a minute or two for your lunch orders." The three men look over their menus.

Larry says, "Andy, after she takes our orders, Aaron has a few comments and questions about our basketball days. I know you want to share Anderson's story and your plans for the service three weeks from Sunday."

Just as Andy says, "Absolutely", the waitress is standing in front of them. All three of them order big meals that are protein rich."

Aaron says, "Andy, I'm such a big basketball fan of yours that I know more about your basketball days, then I do your work as Secretary of State."

Andy laughs and says, "That's refreshing! By the way, what's your height and weight? You look like you would do well on the bench press."

Aaron replies, "I benched 400 lbs. in college. I'm 6'4 and about 240 lbs. I was a short small forward at UT, but I started for them. I was stronger than most opponents, but they were usually three to five inches taller than I was. I read that you benched 600 lbs. in college and held the record for the bench press in college basketball and even among the NBA players."

Andy says, "That's what they told me. I had the same experience in college. I was stronger than my opponents at power forward, but they usually had three to five inches on me. Larry and I played against one team that had a seven foot power forward, but he was only 230 lbs. Unfortunately for my opponent, he wasn't on one of the better teams."

Aaron says, "I was born ten years after you, Larry and your Purdue team won the national championship, but I saw your clips at times on ESPN. Man, you were so strong yet agile on the floor. They said you had an offer from the Celtics."

Andy replies, "That's true. At the end of my freshman year, I didn't want to turn down their offer, but I wanted to serve the country in the State Department."

Aaron says, "I know you earned the Presidential Medal of Freedom.

You were a big inspiration to me in basketball, which has been my life. Of course, the most important thing in my life now is following Christ."

Andy says, "That is what I want to talk about today. It is the most important thing to Larry, to my wife and me and to my cousin Anderson. Tell me when you found Christ and how you met your wife."

Aaron replies, "I found Christ my senior year in high school. Until then, basketball was the most important thing to me. I played varsity at South Point High School in Belmont, North Carolina. We had a good team, but in our sophomore and junior years we couldn't advance beyond the regional playoffs. I was frustrated at the beginning of the season in my senior year.

I went to church on Sunday morning, but I wasn't in youth fellowship. I was invited to a youth outing on a weekend in early October. I accepted Christ during the invitation, and turned my life, academics and basketball game over to Christ. In my senior year, we finally won the regional and made it to the final four. All of my stats improved in assists, rebounds, blocks, points and even steals. Two months before I graduated, the University of Tennessee gave me a full scholarship to play basketball for them. One year we went to the Sweet Sixteen. I've had a good career. I ended up as assistant coach at the University of Georgia and then as coach at Carson-Newman."

Andy remarked, "Excellent testimony and career. How did you and your wife meet?"

Aaron replies, "When I started my sophomore year, she started her freshman year. By then, I was the starting small forward for UT. She went to all the home games, and she began to develop an interest in me, even though we didn't know each other. A male friend of hers knew someone who was a team manager. He said that a freshman co-ed likes me, and she would like to meet me. She was a very attractive co-ed, and we hit it off. By the end of my second basketball season the relationship was getting too heated, and it stayed that way until I graduated.

She didn't get pregnant before marriage, but we missed each other a lot when she was a senior, and I was out of state coaching B ball at a large high school. After she graduated and I finished my first year of high school coaching, we got married."

Andy says, "A lot of young people have similar experiences in college. Did you share your faith with her and find out about her beliefs?"

Aaron replies, "I'm sorry to say that I didn't. I was infatuated with her. Wendy was the first girl that I had a relationship with. I was naïve about relationships, and even though I put Christ first in most of my life,

I realized later that I didn't with our pre-marital relationship. After we married and had our first child, I became a Christian father and tried to become a Christian husband. Until then, I didn't know she was resistant to Christian beliefs. In college, I knew that she liked drinking on a date, but I didn't know that she was an alcoholic or becoming an alcoholic. After she had our first child, I realized that she was an alcoholic, and she still is."

Andy says, "I will be praying for you and your wife. I will go ahead and give you the highlights of Anderson's story and you will hear the complete story in three weeks. I grew up with Anderson, my first cousin. He's five years older, and his family lived eighteen miles north of us. In his seventies, Anderson became more concerned spiritually about his daughter, sister and his best friend, Kenny. He lost his wife just before he turned eighty. A few months after his birthday, he helped his sister financially. She sold her home and moved in with Anderson."

His sister was home one day, when Anderson went for a walk in his woods. He took all of his gear, except his cell phone, which he forgot. His trails wind for miles in almost a hundred and twenty acres of wood. Anderson didn't return at his usual time. His sister finally called his friend Kenny. Kenny advised her to call the police, and Kenny, his friends and the police searched for Anderson before and after nightfall. After a week, they had a funeral without a body. Later, he appeared one evening at his home and visited with his sister. Within a week, he appeared during the day on Kenny's farm. Several days later, he appeared late in the evening at his daughter's house in Indiana."

Andy stops and looks at Aaron, as if he is waiting for a comment. Aaron says, "Wow! What a testimony!"

Andy replies, "Aaron, my cousins and Kenny are level-headed and responsible. They don't tell tall tales, and they don't exaggerate."

Aaron says, "I have no doubt about the authenticity. In fact, I remember the news reports about sightings like this throughout the world."

Andy says, "Yes. We are getting the word out about Anderson's story and the soon coming of the Lord."

Aaron says, "I want to help."

Larry says, "Excellent!

Andy asks, "Are you and your wife coming to the church service on campus three weeks from Sunday?"

Aaron says, "I will be at First Baptist that day, but so far, she hasn't committed to coming."

Larry says, "I told Aaron about what happened to Anderson. I know he wants to hear the story from you and Kenny, but it looks like we will have to wait until we get together that Sunday. Aaron has to be back on campus in about thirty minutes."

Larry finished with his meal, and in less than five minutes Andy and Aaron finish theirs. Andy shakes hand with Larry and Aaron, so Aaron can get ready for his team's practice. He buys a big blueberry muffin for Lydia, then watches Larry and Aaron pull out of the parking lot. He says a prayer for Aaron and his wife, "Lord, guide Aaron in all things, and may his wife see the light of the living Christ." On his way back home, he enjoys another pleasant October day.

He starts thinking about Judy and calling her this evening. Just before he gets to Newport, Andy realizes he needs to call Officer Walling today. When he arrives home, he looks for Lydia.

At first he can't find her, but then he sees her on the back deck tending to some flowers that don't have too much longer before the first frost. He opens the door, and says, "Honeydew, I have a surprise for you!"

Lydia says, "I will be there in a minute or two. When she walks through the door, Andy is in kitchen and pulls out a large blueberry muffin. She walks in the kitchen.

With a broad smile, Andy says, "A super muffin for a super girl!" She smiles; kisses him and says, "Thank you, super boy."

Andy said, "We had a pleasant visit at Perkins, and on the way back, I realized that I need to call Officer Walling today."

Lydia says, "Oh, yes, what happened to the earlier luncheon plans?"

Andy replies, "A couple weeks ago, she couldn't meet, because she was working overtime. I need to stop and call her now"

Lydia says, "It's not 4:00 yet. Maybe she is on an early supper break."

Andy calls her cell phone and she answers. Andy says, "Officer Walling, this is Andy McGraig."

She says, "Please call me, Rachel."

Andy replies, "Is it a good time?"

Rachel says, "Your timing is good. I'm on an early supper break. I came in at 7 a.m. and I work until 6 p.m."

Andy asks, "Do you have long hours every week?"

She says, "Right now we rotate 44 hours a week with 55 hours per week."

Andy says, "Lydia and I want to meet you for lunch or supper."

Rachel says, "This is my 44 hour week, and I could meet you in Gatlinburg for lunch on Friday. I will fill you in on some things going on.

I will send you a text tonight or tomorrow, and recommend a time and location. Can we meet sometime between 11:30 and 1:00 on Friday?"

Andy says, "That's good. I'm sure Lydia is available then. I will look for your text this evening."

Rachel says, "Good. I appreciate you calling, and I'm looking forward to our lunch and meeting."

They hang up and Andy tells Lydia about their Friday lunch with Officer Walling. Andy says, "I'm going to call Judy early this evening. I'm getting excited about inviting her and finding out how she is doing."

Lydia says, "It won't be much longer. It's after 4:00 already, and I will have a light supper for us at 5:00 or a little after."

Andy says, "Good. I will call Judy by 6:00."

Lydia and Andy finish with supper a little after 5;30, and he immediately calls Judy. Judy answers after a few rings and Andy exclaims, "How are you doing, Sweet Pea?"

Judy laughs and says, "Just fine. How is my big brother?"

Andy says, "I've been missing you. What have you been doing?"

Judy in a much more serious tone says, "I've been throwing myself into my work. I like the opportunity of teaching at Purdue. It has been almost ten years, since I sold Dad's house and moved to Lafayette. I miss you and your family a lot."

Andy says, "On a bright note, Lydia and I want you to stay with us during Christmas; two weeks if you want to."

Judy replies, "I would like that. I haven't been to your new house, and I haven't been to the Smokies for a long time. It will make me miss dad, but I always miss dad."

Andy firmly says, "You need a break, and you need to get away and be with us!"

Andy can't see Judy's smile, when she says, "You're right. I will be there for Christmas. I will arrive before Christmas and leave after, but I need to check my calendar book and a few things here. Could I give you the dates in a couple weeks?"

Andy says, "Sure sis, but we want you to stay for over a week. Are you still going to the same church?"

Judy says, "Oh, yes. I've been going there over seven years now. I finally transferred my membership less than a year ago"

Andy says, "Wonderful. We like staying active in church, and we look forward to being with you. By the way, sis, I pray for you every morning. I still remember mom and dad in prayer."

Judy replies, "I do the same. I do miss you a lot. I'm sorry that it has been a long time, since I called."

'No problem, sis. We both miss you, and we're looking forward to being with you. I love you."

"I love you too, Andy. I will call you within two weeks."

Andy hangs up and shares the good news with Lydia.

Lydia says, "I'm so glad that she is coming. It sounds like she might stay for over a week."

Andy says, "I hope so. As you know, she never married, and she stayed in dad's house for five years after he passed away. After mom's early death, Judy and dad became dependent on each other."

Lydia replies, "I know. I'm glad they had each other. It helped them get over the emptiness of missing your mother."

Andy gets up and makes some coffee. It helps him deal with the melancholy after talking about his mom's early demise. When he comes back into the great room, he's feeling better.

He says, "We're getting ready to walk into November, and it's dark by 7:00."

Lydia says, "I know. While the trees are so beautiful, do you want to walk in the woods after breakfast?"

Andy replies, "That sounds perfect. Right now is the peak of the four seasons. It doesn't get any better than this. A good time to start our walk would be around 9:00. How does this sound?

After the walk, we could drive into Newport and have some coffee and ice cream at the Rustic Cow!"

Lydia says, "Excellent idea. Ice cream and coffee sure sounds good."

Andy says, "All coffee shops and restaurants should have ice cream!"

8

Rendezvous in Newport and Gatlinburg

As Lydia and Andy talk about their plans for the day, Andy says, "I need to put a reminder in my calendar book to call Officer Walling, so we can meet her in Gatlinburg. Let's have a hearty breakfast before our hearty walk!"

After breakfast, it's almost 9:00 on the nose, when Lydia and Andy have their jackets on and walking sticks in hand. As they walk out on their back deck, a small patch of fog is still in the top of the trees. As they step off the deck into the back yard, Lydia says, "It feels like 50 degrees."

Andy says, "It probably is, if not a little cooler. It feels good with a jacket on. Look at all the gold and yellow in the hickory leaves."

Lydia says, "Yes, and look how colorful the dogwood trees are at the edge of the yard. The leaves are a striking, pomegranate color."

Andy says, "It's perfect out here; heaven on earth."

As they walk across the yard, they see a chipmunk dart under their shed. They walk into their woods and up the trailhead. Some fog remains, but it is well above the path. There are hickory trees everywhere dressed in their bright yellow and gold leaves. Now and then they pass a cluster of horse chestnut trees. Both Lydia and Andy notice the bigger and older oak trees. They also love looking at the tall loblolly pines that stand tops and branches over the other trees.

After they walk a few minutes, Lydia asks, "When is the last time you saw a coyote back here?"

Andy says, "It has been a good while." He thinks a second and says, "Well over a year ago, wild turkeys were nesting in a clearing with tall grass. It was near the south edge of our woods; maybe 200 yards from here. A coyote was pacing back and forth; not far from the tall grass. I think he wanted a young turkey, but it was broad daylight, and he probably knew that I wasn't far away."

Lydia says, "That reminds me of those yellow jackets you were spraying over two months ago. Did you find out, if a coon or skunk dug up their nest?"

"No. I'm guessing a skunk did it. There is a den not far from the back yard. Skunks come out in the evening and feed at night. I'm only guessing that the burrow was made by a skunk, but I'm not guessing, when I go outside some mornings and smell skunk!"

Lydia laughs and says, "When you smell them, tell me and I will stay inside!"

After they walk about forty minutes, they turn back to the trailhead. Lydia says, "The nice looking trees scattered throughout the woods that have light brown leaves in the winter; what are they called?"

Andy answers, "American Beech. You're right; they're very good looking trees."

As they start going downhill, they admire several small maple trees with radiant colors of red and orange. Now and then a few leaves float to the ground. Because it is so quiet in the woods, they can hear the rustling of the leaves by the cool breeze. At the edge of the woods, they watch tufted titmice fly in and out of the trees.

Lydia proclaims, "That was invigorating!"

Andy replies, "The hike felt great."

As they walk inside, Lydia exclaims, "It's still chilly out there!"

Andy says, "It's nice to be back in the house. We have a few minutes to freshen up, if you're about ready to visit the Rustic Cow."

Lydia says, "I think I will be ready in about ten minutes."

When Lydia comes out of the bathroom, she asks, "Has Officer Walling in Gatlinburg contacted you about the time and location for our luncheon Friday?"

Andy says, "Believe it or not, Officer Walling, Rachel, just sent me a text. She says. "Would 1:00 Friday be good at the Breakfast Restaurant, where I dropped you off after the church daycare tragedy? They have added a lunch menu!" Does 1:00 work for you?"

Lydia replies, "That would be good."

Andy sends her a text. They put their jackets back on and head to Newport.

When they arrive at Rustic Cow, Lydia says, "Look at all of their activities. They have a lot of events." As they walk in inside, they enjoy the displays and atmosphere.

Andy says, "They have a good variety of food. Do you still want only ice cream and coffee or something else?"

Lydia says, "I would like a big bowl of three flavors of ice cream and a large, mild roast coffee."

Andy exclaims, "Me too! Let's order!"

Lydia gets a big bowl with a big dip of chocolate chunk, butter pecan and sea salt caramel.

Andy digs into a big dip of butter pecan and chocolate chunk on a cone. He says, "Since I was a kid, I always liked ice cream on a cone. How could we get more decadent than this?"

Lydia says, "I know. Don't you love it!"

Before they finish the ice cream, Denise, the owner of Rustic Cow, comes over to the table with a smile that fills the room. She says, "You don't like our ice cream, do you?"

Lydia says, "Oh no, we're just acting like it!" They all laugh.

Denise says, "You've become regular customers."

Andy says, "Yes. I think we've been coming here for almost a year. We love it."

Lydia says, "Maybe we could set a time to meet with you here for a few minutes. We would like to tell you about Anderson's story; Andy's first cousin. Do you know that Andy is the former Secretary of State?"

Denise looks at him and with a light in her eye she says, "I thought I knew your face from years past. I would love to hear the story. Just call me a couple days ahead of time, and we'll sit down at a table here. Well, I better get back to work. It's wonderful seeing you again."

Lydia says, "It's always good seeing you."

Andy says, "She's a real nice lady. I'm going to finish this cup of coffee, and I will be ready to go."

Lydia replies, 'Me too!"

On their way home, they stop in Newport at a grocery store to get a few things. Andy says, "Let's not forget mild roast coffee in the K cups."

Lydia says, "Absolutely not. I want to get humus, celery, carrots and chocolate ice cream."

Andy asks, "How did you ever remember to get ice cream?"

Lydia smiles and says, "I wonder."

The rest of the day and Thursday go by quickly. After breakfast Friday, Andy says, "It's hard to believe it's Friday already. In a few hours we'll be having lunch with Officer Walling in Gatlinburg. In two weeks, we'll be with Larry and Kenny at First Baptist in Jefferson City."

Lydia says, "I know Larry's wife will be there, but I hope Aaron's wife comes."

"That's a good thought. I need to pray more for Aaron and his wife these next two weeks."

Lydia asks, "Did Congressman Eastman call you back about the media agent?"

Andy says, "Yes, he sent me a text late Wednesday. He said that an agent, Irwin Cohen, would contact me the first of the week. Jimmy said that Cohen wanted my phone number, since he could probably line me up with some appearances.,"

Lydia says, "That's great news! It will be exciting to learn where he schedules you."

Andy says, "I got up extra early for devotions. I think I will rest awhile before we leave for Gatlinburg."

"Good idea." Lydia says, "I have time to catch up on some correspondence and reading."

They leave for Gatlinburg a few minutes early. Andy always likes to be early.

On their way, Andy says, "Officer Walling, she likes to be called Rachel, told me that their chief encourages them to wear an I.D. badge and a gun on their day off. She said that Homeland Security in Tennessee recommends it for better public safely."

Lydia says, "I would guess that it causes some inconvenience for her, but I'm glad they do it, because of all the crime in this culture."

Andy says, "The good old days were truly good old days. Today, we're living in the troubled new days." Highway 321 stops at the main road to the popular stores in Gatlinburg. They turn left and park two blocks from the Breakfast Restaurant to get a better parking spot.

They walk in the busy restaurant and ask for a table to seat three. Andy tells the hostess, "Our friend, a lady officer, will be here real soon. We want to get the most private table you have."

The hostess says, "That would be a table in the back. Can you wait about ten minutes?"

Andy says, "Sure. We're about ten minutes early."

Andy and Lydia are seated in a few minutes, and Rachel joins them right after they're seated.

Andy stands up and shakes her hand. Rachel says, "I'm enjoying a day off, and I'm glad we could get together."

A friendly and copious waitress takes their drink order. Andy starts telling Rachel about the media, organizations and churches they're reaching out to. When the waitress returns, Andy says, "Put the meals on my tab. What are the popular meals on your new lunch menu?"

The attractive and round faced waitress says, "As you know, we specialize in breakfast food, but we put together three meals for our customers who want lunch between 11 and 2. They are meat loaf with mashed potatoes and green beans; soup of the day, which is potato today, with a grilled ham and cheese sandwich and pork chops with black beans and rice and house salad."

Andy says, "A perfect selection." He looks at Rachel and says, "Ladies first."

Rachel orders the grilled ham and cheese with soup, and Lydia and Andy both order the pork chop meal.

Andy continues with telling Rachel about his cousin Anderson.

Rachel says, "I'm very impressed with Anderson's story and what you're doing to share the gospel and his story."

Andy begins to reply, when the waitress brings their three meals in less than ten minutes. Andy thanks her for the efficient service.

Andy says, "Let me say the blessing, and then we can good start on our meal."

Following Andy's lead, all three begin enjoying their food. Rachel asks, "How do you like their new lunch meal?"

Lydia says, "The food is very good. You can't beat black beans and rice. We have noticed in Charlotte a lot of restaurants offer black beans and rice as a side."

Rachel replies, "When I'm working, I started coming here for lunch about twice a week after I heard about their lunch menu. Of course, they change the soup of the day, but they usually have the other two meals."

Andy says, "We've been enjoying their breakfast food for over a year. They've done a good job on their lunch menu." As Andy puts down his coffee cup, he says, "Tell us what is going on recently with your department and your duties."

Rachel says, "It has been hectic. The hours have increased. Not only are there more security concerns, but we're short of help. A few retired officers are helping us part-time. They have been given some of our routine duties, so we can get our extra work done. I understand that you still have connections with the government and probably receive some classified information. I'm glad you got this table in the back, so I can share some of the things we're being told."

Andy interjects, "I have federal classified clearance, but Lydia doesn't.

If you share any semi-classified information, like local policies, tell us that it is confidential and we'll keep it that way."

Rachel says, "Very good. The fact that I'm wearing a gun and my ID on my day off says a lot. One of the concerns we have is the new gun control bill passed by the socialist controlled U.S. house and senate. If you listened to a non-bias commentator or read a non-bias article, you know the bill is vague. I can tell you that our state legislature and courts are going to revoke the bill as being unconstitutional. We feel confident that Texas, Florida, Indiana and at least fifteen other states are going to do the same. I think a lot of state political leaders are going to promote in the state and nationally: "Take guns away from the good guys, and only the bad guys have them.""

Andy says, "That should be an effective slogan."

Rachel continues, "We know from our department and from Homeland Security that terrorists and other insurrectionists in general are getting bolder and stepping up their crimes. The bias media isn't reporting most of what is happening in crime; especially the terrorism and other insurrection. The other insurrectionists are those who are trying to cancel our culture and dividing our nation. They are still using the race card, when there are no racial issues."

Rachel stops to take a drink of water and finishes the last couple bites of her sandwich.

Andy says, "Take your time; we're in no hurry. When they started the lunch menu, did they add any dessert?"

Rachel says, "Yes, and I'm glad they did. They have apple and cherry pie and vanilla and chocolate ice cream. When I get dessert, I usually get one scoop of chocolate and one scoop of vanilla."

Andy says, "A lady after our own heart! We love ice cream. Lydia, do you want what Rachel orders?"

Lydia says, "Of course!"

Andy laughs and says, "When the waitress returns, I will give her three orders. Speaking of our congenial waitress, here she comes now." The waitress takes the three ice cream orders and heats up Andy's coffee.

Rachel says, "By the way, I want to help you get Anderson's story out, but unfortunately, I have limited time. I could share it with my pastor and give you contacts like the presidents of the Kiwanis and the Rotary Club."

Andy says, "Excellent! We feel that we don't have much time left. Bible prophecy is being fulfilled so quickly now. We are taking on a lot of engagements. I will get your contact information. If I can't fit the organizations into my schedule, I could ask Larry or another one of our friends to speak. Once you talk to your pastor, would he give you at least ten minutes on a Sunday morning to speak?"

Rachel says, "I'm sure he would. After I tell him what you have said, he will probably ask me to give the message." The waitress brings three bowls of chocolate and vanilla ice cream.

After Rachel takes her first bite of ice cream, she says, "Okay, I will try to pick up where I left off."

Lydia says, "Enjoy your ice cream. We can wait a minute. We'll eat ice cream with you!"

Andy says, "While we're taking a break, I will add that dividing our nation is exactly what Hitler did in Germany. He attacked the Jews, then the Catholic and then the Protestants. We had one President that served two consecutive terms not long ago. He was a great divider. He vilified America for its great traditions and accomplishments. He acted like an insurrectionist. I guarantee you that he would not have been willing to lay down his life for our country in one of our past wars. There is not one race in our country that is more racist than any other race."

Rachel says, "How true; the false portrayal of our citizens is sad. The average American citizen is not aware of all the crime now being committed in our country; especially by terrorists and other insurrectionists. It is a movement like the organized Nazis and KGB. Homeland Security in our state is just one evidence of the insurrection by suggesting that our officers wear guns on our day off. We know from our church and daycare attack that peaceful citizens need to be armed."

Andy replies, "I'm glad that the Homeland Security officials in our state are backing up our convictions and our rights. Do you know of anything else that you believe is significant?"

Rachel says, "The crime in the big, socialist run cities is especially bad and getting worse by the day; including Chicago, Baltimore, Philadelphia, New York City, Minneapolis, Los Angeles, Portland, and Seattle. There are too many cities to name. Because of the socialists, we have an open southern border, which is making the problems much worse, including problems with the China virus and other pandemics."

Rachel takes a drink of water and says, "I know none of us are in a hurry, but I just want to share one more thing. I haven't shared anything classified, but anything I share about our department work or assignments here is strictly between both of you, me and the lamppost."

In unison, Lydia and Andy say, "We understand."

"A couple times today, I've mentioned that crime and insurrection is worse than most people realize. Criminals today and terrorists practice one belief: anything goes. They will bomb, burn, shoot, stab, steal and cause any mayhem possible, Police films for years have taught to take a hard look around and, friends, that means anywhere. Keep your cars locked, house locked and lights on. Always be prepared, whether it's quick access to your shoes, your keys, your flashlight, your cell phone and your gun. They will try any type of violence and any type of scam. I'm sure some will get police uniforms and become law enforcement imposters to kidnap; confiscate cars and to confiscate your guns and other valuables at your home. They don't hesitate to kill and commit arson. I know this sounds dire, but be prepared."

Officer Walling continues, "There is one more thing that I think you will want to know, and please keep it confidential. One of our most important assignments is to watch the continuous crowds in the commercial district of Gatlinburg. We look for individuals like narcotic agents scan the crowds at large airports. We do not profile by race. We look for suspicious people, who could be carrying large knives; concealed guns without a permit and even small explosives. We realize that the crowds may diminish with time as this scourge grows. It is a very solemn situation in our society that some associate with end time events." Rachel looks at Andy and Lydia for their reply.

Andy says, "Spot on. Rachel, we love you in the Lord. Thank you for sharing and for all of your sound advice. Let's trade emails before we leave. We will alert each other, if we hear of anything that is real important or urgent. We can also share positive info. about the good news we're sharing."

Lydia says, "We will be praying for you."

Rachel says, "It is an honor to be with you today. Thank you for an excellent lunch and time together. I will write down my email now."

They exchange emails and hug each other. As Rachel walks to the door, Lydia says, "What a courageous woman!"

As Andy and Lydia head back toward Cosby and home, Andy says, "I need to put together a group email to let our group know about our schedules with the media, organizations and churches. Today I will call the Rivera's and get their email."

Lydia replies, "That will be a good outreach system, so they can let their contacts know about the different engagements. In a few days, you will probably know about a national engagement or more."

"Yes. Even though it will take some serious preparation, I'm looking forward to it."

Lydia says, "I'm proud of you. We have talked about going together or me staying at home. I want to be with you, and it has been decades since I've been to New York City or California. I also like being at home."

Andy replies, "You have time to decide."

When they get close to Cosby, Andy says, "I just started thinking about the Rivera's. Why don't we stop at the Rivera's and see how they're doing?"

Lydia says, "That's a great idea!"

In a few minutes, they pull up in front of Rivera's small and attractive, cottage style home.

Andy knocks, and when Gus opens the door, he says, "Welcome, friends. I heard a car door, and when I looked out, I told Gracie that it looks like Andy and Lydia's SUV. Andy shakes Gus's hand, and Gracie walks into the living room and hugs Lydia and Andy.

Gracie says emotionally, "It's so good to see both of you. Do want coffee or hot tea?"

Lydia laughs and says, "You don't have to get us anything."

Grace says. "I insist!"

Lydia looks at Andy and he nods. Lydia says, "Okay, we'll take hot tea, either black or green tea is good."

Gus motions to the couch and says, "Have a seat."

Andy asks, "How are you and your family doing?"

Gus says, "We are fine and Gladis and Tracy are doing well. Our water heater started acting up and I asked a friend this morning to take a look at it. I was hoping he would say the heating element needs replacing, but he said the tank is full of rust. I usually change the heating element, but I'm slowing up. I got a quote on a water heater and installation, but the company wanted over $600 just to install it!"

As Andy says, "That's outrageous. Are the new water heaters still under $400?"

Gus says, "They're about $500 now. In construction, I didn't do electrical installations, and the last water heater I installed was over twenty-five years ago."

Andy asks, "What are you doing in the morning?"

Gus replies, "I don't have any plans, except for solving the water heater problem."

Andy says, "I've installed a couple of water heaters. I can get here about 9:00, and we can take your truck to Newport and get a water heater. Between the two of us, we'll get it installed."

Gus says, "You don't know how much this means to us. You're always helping us."

Andy says, "We're thankful we can do it."

Lydia says, "Gus, I've been thinking about our email list for Anderson's story and our Gospel outreach. Did one of you tell us that Gladis is good with computers?" Gracie comes back in the living room to serve the tea. She hears Lydia's question.

Gracie says, "Yes, she does a lot of work on computers; especially with software. She's at work now, but I will ask her to call you, when she gets home."

Lydia says, "In our country there are thousands and thousands of churches, and we can't reach them all. With the right kind of software or information, maybe we can reach a thousand churches or more rather than just a hundred. We think Andy is going to get one or more invitations to be on national media; possibly television. We want to let as many people and organizations as possible know about the date and time of Andy's media interview."

Gracie says, "I'm excited to hear that. I know Gladis, Gus and I will help anyway we can."

Andy says, "The tea is good, thank you."

The McGraig's tell the Rivera's about the service at First Baptist in two weeks. They tell them the location, and the Rivera's say they would like to attend with Gladis and Tracy."

Andy says, "Arrive about fifteen or twenty minutes before the service. We're expecting standing room only."

Gus says, "Will do."

Andy and Lydia stand up and thank Gus and Gracie for the tea and nice visit. Andy says, "Lord willing, I will see you by nine in the morning."

Gracie and Gus thank them for stopping.

They take off for their country home on a cold and cloudy, November afternoon. Lydia says, "Tomorrow night Daylight Savings Time ends. It has been getting dark before 7:00. On Sunday it will be dark before 6:00."

Andy says, "The years go by too fast and the season go by even faster. Right now it feels like a late December day."

It's late afternoon, when they get home. Andy says, "I'm going to turn on a news channel to see what's going on." Andy sits down and grabs the remote. Right after he finds a news channel, he lets out a gloomy sigh, "Oh, no!"

Lydia walks from the kitchen and asks, "What's wrong?"

"China has released information about a new weapon they have been developing. The Pentagon says they don't have the technology for it."

Lydia says, "Another potential disaster for the world."

Andy replies, "I wondered why the Chinese delegation in D.C. was so bold."

Lydia asks, "What did they say?"

Andy replies, "I can't answer that, because it's classified. I probably said as much as I could say. I can give my opinion. For decades China has been stealing our technology. Their government has no scruples. I would not be surprised, if China in the very near future invades Japan. It is hard to predict what they may try to do toward our country."

Andy gets a call on his cell phone. When he answers, a young lady asks if this is Mr. McGraig. She says she's calling from a Knoxville TV station. She says, "I'm Megan, and I'm the program director. Yesterday Larry Quarles, the former basketball coach at Carson-Newman called and said he was your teammate at Purdue, when you won the national championship in 1965."

Andy says, "Yes, Larry is a friend and we were on the starting five for Purdue."

Megan continues, "I'm only twenty-five and Mr. Quarles said you were our Secretary of State and received the Presidential Medal of Freedom award."

Andy laughs and says, "Yes, I served twice as Secretary of State. My second appointment ended twenty-four years ago. I was awarded the Presidential Medal of Freedom award for my service in the Seven Day Southern Border War; before I served as Secretary."

Megan says, "Very impressive. Thank you for your service. Next Friday is Veteran's Day, We're interviewing a lot of veterans that day and also taking our camera and reporter to the Knoxville National Cemetery. Our scheduled interviews are completely booked for that day. Our regular interviews are fairly short; about two minutes. We would like for you to come the day before and be our special guest. We want to hear your story, and we would like to come back to you during the last half of our program. Of course, we have commercial breaks, but altogether we could spend twenty minutes with you. Your presence will also help us promote our Veteran's Day program."

Andy says, "I would be glad to. I would be glad to answer some questions about my government service and even about my time with Purdue. I also request that the time be limited for those questions, so I could tell my cousin's unique story. It is family centered. spiritual and also a gospel message."

Megan replies, "We want you on the program. We will be glad to work with you. Could we spend the first ten minutes with your story and message? We need to spend at least the last ten minutes with your service to our country. We could take a minute of that to mention your national championship"

Andy says, "That would be fine. I would want a minimum of nine to ten minutes to tell Anderson's story. We could spend the other ten to eleven minutes for the last half of the program."

Megan says, "Excellent. Our first half of the program begins at 3:00. Since you're our special guest, we would like to show your presence a couple times during the first half. Could you be here by 2:15? I will give you our contact number and detailed directions."

Andy writes done the station's info. and gives Lydia the good news as soon as he completes the call. Andy says, "I need to thank Larry for calling them."

Lydia replies, "That's great news. It's already 5:00. Do you want something light to eat; maybe soup and a sandwich?"

Andy says, "You decide. Right now I feel so good that I could eat a seaweed salad."

During supper they talked about the opportunity to be on Knoxville television. Just after they finish, Gladis calls Lydia and says that she could show us how to organize a large group email list. Gladis says, "I could come Saturday or Monday after 5:00."

Lydia says, "Hold on, Gladis. Andy, Gladis says she could come here tomorrow or after 5:00 Monday, Around 4:00 would be good also."

When Lydia tells Gladis that 4:00 would work also, she says, "I will ask mom or dad to watch Tracy, and I will let you know if 4:00 will work."

Lydia hangs up and Andy says, "Tomorrow it will still be light before 6:00. She could see better going back by 5:30."

Lydia says, "Good point. She will let me know the time."

Saturday morning, Andy gets up before 6 to study and pray, and he has breakfast ready a few minutes after 7:00. During breakfast Andy says, I want to be ready by 8:30. I will meet Gus by 9:00, so we can get the water heater and install it."

Lydia asks, "When do you think, you'll finish?"

"I'm guessing by noon, if we don't have a problem. I should be home by 1:00."

Lydia says, "Be careful. I'm going to clean up the kitchen, then shower and dress. While you're gone, I want to pull up our listed email contacts. I mainly want to see who is in there and count them."

Andy says, "Good idea. We'll have a feel for where we are, when Gladis helps us organize a group list."

Andy arrives at the Rivera's a few minutes before 9. Gus is ready to go. He drives his truck to Newport. At the large hardware store, they pick out a 40 gallon tank for a family of four. After the paperwork is ready, and the sale is entered, the salesman says, "With tax and the warranty, the total is $543.40."

Gus says, "That's high for a water heater."

As Andy pulls out his credit card, he replies, "You can thank the New Age Socialist's economic policies for the high rate of inflation."

When the salesman takes Andy's credit card, Gus says, "You're not paying for it."

Andy replies, "Yes, I am. You have other things to spend your money on."

As they walk to the front of the store, Gus says, "With your help and payment, you just saved me over $1,100. How can I ever repay you?"

Andy says, "There is something you can do for me. We need some extra energy for the installation, so stop at a fast food drive thru before we leave Newport, and get us two senior coffees and two ham and egg biscuits."

Gus laughs and says, "I think I can handle that." Within five minutes, they have the water heater loaded and pull out to get the biscuits.

After Gus places the order, he gives the cashier $12.00 for the two biscuits and coffee. He pulls into a parking spot so they can eat the biscuits, then he and Andy head for Cosby.

Gus and Andy take out the old water heater and move it to the side. Andy opens the box, and they both position the new water heater. Gus hooks up the water lines, and Andy wires the heater.

They put the old water heater in the box. Andy says, "Let's slide the box onto your truck now, and tomorrow you can take it to the landfill and just slide it off."

Gus says, "Good idea."

After Gus and Andy slide the old heater on the truck bed, Gus shakes Andy's hand and thanks him. Gus says, "Andy, you don't know how much you mean to me and my family."

When they walk inside, Gracie, Gladis and Tracy greet Andy. Gus says, "Andy, paid for the water heater!" Gracie is in tears and she hugs Andy. Tracy and Gladis also hug Andy.

Gracie asks, "Can you have a cup of coffee with us?"

Andy says, "Sure I can."

When Gracie and Gladis serve the coffee, Gladis says, "I can be at your house by 4:00 today."

Andy says, "Excellent! Lydia and I are looking forward to your help."

After they visit, Andy says, "I told Lydia I would be home by 1:00. Thank you for the coffee and good company."

The Rivera's walk out on their porch. As Andy leaves, they wave to him. Gracie is in tears, and Gus puts his arm around her and kisses her on the cheek.

When Andy gets home, Lydia has tuna salad sandwiches ready for him. She adds lettuce and sets our cottage cheese and carrots. Andy says, "This looks great," and gives Lydia a kiss.

When they get done, Lydia says, "We still have some apples left from our Maggie Valley trip. Do you have room for one?"

Andy says, "I would love a golden delicious or a gala. In a few days we'll have to get more in Cosby."

After lunch, Andy says, "I'm due for a nap. Gladis will be here in two hours. I should get up within thirty minutes, but if I oversleep, please get me up within an hour."

Lydia says, "Will do." While Andy is napping, Lydia reads and dozes off and on. After she dozes longer than usual, she looks at the clock. She thinks, "I better check on Andy. I don't hear him, and it has been almost an hour, since he laid down."

As Lydia walks down the hall, she hears Andy getting up. Lydia walks in the master bedroom and says, "I thought I was going to have to pull you out of the bed."

Andy smiles and says, "We could have a Saturday night smackdown."

Lydia laughs and says, "Gladis will be here in about an hour."

Andy says, "Bring her on! I'm glad she can come and help us. I'm going to splash some cold water on my face and change shirts."

When Andy walks into the great room, Lydia says, "I want to offer her some hot chocolate and a snack. She probably doesn't get out on her own much."

Andy says, "We still have some chocolate from Halloween. We should set that out for her."

Right at 5:00 the doorbell rings. Lydia greets Gladis. She says, "You have a beautiful house. I enjoyed the scenic drive and being out in the country."

Andy gets up and greets Gladis. He says, "We're thankful that you could come and help us."

Gladis smiles and says, "We have never had friends so helpful and nice, as you and Lydia."

Lydia smiles and gives her a hug. Lydia says, "Thank you, dear. We think a lot of you and your family. Before we look at the group email project, we put out chocolate for you, and I'm ready to make you hot chocolate. Do you want cookies?"

Lydia points to where there chocolate is on the dining room table. Gladis says, "What a beautiful long table. I will take two or three pieces of chocolate and just the hot chocolate please."

Lydia says, "While I make the hot chocolate, you and Andy can get started with the computer, if you want to."

Andy says jokingly, "Come into our executive office." When they walk into the office, Andy says, "The computer is at the end of the stacks of papers."

Gladis laughs and says, "Well, the computer monitor is higher than the papers."

Andy says, "After I show you our email contacts, why don't you take the computer seat, and show us what to do."

While Andy pulls up the email list, Lydia brings in the hot chocolate for Gladis. Lydia says, "I will come right back with drinks for Andy and me."

Andy asks, "What are you having, babe?"

Lydia says, "I think I will fix coffee."

Andy says, "I will take the same; with cream please."

Andy makes a comment about the email list, and Gladis says, "I think we're all set for me to pilot you to making a group for a file. I will show you how to enter your emails into a file, and you will be all set."

Gladis sits in front of the computer and shows Andy the steps in creating a group email file.

Lydia brings the coffee into the office. Andy says to Lydia, "I pulled out a folding chair for you."

In another minute, Andy sits by the computer to try what Gladis showed him."

After a few minutes, Andy has entered seven or eight emails into the group file. In an English accent, Andy says, "I think I've got it!"

Gladis replies in Spanish and they both say, "What does that mean?"

Gladis says in English, "I think you do have it." All three of them laugh.

Lydia says, "We can have fun while we work."

Gladis finishes by showing Lydia and Andy how easy it is to place the file in an email.

Andy says, "Gladis, we know several people, who could type emails and put them in their own file. Can they send us their contacts in a file, so we can relay the same message to their contacts?"

Gladis replies, "Absolutely. If you and Lydia need help with typing entries into a file, let me know. I can help, when mom or dad watches Tracy. Even when I'm not at home, mom can help, when dad watches Tracy."

Lydia says, "I can see that we can get our announcements out to a lot more people and organizations than I realized. With seven or eight of us typing email entries, don't you think that we could have a thousand emails or more on our combined files?"

Gladis says, "Definitely. We just need to stay at it daily, if you want to start sending them by a near at hand target date."

Lydia asks Gladis, "Do you want more hot chocolate?"

"No, thank you. I have to go home and give Tracy a bath, then a friend and I are going to see a movie."

They walk Gladis to the door, and Gladis hugs both Lydia and Andy.

They all walk onto the porch, and Andy and Lydia watch Gladis leave.

When they walk back inside, Andy and Lydia are shivering. Lydia say, "It felt like it has dropped to forty or below."

Andy says, "A cold front is coming in tonight. It may get close to freezing."

Lydia says, "It was good to see Gladis this evening. She was a big help."

Andy says, "Yes, she was. It looks like we can go to our own church tomorrow. After dinner we should call Ann, Angela, Davina, Kenny and Larry about the emails."

Sunday morning Andy and Lydia are glad to be back in their own church. They both call their friends about the group email file. When Andy calls Larry, he also thanks him for calling the Knoxville TV station. He gives him the day and time, so he can pass the word. Lydia and Andy have a quiet day; they don't turn on the news.

After breakfast Monday morning, Lydia asks Andy, "Do you think the media agent may call you today?"

Andy says, "He might. I have a feeling he will call tomorrow. I better get a haircut today, if I'm going to be on television. Through the years, I've done a lot of radio phone interviews. We need to develop a plan to get on radio. The phone interviews are easy to do."

Lydia says, "I'm glad you thought of that. We need to begin working on scheduling interviews."

THE GOOD NEWS

On Tuesday morning, Andy dresses right after breakfast. The phone rings by 8:00. Andy answers his cell phone. "Andy, this is Irwin Cohen with American Media Productions. Do you have a few minutes right now?"

"Yes, sir."

Cohen says, "Please call me Irwin. I should be calling you "sir". Do you have a pen and paper handy? I have two engagements for you. They're both in Burbank. I thought that would make it more convenient for you, instead of one on the east coast and another on the west coast."

Andy replies, "I appreciate that. Yes, I have a pen and pad by me."

Cohen says, "First of all, I feel like I should address you as Mr. Secretary. I know about your work in serving our country and being awarded The Presidential Medal of Freedom. I also know about your 1965 Purdue team. I usually don't say this to clients: because I admire your work and achievements, I plan to watch both appearances Your first engagement will be on BSS's "The Slanted View" on Thursday, December 15th. You will be due in their studio by 9:00 a.m. Pacific Time."

Andy says, "I have that down."

Cohen says, "Good. I will also send you a confirmation email with the details. Your second engagement is on GIC's "Night Show" on Friday, December 16th. My agency pays your appearance fee and all your expenses. You will make $2,000 for your appearance on "The Slanted View" and $3,000 for your appearance on "The Night Show". For the twelve days before Christmas, their producers want some Christian celebrities on their shows."

Andy asks, "Do they want to roast me over an open fire?"

Cohen laughs heartily. As he continues to laugh, he says, "If you have lines like that on the air, you'll win the audience. In my email, you'll have all the details about your flight, your hotel and your drive. You don't have to worry about a cab or a rental car. The studios have a driver that goes to the airport and to the hotel. There is a great restaurant at the hotel."

Andy asks, "If my wife wants to go, does the package include her stay, meals and tickets to the shows?"

Cohen says, "Absolutely. Before we hang up, I will give you my email and phone number. We will fly you out on December 14th and fly you back on December 17th. Andy it is a great honor to arrange these engagements for you. I'm a fan and both producers are looking forward to having you on their shows. Thank you for your service. I will be in touch by email. A Kelly on the 15th will give you your check before you leave the studio, and a Clint will hand you your check before you leave the studio on the 16th. I will try to answer any questions now or by email."

Andy says, "I think you covered it well. Do you happen to know how long I will be on the air at each show?"

Cohen says, "Some guests have a two to five minute appearance slot. Other guests who have national celebrity status will stay on the show for twenty to thirty minutes. They will break for commercials and sometimes another guest, but they will come back to you during that time frame."

Andy says, "Thank you, Irwin. I'm glad that Jimmy Eastman and you could provide this opportunity. I forgot to ask about my wife's airfare. I don't want to be cheap, so if she decides to go, I can pay it."

Cohen says, "Andy, it is my pleasure to coordinate these engagements for you. Normally, my company doesn't cover a second plane ticket, but I want to thank you for being an inspiration to many people. If she wants to go, we'll take care of her airfare. Do me a favor, if you would. Get a ticket or program from the Night Show and autograph if for me. I wish you a good trip and successful appearances."

Andy says, "Thank you. Send me your mailing address in the email, and I will mail it to you with my autograph."

When they hang up, Andy makes some notes in his calendar book. Lydia notices that Andy is off the phone. She walks in his office and says emotionally, "Was that the agent?"

Andy smiles and says, "Yes. Two engagements in Burbank on December 15th and 16th."

Lydia's voice rises, "Really? In Burbank? You're taunting me. What are the engagements?"

Andy replies, "The Slanted View" and the "Night Show".

Lydia excitedly says, "Really? Are you kidding me?"

Andy laughs and says, "I always tell you the truth."

Lydia runs over to him and hugs him and knocks him to one side in his chair. "Oh, Andy! How wonderful!"

"The agent arranged it, so you can go with me, including the airfare."

Lydia says, "I would love to, but I need to get the house ready for Judy."

Andy replies, "Get the house ready for Lydia before we leave. We will only be gone three days and two nights. We will return the day before I pick up Judy at the airport."

Lydia exclaims, "You talked me into it!" She hugs Andy again.

Andy says, "Speaking of television, I better start making notes for the interview in Knoxville Thursday."

Lydia says, "Yes, and I need to make a plan for contacting radio stations for phone interviews."

Andy says, "I didn't think about it still being early. I'm going to make a cup of coffee first, then watch a national news channel for a little while."

Andy brings a cup of coffee into the great room. He sits down on one of their two recliners and turns the TV on. The first channel he turns to is talking about what you need to know about Medicare (actually every other channel is talking about what you need to know about Medicare).

He finds a news channel reporting the news. A congressional leader who is not wearing a face mask is saying how important it is to wear a face mask. The commentator interrupts the congressional recording with breaking news. She says, "The head park ranger at Yellowstone is reporting an unusual high volume of seismic activity. The ranger reports that they also had to close the park, because the geysers are spewing hotter and higher levels of water." The commentator adds they will immediately share any updates from Yellowstone.

After Andy studies and makes notes, and Lydia begins her plan for contacting radio stations, they talk about the seismic activity in Yellowstone. Andy says, "Jesus gave us good advice about this kind of thing. I think it's in Matthew 5 or 6." He picks up his Bible from the small table by his recliner. He scans chapters 5 and 6 and says, "Here it is in Matthew 6: 34, Jesus said, "So don't worry about tomorrow; for tomorrow will worry about itself. Each day has enough trouble of its own." (AB)

Lydia says, "Very good; a pertinent lesson in disposition."

After supper, they listen to the evening news. In the opening news story, the reporter says, "Today in Chile a 6.3 magnitude earthquake struck. In Santiago, 46 people were killed and 260 were injured. Bridges and roads were damaged and two high rise apartment buildings. In Japan a 6.6 magnitude earthquake struck. In Tokyo and Chiba 345 people were killed and over 600 were injured."

When they go to the next news story, Andy clicks the mute; looks at Lydia and says in a raised voice. "That's part of the Ring of Fire!"

Lydia says, "I know what you're referring to. I need to look it up again."

Andy says, "You probably know that it includes our west coast."

Lydia says, "Yes, the San Andreas Fault is connected to it."

Andy says, "I'm stunned that the increased seismic activity at Yellowstone happened on the same day as these Ring of Fire earthquakes."

Lydia, "It's very sad news. I'm going back to my computer, and continue my radio station search for possible phone interviews."

Lydia comes back in the great room about ten minutes later. She says, "You received good news from the talent agent this morning, and I just received good news from Gladis and Melissa. I was checking my email before I started my search. They both said they got your appearance time and channel on Knoxville TV to a lot of people, churches and some organizations by email."

Andy says, "Excellent! I appreciate their hard work and dedication."

As they get ready for bed, Andy says, "This day went by like a flash."

Lydia replies, "It did seem that way. It was a day of good news, yet a day of tragedy for many people."

Andy says, "It's one more reminder that we don't have much time to get Anderson's story and the gospel message to as many people as possible."

Lydia says, "Your presentation with Kenny and Larry will soon be here."

Andy replies, "Yes, this Sunday in Jefferson City and the TV interview three days before the Sunday service."

As Andy and Lydia dress for bed, Andy's cell phone rings. Lydia asks, "What time is it?' "9:00; it's Gus; he's on my quick dial." Andy answers, "Hi, Gus."

Gus says, 'Sorry to call you late, Andy, but I thought you would want to know the breaking news on the internet. In Nashville, terrorists bombed a Jewish Synagogue and a large Methodist Church that were a block from each other. Both buildings were destroyed."

Andy asks, "Was anyone wounded or killed?"

Gus says, "No. Someone at the scene said a committee had a meeting at the Methodist Church last evening, but not tonight. Thank God the Synagogue and the Church had no rehearsals or meetings tonight. The news reporter interviewed a State Police Officer about the bombing, and he said there is an increase in crime among illegal aliens."

Andy says, "It's getting so bad that more vigilantes will become active."

Gus replies, "It's something that you should say that. On the late news last night, a breaking news report said that an elderly couple came out of an Indianapolis restaurant and two men and one woman started assaulting them. A shot rang out, and it killed one of the men. The other two offenders ran off. Police think the shot came from a car or from a sniper across the street from the restaurant."

Andy replies, "I'm not surprised. There is still a neighborhood watch in my cousin's neighborhood, where Anderson lived. Did your neighbors start a watch in your neighborhood?"

Gus says, "Yes, the beginning of one. Some of our neighbors met and asked all the neighbors in a two block area to keep all of their outside lights on all night. Some of the neighbors at the meeting agreed to watch from their windows at night. I was told that five of them are taking two hour shifts during the ten hours of nighttime. Evidently, when the first one finishes their shift, he or she calls the next one in line."

Andy says, "Not a bad plan for the beginning of a neighborhood watch."

Gus says, "Have a good night. We'll be watching you on TV Thursday afternoon."

"Thank you, Gus. Have a good night." Lydia gets in bed as Andy hangs up. He tells her what Gus said. They kiss good night and say a prayer together.

When Andy wakes up he is thinking that this is the last full day before his interview on Knoxville television. Lydia, Davina, Gladis, Gracie and Melissa are all busy compiling contacts for Andy's appearances in Burbank and other locations. Andy says to Lydia, "Would you call Gladis and make sure it is alright to show her email during the program tomorrow. I would like for the producer to show our email and hers during the program in case of any errors."

Lydia says, "I don't know her work schedule today. If she's not at home, I will ask Gracie to have her call me today."

Before supper Andy finishes his notes for the Thursday interview. Gladis returns Lydia's call by 6 p.m. and gives them permission to use her email on the program.

By 2:00 Thursday, Andy pulls into the station's parking lot in central Knoxville. He reviews his notes before he gets out of his car. He realizes he can't read notes during the interview, but he has highlights on small index cards. We walks into the station a few minutes early. He is greeted by a young lady, who is smiling from ear to ear. He says, "I'm Andy McGraig."

She says, "I'm Tosha Powell. We're glad you could be with us today. I told my parents and grandparents you would be on the program today; they're big fans of yours."

Andy says, "Thank you, Tosha. It's a privilege to be here."

Tosha says, "Megan wants me to sit down with you and take notes that might be helpful to Allison, our commentator."

Andy replies, "First of all, have her call me, Andy. Many times a person wants to call me Mr. Secretary or Mr. McGraig. I know that Megan has probably shared that the first nine minutes of the interview is an intriguing story that I have to share. The last half we will mention my 1965 championship team; the Presidential Medal of Freedom; serving as Secretary of State and Veterans."

Tosha says, "Yes, sir. I will tell her, and I know she has some of that information. About 2:45 we want to show you a seat so the cameraman can get your picture. Even though you don't appear until 3:30, you will be announced as our special guest today. We also have been announcing your appearance the past two days. At the opening of the show, and at times when we break for a commercial, we will show your picture and tell the viewers to stay tuned."

Andy says, "Sounds good."

Tosha also adds, "When you're seated for the cameraman at 2:45, one of our assistants may use a comb or a little powder, if that is okay?"

Andy smiles and says, "Do I need it?"

Tosha laughs and says, "You look good."

Andy takes a seat for the cameraman and the stylist at 2:45. Before the show begins, he takes a trip to the men's room. From 3:00 to 3:25 he watches the show and enjoys it. At 3:25 Tosha takes him to a seat where he will be interviewed. While the other commentator and hostess is interviewing someone, Allison comes over and greets him.

She shakes his hand and says, "I'm Allison. It's an honor having you today. We're looking forward to the interview and to your story. In four minutes, I will be sitting here and introducing you to our viewers."

Just before the last commercial break ends the attractive hostess takes a seat by Andy. The red light comes on the camera and the cameraman gives Allison her cue. As Allison looks at the camera, she says, "We're honored to have Andy McGraig with us during the last half of our show today. Andy received the Presidential Medal of Freedom after the Seven Day Border War in 1962, and he served as Secretary of State. Our basketball fans will like knowing that Andy was the MVP on the 1965 NCAA championship team with Purdue," Allison looks at Andy and says, "Andy, I feel like I should be addressing you as Mr. Secretary. You have an inspirational story to share with us first, but will you briefly tell us how you became our Secretary of State?"

Andy looks at Allison and says, "Thank you, Allison. Yes, I do prefer to be called, Andy. In 1962, I had an opportunity to serve in the State Department. At the end of my freshman year, the Boston Celtics gave me an offer, but I wanted to serve my country. I trained as a special agent for the State Department. I served two years, then finished at Purdue and returned to the State Department. I served several years as a special agent, then I became a Deputy Secretary. After I served over fifteen years in the State Department, I served two appointments as Secretary of State."

Allison says, "Thank you, Andy, for your service. I realize that you're here today to honor our veterans, who we're honoring tomorrow on Veteran's Day. Before we talk about our veterans and your service to our country, you have a unique and inspirational, true story for us."

Andy replies, "Yes and thank you for the time to share this important story. Allison, we live in a free country." Anderson then looks at the camera as says, "Through our country's history, millions of men and women have laid down their lives for our freedom. Many or most of those men and women were believers in God and freedom. Because of their courage and the freedom that they achieved for us, our nation honored them and all of our veterans and citizens by making "In God We Trust" our national motto. My first cousin, Anderson McCollister, was one of our citizens who loved our country and followed Christ."

"I grew up with Anderson. He was a great friend, family man and business leader. When he retired, he moved to our area He had a country home in Sevier County, which bordered Cocke County. He was a people person and a great help to his family and friends. Allison, you and your viewers have heard the reports of people throughout the world who were visited by friends and family members who disappeared. My cousin, Anderson, was one of those who visited two family members and a friend. He visited his daughter who is a full professor at a respectable university. He visited his sister, who is a retired school teacher. He also visited his best friend, who is a Marine veteran and a retired state police officer."

"I realize that some believers may doubt all of the stories, because they think of what Abraham said to the rich man in hell about Lazarus not visiting his living brothers. I want to remind them, when Christ was crucified, bodies were even raised from the dead and visited people in Jerusalem. We know that Enoch and Elijah never passed away. We also know that Moses and Elijah met with Christ on the Mount of Transfiguration.

I believe that the significance of these appearances is because of the soon coming of Christ and the soon coming of the rapture of the church, which is described in the Bible. We don't have enough air time for me to detail Anderson's disappearance, visits and all that he had to say.

He did tell his friend and relatives to be ready, because the rapture of the church will take place real soon. He also told them that God wants everyone to know this and to know that the only way there is to follow Christ and His Word."

Andy then looks at Allison again and says, "Allison, I don't have time to write a book, because we're trying to get the message out as quickly as we can to as many people as possible. Do you mind, if I share when I will be on two national programs in just three weeks?"

Allison replies, "Please do."

While Allison replies to Andy, he checks his notes. He looks at the camera and says, "On Thursday, December 15th, I will be on "The Slanted View" program on BSS. On Friday, December 16th, I will be on the "Night Show" with Bud Looney on GIC."

Allison looks at Andy and says, "Thank you, Andy, for sharing that powerful message that we should take to heart." She looks at the camera and says, "We have to take a break for our sponsors, and we will be write back with our special guest, Andy McGraig, our former Secretary of State."

Allison looks at Andy and says, "That was a very powerful message, Andy. Thank you for being here and sharing it."

Andy replies, "Thank you for your time and hospitality."

Allison says, "In three minutes, we'll be back on the air. Do you need a bottle of water or anything?"

Andy says, "A bottle of water would be good."

Allison says to a stage hand who is looking on, "Two bottles of water please."

They each have time to drink some water and to get situated for the next ten minutes. The red light comes back on and Allison says to the camera, "We're here today with Andy McGraig, former Secretary of State and resident in the Knoxville viewing area."

Allison looks at Andy and says, "We're looking forward to being with special veterans on our program tomorrow. Andy, how long did you serve our country in the State Department?"

"As a special agent, deputy secretary and two appointments as Secretary of State, I served a little over thirty years. We wanted to move to this area sooner, but I served as a consultant off and on for a number of years."

Allison says, "Tell us about the Seven Day Border War and how you became a recipient of the Presidential Medal of Freedom."

Andy replies, "I was a special agent, who had some special assignments. Overall, my assignments are still classified, but I can tell you my opinion of how they may have decided to give me the Presidential Medal of Freedom. The generals and soldiers did an excellent job.

Lives were lost and those brave men and women paid the ultimate price. I was able to help with some military decisions that probably helped us win a quick and decisive victory."

Allison says, "I have no doubt that your service was vital to the war and victory."

Andy says, "I want to thank all of the veterans for their service. I've had the honor to meet many fine leaders in our government and military."

Allison says, "We have a couple of minutes left before we sign off. Before we announce our program tomorrow, I'm sure many of our viewers would like to know more about Andy McGraig, basketball MVP and national champion."

Andy laughs and says, "That was a long time ago. Everyone on the Purdue team gave their best. Two of the starting five are special friends, John Damber and Larry Quarles. Larry is the former head coach of men's basketball at Carson-Newman, and he played in the NBA. John could play as well as most players in the NBA. When I played basketball in high school, I played against one of the best players in the nation; Mr. Indiana of 1960, Ron Bonham. He went on to win a NCAA championship and two NBA championships."

Allison says, "I just got a text from our producer who says she heard they called you Avalanche Andy. Why was that?"

Andy laughs and says, "Reporters back then said I was agile for a big guy. When I played, I had the record in college basketball and also of those in the NBA for bench pressing the most."

Allison says, "Okay. Now I understand. I'm a basketball fan too. You delivered like Karl Malone, the Mail Man."

Andy replies, "That's the idea. I would like to add that we would like to tell Anderson's story on radio and in churches and other organizations."

Allison looks at the camera and says, "We thank Andy McGraig, our former Secretary of State, for being our special guest today. We thank him for helping us announce Veterans Day tomorrow and honoring our veterans. Join us at 3:00 tomorrow for a special Veterans Day program. Have a great day."

Allison stands up and shakes Andy's hand. She says, "Thank you, Andy, for being on our program. You did a great job today, and I can tell that you served our country well. Please come back and be on a future program."

Andy says, "Thank you for inviting me. It was wonderful being here and sharing with you during the interview."

Allison smiles and says, "God bless."

Andy says, "God bless you."

Tosha appears and hands Andy a card and envelope. While Tosha watches, Andy opens the thank you card from the television staff and looks at a nice gift card that he and Lydia can use in Knoxville or Pigeon Forge. Tosha says, "You did a great job today. Can I get anything for you?"

Andy replies, "How about the bottle of water that I had at my chair?"

Tosha brings him the water. She says, "When you're ready, I will walk with you to the door.' When they get to the door, Tosha says, "Here is my program outline for today. Will you autograph it near your name on the program?"

Andy says, "I will be glad to." He signs it and hands it to her. He says, "It's a pleasure meeting you today."

Tosha says, "My dad served in the army, and when I was young, he was killed in Afghanistan. Do you mind, if I give you a hug?"

Andy says, "Not at all. It is an honor."

Tosha hugs him and Andy says, "Tosha, we have a big God, and he's watching over you and me."

Tosha replies, "Yes, He is. I'm to tell you that when we took a commercial break, we showed the two emails with your picture. Your interview with Allison was very good."

Andy touches her shoulder and says, "Thank you, Tosha."

When Andy gets in his car, he shivers and thinks, "It has gotten a good bit colder, since I've been in the station."

As Andy drives the interstate in east Knoxville, he thinks, "I will be ready for some hot coffee, when I get home." He lowers the volume on his radio and puts in an Alan Jackson CD. The music keeps him alert and he's home in less than an hour.

When he walks through the front door, Lydia is all smiles. She hugs him and says, "You were excellent! I'm so glad that you got the word out to churches, radio stations and organizations."

Andy says, "I either had that reminder in my notes or reminded myself in the last few minutes of the show."

Lydia says, "I recorded the hour program, so we can watch it when we want to."

Andy says, "As I drove home, I got in the mood for some coffee."

Lydia says, "I will fix you a cup with the Keurig. If you want to, stretch out on the recliner."

In a couple of minutes, Lydia brings the coffee to Andy and puts it on the stand by his recliner. Andy sleepily says, "I think I started to doze."

Lydia says, "Good. It will take me a few minutes for the finishing touches on supper. I prepared one of our old standbys: spaghetti and turkey meatballs with parmesan cheese, garlic bread and salad."

Andy says, "Perfect. I worked up a good appetite this evening."

Lydia says, "I will bring your salad in a couple minutes." When Lydia brings the salad, Andy says a prayer."

Just a few minutes after they finish supper, Andy's cell phone rings. He looks at his phone then Lydia; he says, "It's Larry." Andy answers and says, "Is this the TV celebrity?"

Larry laughs and says, "You're the celebrity, but thank you for mentioning me. I hope I didn't call too early. I was chomping at the bit to talk with you."

Andy replies, "I'm glad you called. We finished supper a few minutes ago, and now I'm relaxing on the recliner."

Larry says, "First of all, it was a great idea to show the two emails with your picture. They showed it about three times. If anyone missed it, they can call the station. Secondly, it was a captivating interview. Melissa and I watched the whole hour. You and Allison couldn't have been better. It was good thinking to end the interview with reaching out to churches, radio stations and organizations. When you check your email, don't be surprised to find several invitations in it."

Andy says, "Gladis is a good computer director for us. If she has any invitations in her email, she will probably forward them to me right away. I will check my email before I get ready for bed. Thank you for doing the leg work on setting up the interview."

"I just made a simple call, brother. Melissa and I want to do what we can. With all of the end time signs happening, we feel that the Lord will call us home real soon."

Andy says, "Lydia and I feel the same way."

Larry says, "I'm going to sign off. Get some rest this evening and stay in touch."

Andy replies, "Will do and keep lookin' up!"

Larry says, "I will."

Andy says to Lydia, "It was good to hear from Larry. I'm thankful that he's on our outreach team."

Lydia says, "He and Melissa are a blessing."

Andy looks at the time and says, "I'm glad the evening news has already started. This has been a great day, and I hate to upset the apple cart with more of the bad news we've been hearing."

Lydia says, "I know. When I start to listen to the news, I wonder how bad the report is going to be."

Andy replies, "Thank God we know the one who will bring peace on earth and good will to mankind."

Andy tunes in to some relaxing melodic jazz while they read.

When Lydia gets up and says, "I'm getting ready for bed," Andy says, "I will join you in a few minutes. I need to check my email."

Andy finds two emails from a radio station in Knoxville and another radio station in Maryville.

Both are invitations to join their DJs for an interview." Andy writes down their phone numbers.

On Friday morning Lydia and Andy make plans to get some household errands completed by noon. Andy says, "After lunch, I will check my emails and call the two radio stations."

While they're out, Lydia says, "It's a beautiful day. I'm glad it warmed up a little. Even though we know grilled chicken is better for us, I'm in the mood for fried chicken."

Andy says, "Sounds good to me. Let's get the whole works; fried chicken, cole slaw and beans!"

Lydia laughs and says, "Nothing like splurging at times!"

After they finish their errands, they pick up fried chicken as they head home.

They enjoy their lunch in their dining area and Andy says, "It's nice to have a treat now and then.'

Lydia says, "It is, but I eat too much, when we treat ourselves to fried chicken or to pizza."

Andy says, "I better check my email. If I get more invitations, I will be busy on the phone today."

The first email Andy opens is from Gladis. She writes a short note and says how much she and her family enjoyed the interview in Knoxville. She forwards an invitation from the largest church in the Knoxville area,

Concord Baptist. She also forwards an invitation from the Kiwanis and from the Rotary Club in Knoxville.

Andy thinks, "Now I have five calls to make." As he scans his other emails, he opens invitations from Cokesbury United Methodist and Cedar Springs Presbyterian in Knoxville.

Andy says out loud, "The running total is now seven calls!"

Lydia yells from the great room and asks, "What did you say, honey?"

Andy says loudly, "I was talking to myself and said that I have seven calls to make from seven invitations!"

Lydia cries out, "That's great!"

Before Andy makes the first call, he gets out his calendar book, then he makes a list of the seven starting with those who will reach the most people. He thinks, "I have the engagement Sunday in Jefferson City, then we're in the last week of November. We have to fly to California on December 14th and after we return, Judy will be here on the 18th. As Andy thinks about the number of invitations and time restraints, his phone rings. On his quick dial he sees Kenny's name.

Andy answers, and asks, "How are you doing, Brother Kenny?"

Kenny replies, "Good, my friend. How are you and Lydia?"

Andy says, "We're doing well and getting busy with our outreach."

Kenny says, "I read your email about your two interviews in California. Congratulations! I called the big Christian TV station that is just south of Charlotte. They have shows that are shown nationwide by satellite. There are a couple shows they produce that I thought would interest you. They want you to call them. The station manager knows about your work as Secretary of State. I think they will schedule you." Kenny gives Andy their phone number.

Andy replies, "That's great news, Kenny. Do you want to go with me?"

Kenny says, "I will go with you, but I'm not sure that I want to be on their show."

Andy says, "That's up to you. I would be glad to pick you up, and we could go together."

Kenny says, "Call me and let me know what they say. Are you thinking about a date before your California trip?"

"Yes. I did a TV interview in Knoxville yesterday, and we have already received a lot of invitations. I may need your help and Ann's to fill all of the engagements. They're in the Knoxville area. Your story and Ann's are the most significant, since Anderson visited both of you. Angela lives too far away to make those engagements."

Kenny says, "Let me know the details. If you find out anything today, call me this weekend."

Andy says, "I sure will brother. Let's keep praying for our team."

Kenny says, "I will, my friend. Give Lydia my regards."

Andy says, "I will tell her, and I will call you this weekend."

When Andy gets off the phone, he thinks, "I have about four hours to make eight calls while they're offices are open."

Andy reorganizes his list. The satellite TV station near Charlotte goes at the top of the list.

He knows the two radio station appointments can be done at home with phone interviews. He gets out his calendar book and looks at the last ten days of November, which includes Thanksgiving. He also looks at the first twelve days of December before the California flight.

He puts the churches after the TV station, then the organization and then the radio stations. He leans back and contemplates the list and calls. He decides to make some coffee, then make all the calls before 5:00.

By 4:30, he walks out of his office and looks for Lydia. He finds her cleaning the flower beds outside. Andy says, "I didn't realize that it got over 60 degrees today."

Lydia says, "You were busy in the office, and I couldn't resist getting out in the nice weather."

Andy replies, "I would too. Did you hear me talking with Kenny a few hours ago?"

"No, I heard your phone ring, and I heard you talking to someone."

Andy says, "Kenny added one more invitation to my list of seven. He called the big Christian TV station near Charlotte. I set the date for Friday, November 25th, the day after Thanksgiving. The station is producing one of their own shows that day. It will be telecasted live. I picked that day, because the show airs at 4:00, and the station manager projects a larger viewing audience during Thanksgiving weekend."

Lydia asks, "Is Kenny going with you?"

Andy says, "Yes, but he may decide to not be on the show. If he is free that day, I will pick him up at home. He's on the Waynesville side of Maggie Valley. He's an hour from us, and he is three hours or so from Charlotte. If I pick him up at 10:00, we will have plenty of time for lunch on the way. I'm allowing extra time, since we have to be at the studio by 3:20.

It will be mostly dark, when I drive back to his house. I will probably sleep there and get back around 10:00 Saturday morning."

Lydia asks, "What did you find out about the other contacts?

Andy replies, "All five want me to come and the two radio stations want to do phone interviews with me. I will only have November 28th through December 12th to fulfill those engagements. December 4th and December 11th are the only two Sundays during that time for the three churches. I told all of the contacts that I will call them back to arrange time and dates with them. I think I will ask Larry to fill in for me at the Cedar Springs Presbyterian Church. I remember Anderson or Ann mentioning Concord Baptist and Cokesbury United Methodist."

Lydia says, "Do you have to fulfill those invitations before the California trip?"

Andy says, "It has been over four hours, since I checked my email. Let me check my email, and I will give you an answer."

Lydia says, "I fixed tuna salad for supper. Do you want to eat in a few minutes?"

Andy says, "That would be great. Give me about fifteen minute, and I will be with you."

Andy gets in his email, and the first one is from Gladis. She sent it about ten minutes before he opened it. She has three more invitations in her email. Andy sees four more emails that he needs to open. In those emails he finds invitations from three churches and a Christian radio station in Jefferson City. He writes down the names and contact numbers, then joins Lydia for supper."

After they pray, Andy says, "The answer is "yes". Gladis sent me another email with three more invitations, and I had four more invitations in emails. It looks like we could try to schedule those between Christmas and the end of January. I think I can speak to the Kiwanis or Rotary Club. Do you think you and Ann could speak at the other club? Ann is one of our key witnesses of Anderson's visits."

Lydia says, "I don't see why we couldn't. We were both teachers and use to addressing groups of people."

After supper, Andy decides on tentative dates for the two radio phone interviews, the two churches and for the Kiwanis and The Rotary Club. He calls Larry to see if he wants to speak at Cedar Springs.

Andy tells Lydia that Larry is willing to share Anderson's story at Cedar Springs. Andy says, "They'll be excited to have Larry, when they find out he coached at Carson-Newman and played in the NBA. Do you think we can handle listening to the 6:00 news?"

Lydia says, "I guess we should; we need to get updated."

10

No News Would Be Good News

L ydia and Andy turn on the 6:00 news, and after thirty minutes they almost regret having a reality check. They hear a feature story about several companies in Europe and the United States working on a new method for purchasing goods. One company officer of a northern European company reports that they are experimenting with implanting chips in the right forearms of volunteers. They also have developed a machine that recognizes and records monetary transactions with the implanted chips.

A CEO of another company in Brussels, Belgium, explains they have developed new computer technology that allows them to stamp the human body, so a machine can read the information for transactions. The CEO continues and says that the high tech stamp contains a person's ID and personal information like monetary balances. He says, "We have developed machines that read the stamp. We have imprinted the stamp on subjects' foreheads and right hands. One machine will read the stamp on a person's forehead, if they are under a designated height. The same machine will read the stamp on a person's right hand, if they are over a designated height."

After the featured report, Lydia says, "That's enough bad news for me! It's like listening to a story from the twilight zone. I hope I don't have dreams about the anti-Christ and the Mark of the Beast tonight."

Andy turns off the TV and says, "The Revelation prophecy is coming into fruition. Our society has become so desensitized to violence, abortion killings and things like tattoos that most people won't have a problem with getting their forehead or right hand stamped in the near future.

When it's time to get stamped, many people will say, "That's nothing. I already have tattoos on my body." Of course, some people have tattoos all over their bodies. They might let a person pick the type of image the stamp is displayed in; like design choices for their bank checks. Maybe they will be able to choose between a flower, a dog, a cat or a cartoon character like Goofy or Dopey."

Before they go to bed, they listen to John Hagee and David Jeremiah on television. As they get ready for bed, Lydia asks, "Have you thought about our outreach group having a website?"

Andy says, "Yes. I even thought about calling it andersonsstory.com. Someone else in the group would need to be in charge of the project. I wouldn't have the time to look into it until after January. Gladis is doing a good job. She would probably be best at organizing it, but I don't want to ask her to do more until after New Year's."

Lydia says, "It's a challenge to get everything done that we want to do."

Saturday morning, Angela calls Anderson. She says, "Yesterday, I set an interview appointment with one of the bigger TV stations in Indianapolis. Of course, I told them that I'm a psychology professor at the University of Indianapolis, but I also told them that my cousin, a former Secretary of State and MVP of the 1965 NCAA championship team, is in our group. Naturally they want to interview you also, but I guessed that you were busy through the holidays."

Andy replies, "Well, first of all, Angie, that's great news! Yes, I am real busy with engagements until after January. Once I appeared on Knoxville television, things got real busy."

"Uncle Andy, I'm so glad to hear it. I think about the rapture every day. I really do believe it will happen soon. My thoughts are extremely different now compared to how I thought before I committed my life to Christ. I'm not only going to share Dad's story during the interview, but I'm also going to share that the humanistic philosophy is common in the field of psychology."

Andy says, "God will give you what to say. When is your appearance?"

Lydia says, "It's next Wednesday, the day before Thanksgiving. Their program begins at 3:00. I think they're going to try and give me fifteen minutes."

Andy says, "Set your pre-record for me. When I'm in your area, I would like to watch it. Angela, your dad will be proud of you."

"Thank you so much, Uncle Andy. Have a Happy Thanksgiving. I love you and give my love to Lydia."

Andy replies, "We love you too and Happy Thanksgiving!"

Andy walks out of his office and tells Lydia about his talk with Angela.

Lydia says, "That's wonderful news! Angela is experiencing God's love and convicting power. Will you tell me when you schedule Kiwanis or The Rotary Club? I need to call Ann soon so we can set an engagement with the other club."

Andy says, "Absolutely. I will call The Rotary Club now."

Andy goes back in his office and sets a date with The Rotary Club. He calls the contact person with the Kiwanis and explains how tight his schedule is. He tells their coordinator that his wife and cousin are retired teachers and use to public speaking. He also tells him that his cousin is one of the three people who Anderson visited.

Andy shares the news with Lydia and she says, "Good. I will call Ann now about the engagement, then I will call your contact person and set a date and time."

Andy goes back in his office to think about the service Sunday. Andy calls Kenny to make sure he will be at their house before 9:30 a.m. Sunday. After he talks with Kenny, he touches base with Larry.

Andy says, "I just talked with Kenny and he said he plans to speak no more than five minutes on Sunday."

Larry says, "I'm planning the same thing. If Kenny and I together take less than ten minutes, then you should have fifteen to twenty minutes."

Andy says, "Sounds like a plan. Do you know if Aaron is bringing his wife?"

Larry replies, "I only know that Aaron wants to be bring her. Melissa is planning to come. You always want to pay for everyone's dinner. I have a suggestion. For dinner after church, I want to pay for Kenny's meal and mine and Melissa's."

Andy laughs and says, "It's a deal! After the service, we'll get dinner in Jefferson City or Dandridge. I hope Aaron's wife come. I'm also looking forward to seeing you and Melissa. Over dinner Sunday, we'll catch up on our group email activities. Kenny and I will share about a trip we're taking to Charlotte on the day after Thanksgiving."

Larry says, "Brother, it's always a joy talking with you. Service time Sunday is 10:45. Are we going to rendezvous with the pastor and each other before 10:30?"

Andy replies, "Yes, let's meet in the main foyer by 10:20. We can ask for the pastor before 10:30. What do you think about you starting the message, then Kenny, then me?"

Larry says, "I agree. I'm excited about the service. I will probably be in the foyer around 10:15."

Andy says, "Very good. Lydia, Kenny and I plan to be there early also."

After Andy talks with Larry, he and Lydia catch up on each other's phone calls. Lydia says that she scheduled Ann and her with the Kiwanis on Thursday, December 4th, at 4:00 in Calhoun's meeting room.

Andy says, "Larry and I went over the plans for Sunday. I need to call

Kenny again. The service begins at 10:45. I will ask him to be here around 9:15."

On Sunday morning, Larry, Melissa, Andy, Lydia and Kenny are in the First Baptist foyer at the Carson-Newman campus before 10:20. Larry says, "Aaron will be here early to get an assigned seat. The pastor asked him to sit on the middle, front pew. He said his wife wouldn't come. The pastor wants to meet with Kenny, Andy and me in a few minutes."

The group of friends talk and pray for a few minutes, then they walk into the large and inviting sanctuary to reach the pastor's office. The spacious sanctuary has a balcony and white pews with sides that are squared off on top like those in the traditional Congregational Churches. Melissa and Lydia have a seat near the front, as the three men walk to the pastor's office.

When the men come back into the sanctuary, the church is packed. The pastor says, "The church is almost to capacity. There are over 1,000 people here. The organist is playing the beautiful old hymn, "Great Is Thy Faithfulness".

After the opening ceremonies, the pastor introduces Larry. He says, "Larry Quarles was our head basketball coach for many years, and he led the Carson-Newman men's basketball team to the final four!" The Carson-Newman students in the audience cheer. "Our current coach, Aaron Michaels, is with us today. Aaron, please stand and turn around so everyone can see you." Aaron stands and waves, and the Carson-Newman students cheer and applaud.

The pastor continues, "Larry's MVP teammate at Purdue was Andy McGraig. They won a national championship, and Andy will also be speaking with us today. He is a former Secretary of State. Larry will introduce him and their friend Kenny Goodpaster. Give Larry a good welcome." Applause and cheers erupt again.

Larry walks to the pulpit and towers over it with his tall frame. He says, "Thank you, kindly. I appreciate the great support I had at Carson-Newman for a long time. It is good to be with you today. My wife and Andy's wife are seated near the front. Melissa and Lydia, please stand for everyone." They stand and wave. Larry says, "Our outreach team is growing. Aaron is on our team, and Kenny, Andy and I are here to share with you what we're doing.'

"I have been friends with our special speaker today, since we met at Purdue. Andy McGraig is truth, character and conviction at its best. He served twice as our nation's Secretary of State, and he won the Presidential Medal of Freedom award for his role in the Seven Day Southern Border

War. He was also the best basketball player I knew, and I played in the NBA. Our friend Kenny was Andy's cousin's best friend. Andy and Kenny will tell you Anderson's story today.

About seven months ago, most of us heard some news reports of people in this country and people of some other countries being visited by a friend or relative, who had passed on Andy's cousin, Anderson McCollister, was a dedicated follower of Christ. He was one of those who returned to visit his friend, daughter and sister. Kenny is here to tell you about Anderson's visit. Kenny is a Marine veteran and a retired State Police Officer. He has a farm near Maggie Valley, N.C. Give Kenny a warm welcome."

Kenny comes to the pulpit as the crowd applauds. Kenny says, "Anderson and I were friends for twenty years. He was getting ready to retire from a Fortune 500 company. He was vice-president of their international marketing. Like Andy, he was a man of high character. I received a call from Lydia Ann, Anderson's sister. It was midafternoon; I think in late March of this year. He had gone hiking in his woods, and did not return at the designated time. With two friends, we searched the woods and trails from late afternoon until 10:00 at night. Between 5:00 and 6:00, several officers from the county joined the search. I found his walking stick, but we never found Anderson.

About two weeks later he appeared at my farm without any mode of transportation. I was working outside. At first, I didn't recognize him, because he had just turned eighty and he looked like he was 40. We talked for a couple hours. We went in the house, and we had a diet soda. He had several things to share that he was instructed to tell me. He said he had seen heaven. He also said that too many people are straddling the fence. He said that I should stop following Native American religious beliefs; I'm Cherokee. Anderson said that Christ is the only way. He said I should tell as many people as possible that Christ is coming for the Church real soon."

Kenny continues, "Before Anderson left, he wanted to see the redbuds and dogwoods in bloom. We both love nature, and I had hiked several times with him in his woods. As we walked into a field, he said, "Kenny, walk toward your house. I have to walk toward the middle of the field."

As I walked toward the house with my dog, I looked back several times, and the last time I looked, it appeared that Anderson vanished into thin air." Anderson ends the story and the audience in the sanctuary is spellbound. You could hear a pin drop in the silence.

Kenny says, "Now I want to introduce my friend and Anderson's cousin, Andy McGraig."

As Kenny walks to his seat and big Andy walks to the pulpit, the crowd suddenly erupts in applause.

Andy humbly says, "Thank you. Can we now have an even bigger applause for our Lord Jesus Christ?" The crowd cheers with "Amen" and applauds even louder. Andy says, "Thank you. I hope you open your hearts and minds and are blessed by this testimony and and service today. Anderson and I grew up together. He was five years older. He and his family were our best friends. He was at the top of his class in business at Purdue. He was very successful, a loving family man and a dedicated man of God. Our house is not far from his, but I was doing consulting work with the State Department, when Anderson disappeared."

"After he disappeared, he visited his sister, then Kenny, then his daughter in Indiana. I immediately believed Kenny's, Ann's and Angela's stories. With Kenny, Ann, Angela, Davina, our daughter, and my wife, we organized an outreach group. We have a group email. If you want to receive our emails, please leave your name and email with an usher, who will pass it on to the pastor. Larry or I will get your emails from the pastor."

"Kenny also told me Anderson said that only the Father knows when Christ will rapture the church; as we know from the Bible. God's Word says that the Father knows the day and the hour. Anderson told Kenny that he can't say that it will happen now or in seven months or in fourteen months. He stressed to be ready. Anderson said that we need to follow Christ and his teachings daily. Anderson's warning is that the rapture of the church will happen real soon. Lay aside the sins and cares of the world. We are here to share Anderson's warning of urgency and to remind you of what is prophesied in the Bible.

All of the end time signs are happening. America and the world are crumbling. America is paying a heavy price for its great violation of human rights. Hitler killed 18 million people;. Stalin killed 20 million people and Mao Tse Tung killed 50 million people. American abortionists and their supporters have killed 70 million babies. God is judging America and the world for not following His commands."

"Are you ready? Have you committed your life to Christ? Are you following Christ and His teachings daily? If you need to rededicate your life to Christ; or receive Christ as your Savior or make a commitment today to share this same message with others, please come forward now as the pianist plays."

At the end of the service, it looks like half of the crowd is coming forward. After the service, Andy, Larry and the pastor meet for a moment, and they comment that over five hundred people came forward and made decisions to follow Christ.

Larry keeps his eye on Aaron. When he sees that Aaron is done talking with some of the Carson-Newman students, Larry goes over to him and says, "Can you go out to dinner with us?"

Aaron says, "I would like to, but I want to pick up dinner for us and take it home."

Larry says, "Have a good day. Our engagement at Cedar Springs is coming around the corner."

Aaron smiles and says, "I'm looking forward to it. Good job today, coach."

Larry laughs and says, 'You've gotta shoot'em straight!"

Andy waits on Larry and asks if Aaron is coming with them. Larry says, "No. I think he was disappointed that his wife didn't come. He's going with me to the Cedar Springs Church."

Andy says, "Good. I'm glad he's part of our outreach."

The five team members go to a popular restaurant near I-40. It's located between Larry's home and Andy's home. They have a good time visiting over dinner. Kenny lets his hair down more than usual and doesn't head for Maggie Valley until 3:30.

That evening while Lydia and Andy sit in the great room, Andy says, "Now I have to stop and think about what's next."

Lydia smiles and says, "I know. The Lord is blessing. Gladis has been a big help. I hope we can take time and get with the Rivera's soon."

Andy says, "Me too. It would be nice, if Gus and Gladis could speak at churches in the Cosby area. They make a good father and daughter team. Gladis could begin by telling her story in Gatlinburg and Gus could end the message with Anderson's story and an invitation."

Lydia says, "Let's suggest that, when we get with them."

11

THANKSGIVING 2022

A ndy does the two radio phone interviews on Tuesday and Wednesday. The first one begins at 8 a.m. and the Wednesday morning interview begins at 8:30. One is with the Knoxville bluegrass station that Andy has enjoyed for years. The other interview is with Knoxville's classic rock station.

Lydia is busy planning for Thanksgiving. Davina and her family are coming to their house for Thanksgiving dinner.

Andy catches up on the group emails with Gladis and Melissa. He makes sure Officer Rachel Walling and Aaron Michaels are in the group emails. He calls both Rachel and Aaron to let them know how much he appreciates them being in their group outreach.

Andy also finalizes the appearance dates and times with Concord Baptist in Farragut; Cokesbury United Methodist in Knoxville and The Rotary Club in Knoxville. He organizes his notes for all three appearances.

Lydia and Andy talk about how the news reports are getting worse every day. Lydia says, "The weekend news was bad enough, and this week it has gotten worse."

On Thursday, Davina and her family arrive just after 1:00. For almost three hours they enjoy a feast of traditional Thanksgiving food; sharing memories; telling jokes and humorous experiences and laughing much of the time. By 4:00 Davina says, "We better get back to Crossville; it will be dark soon."

Lydia gets up and says, "I will pack some turkey, dressing, ham and pumpkin pie for you."

Andy laughs and says, "We can all work out extra the rest of the week."

Everyone shares a hug before Davina and her family step out into a light rain. Lydia and Andy follow them to the front porch. As they get close to their car, Lydia yells out, "Be careful! We love you!"

Davina yells back, "We love you too, mom and dad!"

As they pull out of the drive, Lydia and Andy wave. Andy puts his arm around Lydia and leans down to kiss her. He says, "Happy Thanksgiving, sweetheart."

Lydia says, "Oh, Andy, I love you as much as ever."

Andy says, "Me too, honey. It says a lot, when I think about all the wonderful times we had at Purdue and after college."

As they clean up the kitchen, Andy says, "I know we dread to watch the 6:00 news, but I need to catch up with current events."

Lydia replies, "I know. I need to watch too. I will fix some hot tea or coffee for us. It will be in time for the news before we know it."

Andy says, "After the news, I'm going to get ready for the Charlotte trip tomorrow. I want to leave by 8:30, so I have plenty of time to get to Kenny's house."

When they get the kitchen straightened up, Lydia says, "If you want to turn the TV on, go ahead and have a seat in the great room. Do you want coffee or tea?"

Andy replies, "Give me black tea please. Thank you, honey."

When Andy turns the TV on, he realizes that it will be over thirty minutes before the 6:00 news begins. Andy goes ahead and turns it to the news channel. At the bottom of the screen in big red letters is "Breaking News – National Emergency". The first scene Andy sees are flashing red lights and blue lights of ambulances, fire trucks and law enforcement cars.

Andy also sees some military vehicles. There is a reporter at the scene saying something about the Indian Point Nuclear Plant near New York City. He now hears the reporter talking about terrorism and other power plant disasters. Andy thinks about going in the kitchen to get Lydia, but he knows that she will be in the great room soon enough.

Just before Lydia brings the tea, the news station switches back to the anchor in the news room. He says, "We are still getting new reports about the concerted attack by terrorists on our nuclear power plants. Over 30 million people are without power right now; about ten percent of our nation's population. If you're just joining us, terrorists today attacked at least half of our nuclear power plants and about fifty nuclear reactors."

Lydia walks in the great room; stops and looks at the TV and says, "What's going on, honey?"

Andy says, "Terrorists today attacked about half of our nuclear power plants."

Lydia says, "Oh, no." Trembling a little, she sets Andy's tea down and has a seat in the other recliner.

The reporter continues, "We understand that the plants they attacked were near some of our biggest populations. Some of the cities with big populations that have been hit hard are Chicago, Dallas, Fort Worth, Houston, Minneapolis, the Chicago area, Miami, the New York City area, Philadelphia, New Orleans and Phoenix. New reports keep coming in every few minutes. The reported death toll so far is over 9,000. The reported wounded including radiation exposure is over 30,000. Those killed and wounded include terrorists, military, security, law officers and citizens."

So far, it is estimated that over four thousand terrorists descended on roughly thirty nuclear power plants and fired on security and electrical stations. They fired shoulder-launched rockets, which are bunker busters. The also fired mortars into the cooling towers. Fires broke out with nuclear meltdowns in every plant they attacked."

Andy turns down the volume on the remote a little and says, "In some respects this is worse than the beginning of the Seven Day Border War." He turns the volume back up and pushes the record button.

The commentator is saying, "The attacks began between 3 a.m. and 6 a.m. Eastern Time. We were not able to piece together the enormity of the report until mid-morning today. Some of what you here are brand new reports. Some of the killed and captured terrorists have been identified. Many are illegal aliens. Some of the illegal aliens have ties to Isis, Al Qaeda and the Taliban. The authorities believe other terrorists are tied to the Mexican Drug Cartel. Most of the terrorists are Latin and Middle Eastern; some are African."'

Lydia asks, "Did the attacks just happen between three and six this morning?"

Andy replies, "It sound like the attacks began between three and six. We don't know yet how long the fighting lasted. It could have been noon before all of the terrorists were contained. The courageous fire fighters will be fighting blazes for a long time."

Lydia says, "I know we want to find out more about what is happening, but it's so grim; almost apocalyptic."

Andy replies, "It is very disheartening. It's so catastrophic, that it compels us to turn the TV off, but the problem doesn't go away. We can go to bed, when we want to. They will be running this coverage all night and all day tomorrow. We are fortunate, if the plants near Knoxville, Chattanooga and Charlotte weren't attacked."

Lydia and Andy watch the coverage as long as they can. One of the last things they hear the news anchor say is a summary of the disaster: "The

Chicago area was hit especially hard, including Joliet and Milwaukee. Philadelphia, the New York City area and a number of Atlantic coastal towns, including Miami, were also hit hard. Reports are still coming in about casualties in Dallas, Fort Worth and the Phoenix area. Some government leaders and law enforcement officials are already criticizing the New Age Socialist administration for weakening Homeland Security. One Traditional American Party senator said, "We are shocked by the administration's lack of leadership in keeping Homeland Security strong and vigil."

Before Andy goes to bed, he calls a friend who retired from Homeland Security, but still does consulting work for them. Andy says, "Jack, this is Andy McGraig. How are you doing?"

Jack replies, "I'm fine, Andy. It's good to hear from you. I wish it was under better circumstances."

Andy says, "This terrorist attack is horrible. Like some of our congressmen, I'm greatly disappointed that the terrorists could inflict so many casualties and other losses. It's worse than 9/11 and the beginning of the Seven Day Southern Border War."

Jack says, "Absolutely, Homeland Security and plant security got caught with their pants down. The socialist so-called leadership is so weak that it's a disgrace. Now we have to pick up the pieces. It's a tragedy for the nation and an embarrassment to Homeland Security."

Andy says, "I still receive some classified information, but since retirement I don't have general clearance."

Jack says, "Since you're a former Secretary of State, I can share some things. You can guess that the aftermath is a mess; not to mention all the casualties. The news media has not yet been informed of nearly all the casualties and wounded. The destruction is very extensive. It's an absolute catastrophe."

Andy says, "We are fortunate that the Knoxville and Charlotte plants were not hit. I have a media appearance in Charlotte tomorrow afternoon, I'm going to call the station before I leave. As far as you know, is the route from Knoxville to Charlotte normal?"

Jack says, "Yes, as far as I know, Andy. I would also call the state police in Tennessee and North Carolina before you leave."

Andy replies, "Absolutely. Is there anything else that I should know at this time?"

Jack says, "Keep your family safe; keep an eye out; keep praying and call me anytime."

Andy says, "Thank you, Jack. Keep your family safe too. I will certainly be praying."

By the time Andy gets to bed, Lydia is asleep. He sets the alarm early, so he can call the state police, the station and Kenny before he leaves.

In the morning, Andy takes a shower and then makes the calls. Everything checks out, and Kenny is looking forward to the trip. Lydia is in the kitchen and says, "I heard you on the phone, so I made breakfast, since you're leaving early. I didn't turn on the news, because we know the report will be worse than last night. I'm sure Kenny will fill you in on the way to Charlotte."

"You're right. Kenny will have an update for me and thanks for fixing breakfast. During breakfast, Andy confirms with Lydia that he will have to sleep over in Maggie Valley and will be home around 10 a.m. Saturday. Andy takes a change of clothes and heads out early to Maggie Valley.

He pulls into Kenny's farm about fifteen minutes early. Scooter comes out to meet him; barking and tail wagging. Kenny is on the porch with a cup of coffee in hand. "He yells, good morning, my friend. Do you want a cup of coffee?"

Andy says, "Yes, I could use a cup before we head to Charlotte." When Andy follows Kenny into the front room, he sees the old upright piano and smells the pipe tobacco that Anderson talked about. Kenny hands Andy a steaming cup of coffee. Kenny says, "Have a seat. I want to check Scooter's food and water, since she will be inside all day". Kenny then sits down with Andy to finish his coffee.

Andy says, "The news was so shocking last night, that we didn't listen to the updates this morning."

Kenny says, "On the way to Charlotte, I can give you the updates. It's horrific."

They leave right at 10:00. Andy tells Kenny the route he plans to take, and Kenny is in agreement. After they merge onto I-40 West, Kenny says, "I can tell you now what I heard on the news this morning."

As they travel I40 to I26, Kenny and Andy talk about the attack on America's nuclear plants. Kenny says that more than 20 million people are still without power. He says, "They are still saying that the hardest hit states were Illinois and New York. They're reporting that the hardest hit large cities were Chicago, New York City, Philadelphia, Miami, Dallas and Forth Worth. A lot of Atlantic coastal towns were hit hard as well as Joliet and Milwaukee. The current reported casualties are over 14,000 and over 50,000 wounded, including radiation burns. The destruction is off the charts. They hit thirty nuclear plants, but some of them had two reactors. The damage to the plants and reactors is over $160 billion. The other commercial and residential damage is not included in the estimate."

Andy shakes his head as they head down I-26, which goes to Columbia, S.C. He says, "A terrible catastrophe doesn't even describe it." When he gets to the Forest City, N.C. exit, he turns east onto Highway 74, which passes the edge of Forest City. They turn onto I-85 North and head to Charlotte. As they get close to Charlotte, a newer by-pass takes them southeast to Pineville, near South Carolina.

After Andy drives almost three hours, Kenny says, "Pineville is a good place to stop for lunch, and it's close to the TV station."

Andy says, "We have well over an hour for a lunch break. I can use the rest and pit stop."

Kenny asks, "What kind of food do you want? There are a lot of choices here."

Andy says, "Do they have something like an Applebee's?"

Kenny says, "They have Applebee's, and I think I remember where it is."

The two for $25 meals with an appetizer are now two for $40. Kenny says, "You drove, so I want to pay the tab."

Andy replies, "Thank you, Kenny. It's nice to get a break from the road."

They take their time visiting and eating. Finally they decide to leave, even though they'll be at the station early. Andy says, "I'll stop for gas now, since we're going just south of Pineville."

The program coordinator meets them near the entrance. He shakes their hands and says. "I'm Bruce. Since you're a little early, I will bring you some water or coffee. The producer of the program wants to go over his program format in about twenty minutes."

A little after 3:30, a short, lean and energetic middle-aged man greets them and says, "I'm Frank Edwards. Let's have a seat at a table in the next office."

He asks Kenny to be on the program with them. Frank says, "Kenny. Andy will be sitting closer to the host, Chuck Reynolds. Most of the time, the camera will be fixed on them. Before the half-way point, the host will ask you to share Anderson's visit with you. Once you log close to three minutes, the cameraman will signal that you have one minute left. He will also give you the final ten second signal."

Kenny replies, "I will be glad to do that."

When Frank leaves them to get ready for the show, Andy asks Kenny, "Do you feel like you're under a time restraint?"

Kenny replies, "Not at all. I wasn't planning to be on the show, but I think it will be a good thing."

Andy says, "Absolutely! You, Ann and Angela have powerful testimonies."

A few minutes before 4:00, they're seated on the set for the program. A stage hand checks their appearance for hair and straight collars. She says, "Believe it or not, we have to check for unbuttoned shirt buttons."

Andy says, "We shouldn't be unprepared!"

Kenny's and Andy's presentation is similar to what Andy shared in Knoxville and what Kenny and Andy shared in Jefferson City. Before and after the show and during the break, they show Andy's picture with the two emails.

On the way home, they find a FM news station. The reporter says the national guard have been dispatched to every nuclear power plant in the nation. They have expanded the security perimeter around every nuclear power plant. Traditional power grid companies have also been alerted to expand their perimeter security. The military is on high alert.

Kenny says, "Our military and other national security have been too reactionary and not proactive."

Andy replies, "Definitely. I know you have a lot of experience from the Marine Corps and from the state police."

By the time they drive past Forest City, the sun has set. They stop at Hendersonville for a sandwich. By the time they get to Kenny's farm, it's almost 8:30. When Andy puts his car in park, he says, "Thanks for letting me stay over. It would have been a strain to make it home"

Kenny says, "You are welcome anytime."

When Kenny opens the front door, Scooter is in full gear. She barks and jumps on both of them and dashes into the yard. In a few minutes, Kenny lets her in. She stays wound up for about fifteen minutes; jumping, barking, whining and wanting to be petted.

Kenny and Andy retire about an hour later. Kenny asks, "When do you want to get up?"

Andy says, "I told Lydia I would be home about 10:00. I think I will leave about 8:30 and get up by 6:30. It takes a while."

Kenny laughs and says, "I know about that. I will have breakfast ready at 7:00. Do you like bacon and eggs?"

Andy says, "Sure. Can I help with the coffee or anything?"

Kenny says, "You're my guest. I will have everything ready."

During breakfast, Kenny and Andy have an enjoyable visit. Kenny talks about some of his memories from the Marine Corps and from the State Police, and Andy shares some of his State Department memories.

Just before Andy leaves, he reaches out his big hand and shakes Kenny's hand. He says Kenny, you're a wonderful friend and brother in Christ."

Kenny humbly replies, "I feel the same about you, Andy."

Andy leaves behind Kenny and the farm where Anderson visited. He's ready to return home and see the love of his life.

He pulls in the drive right before 10:00, and he see Lydia on the front porch. He gets out, and Lydia yells, "I thought you would be here any minute!"

Andy and Lydia hug and kiss each other. She looks up at him and says, "You and Kenny did a great job. I have a surprise for you."

Andy smiles and says, "What's that, honey?"

"For roughly two weeks, I've been submitting individual's names, churches and organizations to Gladis and Melissa. They have both been adding the same to their group emails. They told me while you were gone that we have a combined list of almost 1,000 emails."

Andy says, "That's outstanding!"

Lydia says, "That's not all. The day before you left, Melissa and Gladis sent out their group emails about your appearance and Kenny's on the Christian TV network. Over three hundred of the email recipients sent a reply and said they would be watching. As you know, the TV station posted your picture during the program with your email and Gladis's email. I doubt if you have checked your email yet, but Gladis just called and said a dozen churches, Christian radio stations and other organizations have invited you to come and speak. She forwarded the emails to you."

After a few minutes, Andy checks his email and goes in the great room to tell Lydia that besides the emails from Gladis, he has over fifteen new invitations.

Andy says, "I don't know how we could make so many appearances in the next couple of months. Even with everyone in our group helping, it would take over three months. Aaron and Gus and Gladis might be able to do a few, but in the future, we might want to have some classes for speakers, so we can schedule more engagements." Lydia replies, "Yes, I think classes for more speakers might be the answer. I'm sure Davina could do some of the engagements."

Andy remarks, "How could I be so dense? You and Davina could do quite a few of the engagements. I can't believe I overlooked my own wife and daughter team!"

Lydia laughs and says, "You've been busy. Ann and I can do some. We're doing one next week."

Andy says, "I wish I could go and listen. On the way back, Kenny and I heard the about the deployment report on the National Guard. Have there been any other national emergency reports or alerts?"

Lydia says, "That's the only one I know about."

Andy and Lydia with Larry's and Melissa's help coordinate what engagements they can. The distance of the radio stations is no problem; they do phone interviews. Most engagements over an hour away, they don't want to delay, but they're compelled to.

The Kiwanis provide barbecue pork sandwiches for everyone at Calhoun's in Knoxville on Thursday, December 1st. Ann and Lydia have a good response at the Kiwanis meeting. When they return home, they call Davina and Melissa and encourage them to schedule themselves for some of the pending engagements.

Andy and Lydia are so busy with their group emails and fulfilling all the invitations possible that time begins to slip away from them. Early Wednesday morning, December 7th, China invades Japan. The United States protests, but the federal government is so weak under the New Age Socialist Party, that the socialist President tells the Pentagon to only defend Japan, Okinawa and Taiwan; do not attack. When they hear about the attack, they turn on the news. The reporter says, "At 5:30 a.m. Eastern Standard Time, China used the coastline of North Korea to attack Japan near Akita, which is in the central region of Japan on its western coast. So far, China's other main attack has been a barrage of missiles fired on Sendai in southern Japan, which contains the two active nuclear reactors in Japan. The Prime Minister of Japan is pleading with the United States government to retaliate by firing missiles at China's command center on the coast of North Korea."

The reporter continues, "As an ally of China, Russia has been silent about China's attack on Japan." Andy turns the volume down and says to Lydia, "This has the potential of escalating into a WWIII. With North Korea being involved in the attack, South Korea will probably get involved. It is anyone's guess at this time, if Russia will get involved and if the United States will declare war on China. We have a lot of military bases in Japan, Okinawa and Taiwan. Andy turns the volume back up when the reporter says, "We just got word that China has landed an estimated 200,000 troops on the coast of central Japan."

Lydia and Andy listen to the reports for an hour. Finally Andy mutes the TV and says, "We're gonna have trouble right here in River City."

Lydia soberly says, "Yes we are; including wars and rumors of war; earthquakes, pestilence and famine. We need a break. I'm going to fix some coffee."

Just before Lydia brings the coffee, Andy's cell phone rings. He calls out, "I think I have a call from D.C."

Andy hears a familiar voice when he answers, "Andy, this is Will Jones, Under Secretary at the State Department."

Andy says, "Yes, Will. I recognize your voice. Other than the mess that China is making in the East, I hope you're doing well."

Will replies, "Yes, I am, Andy; the same to you. The Secretary wants to know your assessment of the invasion. There is some division in the Pentagon, but not much. Eighty percent of our generals want us to attack China, but our current President is listening to the other twenty percent. Almost all of the head leadership here knows your reputation for accuracy. We are hoping that your report will help sway the President."

Andy replies, "Will, my report is no different than what McArthur or Patton would say, if they were living today. We must meet force with force. If we give an inch, they'll take a mile."

Will says, "We knew your assessment would be the same as the eighty percent. We had to make it official by calling you. Is it alright, if we give your number to the Joint Chiefs of Staff in case anyone wants to confirm your report?"

Andy says, "Absolutely. Give it to them. If anyone has a doubt about the situation, have them call me."

Will says, "Thank you, Andy. We appreciate your input. I will give your answer to the Secretary right away."

"Give him my regards, Will."

Lydia comes in with the coffee and asks, "Was that the State Department?"

Andy says, "Yes, they're trying to get all of their ducks in a row."

12

SMOKY MOUNTAIN HOME

In a world of uncertainty, Andy and Lydia understand that a Smoky Mountain home does not guarantee safety, but living close to the Smokies lends a hand to the feeling of hope, peace and security. As Lydia and Andy share their blessings at bedtime, Andy says "The Smokies are a great blessing of God." To the White House's chagrin, the day after the invasion, South Korea declares war on China and starts firing missiles at China's command center on the North Korean coastline.

Four days after China's shocking invasion of Japan, Russia announces its own astonishing declaration. A Moscow spokesperson says, "Russia's Parliament wants the world to know that our intelligence has proved that China has launched a new pandemic virus that we've labeled the "Mortem Virus". It is ravaging southern Russia. Since this horrific biological warfare is of the worst kind, we revoke our alliance with China and declare war on The People's Republic of China.

As soon as the Pentagon hears the news, the Joint Chiefs of Staff unanimously agree on an occupation of Hong Kong. The President is pressured to declare war on China and to order the occupation of Hong Kong by U.S. Marines and backed by the U.S. Navy and the U.S. Air Force. Immediately after the Marines occupy Hong Kong, two U.S. Army Divisions of 30,000 soldiers are deployed in Hong Kong to back up the Marines. Air support is supplied by the U.S. Air Force Base in Taiwan.

On December 12th, Russia occupies the Chinese border city of Mazzhouli. Russia has already cancelled all trade with China. The populous city of Mazzhouli handles most of China's trade with Russia. In Mazzhouli are 2 billion dollars worth of export products that were bound for Russia.

The Russian troops confiscate all of the products and seize currency at all of the city's banks. Retail store valuables like gold, silver, arms and ammunition are seized. Russia surrounds the city with two hundred T-14 tanks (equipped with anti-aircraft missiles), T-90M and T-72 tanks. In the next week, 100,000 Russian troops completely barricade the city and Russian MIGs are deployed at the Mazzhouli airport.

Early morning on Tuesday, December 13th, Andy sets down his Bible after he finishes devotions He begins to get a little apprehensive about their California flight and his engagements for the two shows in Burbank. He thinks, "After breakfast, I need to call Irwin Cohen to make sure everything is still a go for our flight and California appearances."

By 9:00 Andy calls Cohen and says, "This is Andy McGraig. I 'm calling to confirm the flight and the two engagements for December 15th and 16th."

Cohen says, "Everything has been confirmed. We're looking forward to seeing you on "The Slanted View" on the 15th and the "Night Show" on the 16th. Let me know if you need anything, Andy."

Andy replies, "Thanks so much."

When Andy gets off the phone, he finds Lydia drinking her second cup of coffee in the great room. Andy says, "It's a go! I guess it shows how obsessed Americans are with news and entertainment. We have a national emergency with terrorists bombing our nuclear power plants, and soon after we find out that China has released another pandemic upon the world. America declares war on China, and America's entertainment venue is going strong"

Lydia replies "It's sad. Americans are fixated on entertainment. Many Americans are preoccupied with TV, movies, the internet, video games and gambling."

Andy says, "Our flight leaves the Knoxville airport at 3:12 p.m. and we land at the L.A. airport at 4:40 p.m. Pacific Time."

Lydia replies, "Wow. It's almost 9:00. I better start getting things ready. When do you plan to leave for the airport tomorrow?"

Andy says, "If we leave by 12:30, we should have plenty of time for check-in."

Lydia says, "Since it's a Wednesday, and we're still eleven days from Christmas, it shouldn't be too busy."

Andy says, "Since we're leaving from the Knoxville airport, we're flying into the L.A. Airport instead of the Hollywood Burbank Airport. We're staying at the Hilton Garden Inn, which is near the studios. I looked at their facilities on line. You'll like it. Will you call Melissa this morning about sending the group emails for the 15th and 16th engagements? The Slanted View" is on BSS at 4:00 p.m. EST on the 15th and the "Night Show" is on GIC at 11:30 p.m. EST on the 16th. I will call Gladis with the info."

Lydia says, "Please write it down for me, and I will call her within the hour."

Andy replies, "I will. I just realized we haven't put Tennessee Readiness in our group email. I'm sure Carey and Sonja will get the word out as well as anyone."

Lydia says, "You're right. We've been busy, but we should have thought about our church friends long before now."

Andy adds, "And they have the perfect prepper business. There is nothing like being prepared! I'm calling Gladis now. We'll get Sonya, Carey and Tennessee Readiness in her group email. Our pastor asked me to share Anderson's story the day after we return from California. I'm going to call Sonya and Carey. I know they will want to hear his story."

While Lydia calls Melissa with the California dates, Andy calls Gladis, then Carey and Sonya. He talks with Carey and tells her about the group email and what their outreach group is doing. He gives her the California dates and times and says, "I hope you can watch the shows."

Carey says, "You bet I will. I know Sonya will want to see them too"

Andy says, "Our pastor wants me to share Anderson's story at our church Sunday. We return from California the day before, but we will be glad to be back in our own church.

Lydia and I have to leave for the Knoxville airport by 2:00 Sunday. My sister's flight arrives at 3:24."

Carey says, "Hopefully, the service will dismiss by 12:30 to give you and Lydia a little breathing room. We would like to see you and Lydia for a few minutes after the service."

Andy replies, "We'll be looking for you. Give Sonya our best."

Carrey says, "I will. We'll be praying that you and Lydia have a safe trip. I will be praying for you during the broadcasts."

Andy says, "Thank you, Carey."

When Andy hangs up, he thinks to himself, "What a beneficial business they have. In Cosby the two people that really know about being prepared are Sonya and Carey."

While Lydia is packing, she says, "Are we going to take in any shows while we're in the Hollywood and Burbank area?"

Andy says, "What about "The Slanted View" and the "Night Show"?"

"Funny."

Andy can't help but laugh. He says, "We'll decide on sightseeing or something special. We have a driver from the studio picking us up at the airport and taking us to the hotel. By the time we get checked in, it will be 6:00 or later, which is 9 p.m. our time."

Lydia says, "That's true. Maybe a light supper is the answer for Wednesday evening."

Andy says, "Thursday we'll have from morning until mid-afternoon. On Friday, it's suppose to be sunny with a high of 63 degrees. We'll have all day, but we'll need a senior nap before or after supper. The "Night Show" begins at 11:30 p.m. and we have to be there at 10:30."

Lydia asks, "What is the flight schedule for Saturday?

Andy says, "Our agent knew we would be up late, so he booked us for a flight at 12:30 p.m. PT. We land at Knoxville around 8:00 p.m. EST."

Lydia remarks, "Jet lag!"

Andy laughs and says, "How true it is. It's hard to just sleep off jet lag, but Saturday night we'll have time to sleep as much as ten hours."

Lydia says, "I know you won't stay in bed for ten hours."

"Even though the service doesn't begin until 11:00, I want to shower by 8:00 to help me get alert. It may not be a three dog night, but it will definitely be a three coffee morning."

Lydia says, "I'm really looking forward to it. In any free time today, we'll have to get some ideas of what we want to do Thursday morning and Friday."

Andy says, "I'm also looking forward to it. I'm so glad you can go with me."

Lydia goes over to big Andy and hugs him and kisses him. She says, "I love you."

While Lydia and Andy pack and check the house and their agenda, they have a light lunch. They're done with everything by 4:00. Andy orders a pizza. After supper they watch the evening news. They hate the depressing news, but they're compelled to get an update. The reporter actually announces a good update. After a week of fighting the Chinese invasion in Central Japan, the U.S. Air Force with Japanese ground troops and U.S. Marines contain the Chinese advancement. The reporter says the Chinese are now fighting a defensive battle. He says, "Over 60,000 Chinese soldiers have been killed. It is estimated that over 70,000 have been wounded. Intelligence expects the Chinese ground troops to withdraw. Unfortunately, the Chinese have started firing missiles into major Japanese cities, including Tokyo."

Wednesday morning, Andy reluctantly gets up after a trying and tiring day. He isn't looking forward to the long flight today, but he is looking forward to being in California for the two national shows. Since they're not leaving the house until 12:30, he has time for devotions and fixing breakfast. Before Lydia gets up, he starts preparing a traditional breakfast of fried eggs, turkey bacon and toast with apple butter, of course. His beautiful wife comes into the kitchen just as he puts the toast in the toaster.

Lydia says, "Good morning, honey. It looks like you're taking care of me again."

Andy kisses her; smiles and says, "Always."

Lydia gets their coffee while Andy butters the toast and takes their breakfast to the dining room table. He says, "I thought we would enjoy breakfast more at the table before we a news update."

Lydia says, "Absolutely. No noise over breakfast."

They pray and enjoy the blessing of a good breakfast.

When they finish, they take a second cup of coffee to their recliners and turn on the news. They are appalled by what they hear from the news anchor. When they tune in, he is saying,

".... the Pentagon believes Iran and Lebanon declared war on Israel during our early morning hours. We have not received the exact time, since the Pentagon is preoccupied with China. At 7:15 a.m. Eastern Standard Time, Israel and the Sunni nations of Saudi Arabia and Egypt declared war on Iran and Lebanon. So far, Iraq has remained neutral. Overnight Iran has gone from rattling swords to firing deadly missiles on Israel, especially on Tel Aviv. The iron dome has been partially effective. Israel says their death count has been almost three hundred. Immediately they fired missiles back at Iran, but Iran has not disclosed their casualties."

Lydia turns the volume down and says, "God help us."

Andy says, "Yes, and help Japan and Israel. Just a couple of days ago you said, "wars and rumors of wars"."

Lydia remarks, "Pestilence is getting worse and earthquakes. If inflation keeps rising, famine will get worse."

Andy says, "The droughts in Africa are getting worse, and war will give rise to more famine."

After a moment of silence, Andy says, "This is not a very cheery way to get ready for our California trip. I'm going to get in the shower."

Lydia says, "I'm going to straighten up the kitchen, and do a once over in the house."

Andy says, "I will pack everything in the SUV by 12:00, and we'll head out by 12:30."

Lydia replies, "Aye, aye, Captain!"

Andy laughs and says, "Swab the deck, matey!"

The Captain and his First Mate leave at 12:30 on the nose.

After they check in at the airport and go through security, they have plenty of time to get coffee and a sandwich. Cohen had his assistant to reserve tickets on the two-seat side of the plane. The call for boarding is at 2:45. When they find their seats. Lydia sits by the window, and Andy sits by the aisle, since he is a wide body. He also has to stretch out his legs and feet, when he can.

Once they're in the air, it's smooth sailing. After the first hour, both Andy and Lydia get up to use the bathroom. After the second, third and fourth hours, Andy still has to get up to stretch his long legs. He acts like he's walking to the bathroom, so he can stretch his muscles.

Andy is relieved, when the big jet lands about 4:40 p.m. at the Los Angeles International Airport. All passengers are glad, when they can get up and leave the airplane. After Lydia and Andy get their luggage, their agency's driver locates them. He has a sign with their names and introduces himself. Lonnie says, "Mr. Cohen's staff told me that you're staying at the Hilton Garden Inn in Burbank. The traffic is not bad at this time on Sunday, so we should be there in an hour."

Andy says, "We appreciate it. Out of Knoxville, we can't get a straight flight to the Hollywood/ Burbank Airport."

As they walk to Lonnie's car, he says, "Coming back will take a few minutes longer. I will have to pick you up by 9:30 Saturday morning, so you'll have enough travel time and check-in time."

On the way to the Hilton, Lonnie asks about his Purdue team and work as Secretary of State. Lonnie also has an intriguing story. He says, "I was a stunt man for Universal. By the way, that's a nice tour in Hollywood; about ten minutes from where you're staying. I worked as a stunt man for fifteen years. Long before I had a career ending injury. I knew about the Cohen agency from celebrities. After I got out of the hospital, I was given Cohen's number by a celebrity friend. I called him and he said that he's heard good things about me. He offered me a full-time job. He pays me well, and I've been working for him for over twelve years."

Lydia says, "Blessings from above. God has taken care of you."

Lonnie replies, "Yes, He has."

Within the hour, they pull up in front of the beautiful Hilton, and Lonnie gets their luggage. He makes sure they get checked in and he says, "Andy, I will be here by 9:30 Saturday morning. One of the staff members from each network will pick you up and bring you back from your two engagements."

Andy says, "Thank you, Lonnie. It's a pleasure meeting you."

Once they get in their room, Lydia flops down on the bed. She says, "Whew, what a trip!"

Andy says, "Why don't we rest about thirty minutes; freshen up, then have supper here at the Hilton."

Lydia says, "Sounds good to me. If I go to sleep, wake me up by 6:30."

They go to their room right after supper. Andy says, "I think we're both getting sleepy."

Lydia says, "We are. I enjoyed supper. Their restaurant is comfy. By the way, have you ever watched "The Slanted View?"

Andy smiles and says, "No. I've just heard about it."

Lydia says, "The co-hosts, Wimpy Iceberg and Yoyo Haras can get verbally aggressive. I know you can hold your own. I just wanted to let you know ahead of time."

Andy says, "No worries. I can be assertive, if I need to be."

Before bed Andy says, "I checked online and with Lonnie about what we could do in this area. Both Lonnie and the internet recommend three places that are five to fifteen minutes away from us in Hollywood. The three suggestions sound good to me: the Universal Studio tour and entertainment park; Grauman's Chinese Theatre and celebrity walk and Warner Brothers Studio Tour."

Lydia smiles and says, "I think we'll both enjoy all three excursions."

Andy says, "Early tomorrow, I will probably get a call about our pick-up time for "The Slanted View". Since we have to be in the studio by 3:00, they will probably have their driver pick us up around 2:30. Since we have more free time Friday than tomorrow, maybe we should go to Universal and Grauman's on Friday and to Warner Bros. on Thursday."

Lydia says, "The right man with the right plan! I think that would be best. They went all out on our accommodations by putting us in one of their suites. You have a nice desk area for your studies and devotions."

Andy replies, "Yes, Cohen has been very generous. The least I can do is send him a thank you card, when we get home. By the way, please remind me to get a brochure, ticket or something from the "Night Show". Irwin wants me to sign it and mail it to him."

Lydia says, "I can handle that. I will put a reminder on my phone's notepad."

Both of them are weary from the flight. They go to bed by 9 p.m.

By 6:30 in the morning, Andy finishes devotions. He starts making notes of things he wants to share on today's show. While Andy finishes his notes, Lydia gets up and takes a shower.

As soon as Lydia finishes in the shower, Andy gathers his clothes for the day and walks toward the bathroom. He says, "As soon as I shower and dress, will you be ready for breakfast?"

Lydia says, "I'm getting hungry already."

After breakfast, they ask the front desk clerk to call a cab for them. Andy says, "Ask their driver to pick us up at 9:00."

Before 9:00, they step outside to wait on the cab. It's a sunny day in California. By online reservations, the Warner Bros. receptionist has them scheduled for the 9:45 guided tour. The young, tanned receptionist says, "The tour ends at 12:30, and the guide will give you a coupon, that you can use in our restaurant for lunch."

Warner Bros. has several open shuttles lined up. Each driver is also the guide. When Andy and Lydia board the shuttle, they hear a booming voice that says, "Are you Andy McGraig?" As they walk to a seat, Andy looks down and sees a big man and his wife already seated. As Andy says, "Yes I am," Andy and Lydia sit across from them.

The man says, "I'm Pete Leigh from Purdue, and this is my wife, Veronica."

Andy says, "I remember you! You were the one guy on campus as big as me! This is my wife, Lydia."

Pete says, "I remember you in the weight room benching 600 lbs. My football teammates, and I were amazed. I benched 450 lbs. which was more than my teammates. Man, we had a great basketball team with you and Larry Quarles at the helm. What a year; my first year at Purdue and our basketball team wins the national championship."

As Andy and Pete catch up on old times, the driver welcomes his group and announces their first stop for the tour. He says, "Warner Bros. has preserved some studios, where block buster movies were made by legendary stars, including Mary Astor, Errol Flynn, James Cagney, George Raft and Bette Davis. Our tour today begins at those studios."

As they leave for the historic studios, Andy asks, "What did you do after you left Purdue?"

Pete says, "After I graduated, I played twelve years for the Los Angeles Rams as a tackle. We moved to San Diego, and after thirty years of building a commercial real estate business, I sold it to a national conglomerate that deals with land, commercial and residential real estate. Now we enjoy traveling and being active at David Jeremiah's Shadow Mountain Church."

Andy says, "I love to listen to David Jeremiah. I think we're having lunch at Warner Brother's restaurant after the tour. I have a special story to share with you. Will both of you join us?"

Pete looks at his wife and Veronica says, "We would love to. It will give us ladies a chance to visit."

Lydia laughs and says, "Amen!"

During the tour they walk into several studios and see some elaborate outside sets. At one stop they see Sam Worthington walking into an office. The last three studios they walk through are in use. The list of actors and actresses who use them read like a list of the rich and famous, including Kevin Costner, Clint Eastwood, Julia Roberts, Tom Hanks, Will Smith and Matt Damon.

Just after 12:30, Lydia, Andy, Pete and Veronica stay on the Warner Bros. lot for lunch. Andy shares Anderson's story with Pete and Veronica. When Andy finishes, they are both overwhelmed. Pete says, "I have never heard a true story that is current and yet so remarkable."

Veronica says, "It's astounding and credible. We heard some of the news stories over six months ago, about people who seemingly had passed on, but they were visiting friends and relatives."

Pete looks at Andy and Lydia and says, "I know David Jeremiah personally, and I'm guessing that he will want you to speak to our congregation."

Pete and Andy exchange phone numbers and emails, and Veronica and Pete invite them to their home in San Diego on their next trip to Southern California.

Lydia and Andy catch a cab to the hotel. When they get in their room, it's almost 2:00.

Andy says, "The BSS driver sent me a text and said he would pick us up at 2:40. I better lay down for a while."

By 3:00, the BSS driver escorts Lydia and Andy into their building. They meet, Kim, the program coordinator. She says, "We are glad that you could be with us today. "The Slanted View" studio is on the second floor. I will take you to a dressing room, where you and your wife can relax. Andy, your make-up person, Tiffany, will come in with her styling supplies about twenty minutes before the program begins. You go on the air at 4:30, and you will be sitting with our co-hosts, Wimpy Iceberg and Yoyo Haras, until 5:00. Tiffany will come and get you, Andy, at 4:24.

She will take a minute for a final touch-up, then walk you to the wings. You will be directed to a chair on the set, when they break for a commercial."

Tiffany escorts Lydia to a studio seat near the stage. During the first half, they announce Andy as the former Secretary of State, the recipient of the Presidential Medal of Freedom and the MVP and team member of the 1965 NCAA Basketball Champions.

Right at 4:30 they seat Andy on the set and after the break they welcome him. Wimpy says, "We want to show the audience and viewers at home the picture of you dressed as a Purdue Boilermaker."

When they show Andy's picture from 1965, several ladies in the audience whistle and cheer.

Andy says, "Take it easy; my wife is in the audience."

Yoyo looks at the cameraman and says, "Let's get a picture of her."

Everyone applauds and Wimpy says, "She's beautiful."

Yoyo looks at Andy and says, "I bet you were a heartbreaker at Purdue."

Andy says, "Lydia doesn't know; I married her!" Everyone laughs.

The co-hosts talk with Andy about his two stints as Secretary of State. They also ask how he became a recipient of the Presidential Medal of Freedom. They're intrigued about his early work as a special agent. After the mid-break for the last half hour show, Wimpy says, "I understand you have a special story to share with us."

Andy reminds the audience of similar events that took place throughout the world. He shares Anderson's story with the studio audience and the viewers. When he finishes, everyone appears to be stunned for at least ten seconds. Finally, Yoyo says, "Now we'll break for a word from our sponsors."

During the break, Wimpy says, "Very captivating, Andy."

Yoyo says, "I don't know what to think."

After the commercial break, Yoyo says, "Andy, I heard you're an evangelical."

Andy replies, "I am. Are you prejudiced?" (The audience chuckles.)

Yoyo is taken off guard and says, "What do you think?"

Andy says, "I don't know. Do you?"

Wimpy laughs and says, "He's got you there, Yoyo."

Yoyo tries to regain face and says, "I just wanted to know your beliefs."

Andy replies, "You don't persecute Christians, do you?"

The audience laughs and Wimpy says, "Enough of this. I can't help but laugh myself. Andy, we're almost out of time. Thank you for being with us today and sharing your cousin's story."

When the director gives the "signed off" cue, Wimpy looks at Yoyo and says, "Girl, you better take a long bubble bath." She walks over to Andy; shakes his hand and says, "Andy, it has been a pleasure. Your career and life are very impressive."

Andy thanks her and meets Lydia. Lydia says, "You were wonderful, big boy," and she kisses him.

Andy's hostess, Kim, comes and thanks him and gives him an envelope with his check.

The studio driver takes them back to the Hilton, and they have a peaceful dinner at the hotel restaurant. They spend a quiet evening in their suite and make it an early night.

The next day after breakfast, they take a cab to Universal Studios and their amusement park. They get a kick out of seeing Laurel and Hardy in a restored Model A Ford on a studio designed street. Laughing, Lydia says, "They look just like the real comedy team, and they have all the antics to go with it."

Both Andy and Lydia like the make- up show that specializes in demonstrating the preparation for horror show make-up and scenes. Lydia says, "What a hoot!"

They even take in a couple rides and go on the "World Famous Studio Tour", which gives them the experience of being on the sets of live action filming. While they enjoy the fun at Universal Studios, Lydia eats cotton candy and Andy has a pineapple ice cream cone.

They have a late lunch at Grauman's Chinese Theatre, then they take their time looking at the walk of celebrity stars. Andy says, "It will be close to 5:00, when we return to the hotel.

I need to rest, when we get to our room."

Lydia says, "Maybe we could have a late supper about 7:00."

Andy says, "Good idea. We can relax after supper. I want to take a shower by 9:00, so I will be fresh for the late night interview. The GIC Studio driver is picking us up at 10:30."

Everything goes as planned, and their GIC driver gets them to the bustling studio by 10:45.

The driver escorts them inside to their host, Xavier. He shows Lydia to the show's theater; equipped with concessions near the entrance. After he shows them Lydia's seat (near the front of the stage), he takes Andy to a corridor area lined with dressing rooms. Xavier says, "The make-up stylist will be here within fifteen minutes. You have an hour before you're escorted to the stage area. Do you want a drink and a snack?"

Andy says, "A bottle of water please."

After Xavier brings the bottle of water, he says, "After the show, I will meet you here or on the stage."

The dressing room has a TV and remote. Andy tunes in to a melodic jazz station.

The make-up person arrives a little before 11:30. She says, "I'm Andrea. I'm running a little late, because we have several guests slotted for the first thirty minutes. I understand that you're the main guest for the second half of the show."

Andy says, "That's what I understand. Can you do anything with my face?"

Andrea laughs and says, "You look good. I have several minutes, so I can give you my best attention."

After Andrea finishes, Andy listens to music for another twenty minutes, then the stage hand comes in. He goes over the program for the last half of the show. He says, "Mr. Looney will welcome you and introduce you to the audience at midnight. Before the end of the show, there will be three commercial breaks. Midway a comedian will have a three minute spot, but he will leave the stage. You will be the only guest seated by Bud Looney. You and Mr. Looney will have have a total of eighteen minutes in three segments for the interview and conversations. He knows the story you're sharing will take about five minutes. We have you down for telling the story in the second segment.'

Andy says, "Sounds good to me."

When they walk to the wing of the stage, Andy has about two minutes before he sits by nationally known TV host and comedian, Bud Looney.

After the commercial break, Bud Looney says, "I want you to welcome our two term Secretary of State, Presidential Medal of Freedom recipient and MVP of the 1965 NCAA Basketball Championship team. Mr. Andy McGraig!" The audience gives Andy thunderous applause, and Looney gets up and shakse Andy's hand just before they take their seats.

Bud says, "Andy, its great having you for the last half of our show tonight. Our staff has prepared a short video that I think you and our audience will like. First, let me confirm and share a few things. We learned that while you went to Purdue you could bench press 600 lbs. We found that you were the only one who in college basketball and those in the NBA, who could press 600 lbs."

Andy says, "Yes, I pressed 500 lbs. in high school and 600 lbs. in college.'

Looney says, "It looks like you could still press a lot."

Andy replies, "I can still press 400 lbs." The audience applauds.

Looney says, "Remarkable. Our staff found that when you played at Purdue, sport writers were calling you the linebacker of basketball. We also learned that you were the best freshman player in the nation, and at the end of your freshman year, the Boston Celtics offered you a lucrative contract."

Andy says, "That's right, but I wanted to serve my country. I was trained as a special agent for the State Department after my freshman year, and when I returned to Purdue in 1964, I had another year of basketball eligibility. I had the great opportunity to play with four of the players, who were my teammates in my freshman year. We were team players."

Looney says, "Excellent. We're ready to show a clip of you playing in the 1965 final.

Everyone watch the big guy, number 40, drive to the basket."

As they watch Andy drive to the basket, the audience cheers as his opponents move out of the way. Andy dunks the ball and shakes the backboard."

Looney laughs and says, "Wonderful! That's why we hear your fans shouting, "Avalanche Andy! Now we know why they called you the linebacker of basketball. After the final, one sports writer wrote, "As McGraig drives to the basket, his opponents move to each side like the parting of the Red Sea." Looney continues, "You know, Andy, two great NBA players, who followed you, remind me of you; Karl Malone and LeBron James."

Andy says, "Thank you, Bud."

Bud says, "Basketball is a game, but being Secretary of State is serious business. We're going to talk with you during our last segment about your role in the Seven Day Border War and your two stints as Secretary of State. After this commercial break, Mr. Andy McGraig, has a special story to share."

When they come back on, Bud Looney announces their comedian guest. After his three minute skit, Bud says, "Andy, tell us about your cousin's story."

Andy shares Anderson's story and how he visited his sister; his best friend and his daughter after he disappeared. When he finishes, Looney says, "I heard the reports earlier this year about others in different countries who had a similar experience. It's hard for me to believe."

Andy says, "Are you a follower of Christ?"

Looney says, "I believe he was a great prophet, but I'm not a follower."

Andy says, "Christ, the prophets, the apostles and many others like Anderson have warned us to be ready. The Lord is coming real soon."

Looney says, "But I believe I'm a good person, and I believe in social justice; do you?"

Andy replies, "Social justice is God's justice. It's defined from Genesis 1 to Revelation 22."

Looney says, "It's hard to believe everything in the Bible, like the teaching on hell. I don't believe in a hell."

Andy says, "You may have a firsthand experience; sooner than you think." The audience laughs.

Looney smiles and says, "Are you after my job?"

Andy says, "No, I have to be accountable for what I say."

Looney and the audience laugh. Looney says, "You've stolen my show!" He looks at the camera and says, "We will be right back with our very capable guest, Andy McGraig. He will tell us what it's like to be Secretary of State and to receive the Presidential Medal of Freedom." The audience applauds.

After the last segment, Looney thanks Andy on the air for being an excellent guest. The live audience gives a big round of applause. After they go off the air, Looney says, "Andy, you are one of the best and most challenging guests I've had. Thank you for coming."

Andy says, "Thank you, Bud. It's good to meet you. I hope you pray; read God's Word and invite Christ into your life. He really is coming very soon."

Bud thanks him again and says, "I will think about it seriously."

Lydia walks up to the stage and says to Andy, "No one could have done better."

Andy says, "Thank you, gorgeous," and he gives her a kiss.

The stage hand escorts them back to the dressing room. He says, "Xavier will be here in a few minutes. Do you need water or anything?"

Andy looks at Lydia and asks, "Do you want a water?" She nods her head. Andy says, "Two bottles of water please. Would you do me a favor and get two programs or two of any document that has the show's name and date?"

The stage hand replies, "I can do that."

Andy looks at Lydia and says, "Irwin Cohen wants me to autograph a program and mail it to him."

Right after the stage hand brings Andy the water and programs, Xavier knocks and comes in.

He says, "Excellent job tonight. You could make a living at this. I have this for you." He hands Andy a white envelope with the name of the show and address.

Andy looks in the envelope and says, "Thank you, Xavier. It was a pleasure being here and meeting you."

Xavier says, "I will show you the way to our front lobby. Our driver will be waiting for you."

They go directly to the cab and their hotel without any delay. Andy gives the driver a tip and thanks him. Lydia asks, "Do you know its 1:30 a.m.?"

As they walk to their suite, Andy laughs and says, "I knew it was a little later than our 9 p.m. bedtime."

Lydia asks, "Did you know who the special guest was in the first half of the show?"

Andy says, "I didn't notice."

"Jim Carrey."

Andy replies, "Wow. I bet he was entertaining."

Lydia says, "He's still a riot."

As Andy changes into his night clothes, he says, "7:00 is going to roll around fast. I will shower at seven. We should probably have breakfast about 8:00. I want to come back to the room to organize my luggage. Just before 9:30 we can take our luggage to the lobby and check-out"

The driver is right on time and at the big L.A. International Airport, he helps Lydia and Andy with their luggage. When they go inside the terminal, Lydia exclaims, "Look at all of these people!" On Saturday, the week before Christmas, people are traveling to and coming from all parts of the world."

Just after the pilot makes an announcement and tells the passengers to fasten their seat belts,

Lydia says, "After just three days, I already miss our Smoky Mountain home."

13

FROM CALIFORNIA TO SMOKY MOUNTAIN LIVING

Lydia and Andy sleep most of the way home. Just before they touch down, they see the majestic Smoky Mountains. The taller mountains are snow-capped. After the jet lands, Andy says, "It sure feels good to be back in Tennessee."

After they get their luggage at baggage claim, they walk to the extended stay parking lot. They go through the gate to pay the parking ticket. Lydia says, "It has gotten colder here." Andy looks at the temperature on his dash.

Andy says, "Its 40 degrees now, which means it could get to freezing or below tonight. Even though its 8:00 p.m. already, I need to call Judy tonight and double check her flight arrival."

Lydia says, "9:00 isn't too late to call. I sure will be glad to see her. Will you be okay with telling Anderson's story at our church tomorrow?"

Andy replies, "No worries. It has become second nature to me."

They get on Cosby Highway and turn on Rocky Flats Rd. to their turn off. Andy calls Judy right away, and he's delighted that she answers. Andy says, "I'll be at the airport early. We can't hardly wait to see you."

Judy says, "Me too. The airline says my flight will arrive at 3:05."

Andy signs off and feels like he's stumbling to the bedroom after all the activity and jet lag. They don't have to be at their church until 10:45, but Andy sets his alarm for 6 a.m. so he will have plenty of time for devotions, breakfast and a shower to revive himself.

The small country church is packed out. Andy meets with the pastor at 10:45, and they pray together. Andy sits with Lydia on the front pew. The pianist is playing beautiful Christmas arrangements. Christmas is next Sunday. The pastor opens the service with prayer. A talented duo lead the song service. They open with "O Come All Ye Faithful".

After the congregation sings, "Angels We Have Heard on High", the pastor introduces Andy as today's speaker.

Andy says, "We are here today, because we are united in the One, who redeemed us and told us that we are one as He and his Father are one. I have a story to share about my first cousin, Anderson, who lived in this area. Some of you knew him. Anderson's story tells us to be prepared, because the Lord is coming for His bride real soon. We have an outreach team, that is getting the message out in group emails. Some of you know that I was at two events the past few days sharing Anderson's story. We have an offering plate at the exit. If you want to be on our email list, please put your email address in the plate as you leave.

Matthew 24: 3-44 (NIV) tells us a lot about the society and world we live in. Jesus speaks to us in the whole passage. In verse 12 He tells us that in the last days: because of the increase of wickedness, the love of most will grow cold. Jesus says that there will be nations warring against each other, and he says there will be famine and earthquakes throughout the world. He says that many will be deceived. He continues to tell the apostles about the end of the age and the signs of His coming. In verse 3, He says that many will turn from the faith. In verse 13, Jesus says that those who stand firm to the end will be saved.

In verse 40, Jesus is even more specific about what happens at the end of our world, as we know it: "Two men will be in the field; one will be taken and the other left." Jesus continues his prophecy in verse 41: "Two women will be grinding with a hand mill; one will be taken and the other left." Jesus said in verse 44 that He will come at an hour you do not expect Him. Jesus emphasizes that we must be prepared. Those who are not prepared will be shut out."

Andy continues and shares Anderson's story. When he completes the story, Andy says, "Anderson emphasized to his sister, best friend and daughter that we must be prepared. He told them to share the good news of the gospel, and to tell everyone that the Lord is coming real soon for His church, The Bride of Christ. We are in a world that is upside down with earthquakes, wars, pestilence, famine and a great falling away from the church. I can't over emphasize the importance of being ready. If you are willing to share the good news and to tell the world of His soon coming, please come to the altar now and make that commitment."

As the pianist plays "Have Thine Own Way, Lord" in the background, it appears that everyone in the church comes forward. The pastor, Andy and several lay leaders talk and pray with many, who have come forward to follow Christ and to rededicate themselves. Andy shakes hands with men, women and children, who came to the altar. As the congregation begins to thin out, Carey and Sonya come up to Andy and Lydia, Sonya says, "The service meant a lot to Carey and me; thank you." They both hug Lydia and Andy.

Carey says, "We would like to invite both of you to our Christmas party at Tennessee Readiness. It's this Wednesday, December 21st, at 3:00."

Andy says, "I'm sure we can both be there." He looks at Lydia, and she nods her head. Andy continues, "Do you know Gus and Gracie Rivera?"

Sonya says, "We know Gus. He's a real nice guy and a prepper."

Andy says, "We're friends and they're in our outreach group. Do you mind, if we bring them? By the way, my sister will be visiting. I would like for you to meet her."

Carey says, "Bring them, and don't bring anything. We'll have plenty!"

Sonya says, "Great service. We'll look for you around 3:00 Wednesday."

Andy and Lydia say they are looking forward to it.

As they leave the church, Lydia says, "Is Judy meeting us for an early dinner?"

Andy says, "She plans to eat lunch about 12:30. I asked her about dinner. She asked if we could pick up something on the way home, and have a light supper at our house. I wish she would move near us. She could have retired eight years ago."

"I'm sure she has had a good income for decades. She could probably afford what she wants. It would be nice, if she found a home and some land she likes off Rocky Flats Road or somewhere in the Cosby area."

Andy says, "I agree; that would be nice."

It's already a few minutes before 1:00, so Andy and Lydia decide to eat out, so they can be at Knoxville's McGee-Tyson Airport before 3:00.

As they get ready to leave the restaurant, they order coffee to go. The temperature is starting to drop during the day. They've enjoyed some weather in the sixties recently, but at 2:00 it's only 45 degrees. Lydia says, "Do you think we'll have a white Christmas?"

Andy says, "It could happen. It's forecasted to be below freezing tonight."

When they come to the passenger arrival area, Andy looks at the Arrival and Departure Board. He says, "Her flight is on time. By the time she waits for other passengers to leave the plane, she should be here in fifteen to twenty minutes."

While they wait for Judy, Lydia and Andy take in some people watching and drink their coffee. All of a sudden, when Andy yells, "There she is," Lydia jumps. Andy quickly walks toward Judy; picks her up and gives her a gentle bear hug. After Judy recovers form Andy's hug, Lydia hugs her.

Lydia says, "It's a joy to see you. It has been too long."

Judy says, "I know. I'm glad we're together; especially at Christmas."

Andy says, "Well, Sis, let's get your luggage and hit a drive thru."

When they're ready to leave the airport, Andy says, "What are you in the mood for?"

Judy says, "Fried chicken! Usually I eat grilled chicken, but we grew up on fried chicken."

Andy says, "How true it is. There's a drive through chicken place just east of Knoxville off I-40." After Andy takes the chicken exit, they order the works: fried chicken, pinto beans and cole slaw. "Sis, I couldn't wait until you arrived. Do we have you for two weeks?"

Judy says, "Close to it."

Lydia says, "Are you thinking about retiring?"

Judy laughs and says, "I've been thinking about retiring for the past seven years, but I'm seriously thinking about it next year, after May.

Andy says, "We would love to have you nearby."

Judy says, "By the end of May I will be done with classes and grading. If you hear of some good buys with land by early spring, let me know. I would love to be near you and the Smokies."

Andy enthusiastically says, "Now we're talkin'! We'll keep our eye peeled and let you know the location and address. The pictures of the houses and their features and property should be on the internet."

It's twilight by the time they get home. Andy turns on the propane fireplace, and Lydia places the food and dinnerware on the table. Andy turns the radio to Christmas music, and they sit down to pray. They have a good time talking during supper.

After they finish eating, they're still at the dining table talking and laughing, when Andy's cell phone rings. Andy answers and says, "Hi, Larry, I saw your name from my contact list."

Larry asks, "Am I calling at a good time?"

Andy says, "Yes, my sister is here, and we just finished supper."

Larry says, "Melissa and Gladis didn't want to call earlier, because of your long trip. Speaking of that, brother, you did a great job. I also appreciate you mentioning our fellow freshman players, who became a major part of the team our senior year. I've been on pins and needles today, because I didn't want to call too early. Have you checked your email yet?"

"No, we were wore out when we got home Saturday night, and we've been busy all day today." Andy gets up and says to Judy and Lydia, "I'll be back in a few minutes."

Larry says, "I understand. You have more than a full plate. Melissa was also anxious about calling you. Brother, when you see your emails, it's going to knock your socks off. The invitations are pouring in. They're coming from the Atlantic to the Pacific."

Andy says, "Wow. I'm at my desk now and going to my email."

Larry says, "Gladis was also anxious about you seeing your email. I told her and Melissa that I would call you this evening. I'm sure you're going to need help, since there are so many invitations."

Andy says, "I'm in my email now. I'm starting to see that the invitations are many and from all over the country. You're right. We'll need everyone on the team who is willing and able to help fulfill these invitations. Our group can't fill all of them, because a large number are hundreds of miles away."

Larry says, "You have your hands full. Let me know, when I can help."

Andy replies, "During the Christmas and New Year holidays, let's think about how we can organize this. I can do most of the radio invitations, since I do interviews over the phone. I think I can acknowledge some of the emails before Christmas and New Years. I wouldn't want to schedule until after New Years. Let's get the word out to our group that we need to meet right after the first."

Larry says, "Good idea. To switch gears, brother, have you heard any news since yesterday?"

Andy replies, "No. Actually, I've heard very little news, since we left for California. I didn't want to take the chance of getting distracted from the goal of our engagements."

Larry says, "I totally get it. You will need to sit down, as I tell you what is happening to Iran and China. Major earthquakes have hit both countries. They have also hit Tehran and Beijing. U.S. Intelligence reports that over a million people have died in China, and almost a million people in Iran."

Andy replies, "He's coming soon. I think we're ready. Do you feel like you and Melissa are ready?"

"Absolutely. Melissa and I talk about it often."

Andy says, "Thank you so much, brother. I'm going to share the news with Lydia and Judy. We'll talk soon. Call any time."

Andy goes to the great room and tells Judy and Lydia about Larry's call."

After Andy fills them in, Lydia says, "We better be ready."

"That's just what I told Larry!"

Judy says, "I think I'm ready. I'm sure going to do some hard praying before I go to sleep tonight."

Andy says, "We all should."

After they visit a long time, Judy gets tired from her trip and Lydia and Andy are still getting over jet lag. Andy and Lydia say good night to Judy and give her a kiss on her cheek. Lydia says, "I have our guest room all fixed up for you. There are plenty of towels, a robe and a bathroom next to your room. You probably know that Andy fixes breakfast early. We will probably eat between 7 and 7:30."

Judy says, "Thank you. Have sweet dreams."

Andy is up early as usual and has devotions. He wants to fix something special for breakfast, but he goes with the ole' standby; eggs, turkey bacon, toast and jelly. He sets strawberry and natural grape jelly and apple butter on the table.

As they finish breakfast, Andy leans back and says, "Sis, we have not listened to the news for days. We've been super busy until now. Is it alright, if we get caught up?"

Judy replies, "You're in for a big surprise or shock. I wish I could take a five day break from it. I want to listen to the news, but it's depressing."

While Lydia clears the table, Andy gets the remote and says, "Larry told me about the deadly earthquakes in China and Iran. Are some of the other current events better or worse."

Judy says, "Worse."

Andy asks, "Babe, are you ready to join us?"

Lydia says, "Give me thirty seconds."

Judy and Andy have a seat, and Andy says, "I'll go ahead and turn it to the news channel." Lydia comes in the room drying her hands and has a seat.

The news reporter is just beginning an update on Yellowstone. He says, "Today, the head ranger at Yellowstone said the National Park remains closed due to increased seismic activity.

He also said the geysers are extremely hot. Anyone within forty yards can get severe burns.

China and Iran have finally released a casualty and injured report from the earthquakes. China reports 1.3 million killed and 2 million injured. Iran reported 930,000 killed and 1.2 million injured. U.S. Intelligence reports more casualties than either country reported.

The new Mortem Plague released by China now enters its second day on the west coast. California, Oregon and Washington are reporting that the number of Mortem cases has more than doubled, since 5:00 p.m. Pacific Time.

Before the commercial break, the best news we can report is that China has slowed its aggression toward Japan, since the catastrophic earthquake. The Pentagon reports that U.S. Forces with the aid of Japan and Taiwan are actively bombing military installations inside China. Russia has continued its advancement in northern China."

When the news channel goes to a commercial, Andy turns off the television. Andy asks, "What do you think?"

Lydia says, "I think it's terrible, and we haven't heard about several other major problems in our country."

Judy says, "I have one word: depressing."

Andy says, "I want to be optimistic, but the reports are very sad."

Lydia says, "Fortunately, we can be optimistic in our faith. Why don't we see what Lydia Ann is doing? Maybe we can take a walk with her on the trails, then take her out to lunch."

Andy looks at Judy and says, "Are you up for that?"

Judy says, "I would love to see Ann. I'm going to hop in the shower while you call her."

The four friends walk Anderson's trails for an hour. They do some bird watching along the way. They enjoy a mild and sunny morning. Judy says, "In two days it will be the first day of winter. I love being back in Tennessee."

Lydia says, "I wonder, if we'll get a white Christmas?"

As they get close to the trailhead, Andy replies, "I looked at the forecast yesterday. The two nights that get below freezing, there is next to no precipitation during the day. The one day before Christmas with some precipitation has a high of 62 and a low of 41.

Lydia says, "You never know, when Mother Nature will change."

They walk down the trailhead to Ann's house. They take Judy to Gatlinburg, so she can go to the Great Smoky Mountains National Park and the Sugarlands Visitor Center. They stop for a sub and soda in Gatlinburg before they enter the park.

Judy says, "I love looking at the nature display and walking around the old settlers' buildings at Sugarlands." They also take a drive to enjoy the woods and the mountain scenery. They don't stop for a hike, since they already had a long walk this morning,"

Once they finish their drive in the Smokies, Andy announces, "It's 2:OO and time for a nap!"

Judy laughs and says, "Okey dokey, old man."

Andy asks Ann, "Do you want to join us or go home?"

Ann says, "I think I need a nap too, but I'm ready to go home."

Lydia says, "Home sweet home. There's nothing like going back home, like we did two days ago from California."

Andy and Lydia take Judy and Ann to the Smokies

14

A CHANGE IN THE FORECAST

Tuesday morning Andy says, "I need to call Gus and see if he and Gracie can go with us to the Tennessee Readiness Christmas party."

Lydia says, "While you talk to Gus, I need to call Davina and make sure that she and her family can be here Sunday for Christmas dinner at 1:00."

Andy says, "Did you ask Ann if she can stay with us Christmas Eve?"

Lydia says, "Yes. She will be here by 5:00 for our Christmas Eve dinner, and she can stay until 9:30 Christmas morning."

Judy walks in the room while Lydia is talking about Ann. She says, "I'm so happy that the four of us can spend Christmas Eve together."

Andy teases Judy and says, "You are the celebrity guest."

Judy replies, "Where is my crown? Sorry that I didn't get up early for breakfast."

Lydia says, "Get anything you want: eggs, muffins, toast or cereal. I will show you where everything is."

Judy asks, "After I have some cereal and toast, do you mind if I watch the news? I know it's a downer."

Andy says, "Help yourself. I have to make a call, and I will join you in a few minutes."

When Andy calls Gus, Gracie says, "I'll get him for you, Andy." When Gus comes to the phone, he says, "Carey and Sonya at Tennessee Readiness invited the five of us, which includes my sister, to their Christmas party, which is tomorrow at 3:00. We want to pick up you and Gracie."

Gus says, "Gracie is right here; I'll ask her" In a few seconds, he says, "Yes, we would love to go. Gladis had vacation time coming, so she is off from work until January 2nd. Tell Gladis that when we bring you back from the party, we would like to see her and Tracy. On Christmas day, around 4:00, we would like to bring them some presents."

Gus says, "I will be happy to tell her. I know she and Tracy will be looking forward to seeing you and Lydia."

Andy says, "Good. We'll pick you up at 2:45 tomorrow."

Andy goes back to the great room and sits down with Judy to watch the news. Andy says, "It's great being with you again."

Judy replies, "I love being here."

As they listen to the news, it progressively gets worse. The news anchor interrupts a reporter with breaking news. The anchor says, "China just released a warning to the United States and Russia. The Chinese spokesperson said that China would release its new secret weapon against Russia and the United States, if Russia does not withdraw its troops from northern China immediately and if the United States does not withdraw from Hong Kong immediately. The Pentagon has not given a public response yet. However, Russia's spokesman for the Russian Prime Minister and the military said, "If we see that China has released anything unfamiliar to us, we will hit every major city in China with nuclear weapons, and wipe China off the face of the earth."

Russia reported late yesterday that China's new Mortem Plague has already killed over 250,000 people in Russia." The anchor ends with, "We'll be right back." Judy mutes the volume and asks, "What do you think, big brother?"

Andy replies, "When we hope things get better and believe it can't get much worse, it gets worse."

Lydia sits down and says, "I heard most of the last report. I guess I'm stunned."

Andy says, "I would guess that the words, "end of the world", are coming to more people's minds."

When the news program returns, a sign at the bottom of the screen in big red letters reads, "Breaking News". Most viewers would assume the same story about China will be repeated or elaborated. The anchor says, "The worst job of any reporter is to follow one shocking story with another shocking story. It is my dubious duty to do that at this time. Seismologists are concerned about earthquake activity along the Ring of Fire, which circles the Pacific Ocean. It includes Indonesia, Malaysia, Japan, New Zealand, Mexico, the United States, Canada and Russia. Just two hours ago, at 8 p.m. Australian time, an 8.9 earthquake was recorded between Indonesia and Australia. It is nighttime in Australia, but deaths have already been reported from Indonesia to Australia. At the same time, seismologists in California are reporting a lot of earthquake activity.

California seismologists are in touch with seismologists from Australia to Canada to learn the scale of the earthquakes. Stay tune for updates." They go to a commercial break.

After a moment of silence, Andy looks at Judy and asks, "Are you ready to turn it off?"

Judy softly says, "Absolutely."

Andy says soberly, "Things have obviously gotten worse. I read a long article about the Ring of Fire this year. It contains 90% of the world's volcanoes and 75% of the world's earthquakes. The largest tear in the earth's crust is in the Banda Sea floor, which is between Asia and Australia. I think the article said the tear or gap covers about 23,000 sq. miles, which is almost the size of West Virginia. The gap is 4.3 miles deep."

Lydia says, "No pun intended, but that is earth shaking. How do you remember all of those facts?"

Judy says, "I wondered the same thing, when we were kids. I know if he hadn't received a full basketball scholarship to Purdue, he would have received a full academic scholarship."

Andy continues, "What he just reported is potentially the biggest sign of the end times to date.

If enough of the earthquake epicenters have a large seismic reading, the results would be of epic proportions. It would result in a worldwide catastrophe of death and destruction."

Judy says, "I would hide my head under a blanket."

Lydia says, "All we can do in a situation like that is pray."

Andy says, "God gives us fair warning in His Word. He gave us more than fair warning, when people like Anderson appeared to friends and relatives worldwide. From all of the terrible things that have happened recently, we shouldn't be too surprised, when hear the next appalling report."

In the afternoon, they walk in their own woods with Judy. Andy says, "Sis, where do you think I should put in some more trails."

Judy hesitates a second and says, "Well, you have plenty of room! How many acres are here?"

Andy replies, "One hundred and forty. Years ago, I sold sixty acres to Anderson."

Judy asks, "How many trails do you have now?"

Andy answers, "A long one and a couple of short ones."

Judy laughs and says, "You might be 100 before you can finish trails on all these acres."

Andy smiles and sarcastically says, "Thanks for your advice." In another second he says,

"Look there!" He points his finger to a tree about twenty-five yards ahead of them. "Look close. It's on the side of the trunk, and you can see the sunlight shining on the back of its red head."

Judy says, "Wow, that's a big bird."

Andy says, "It's the big Pileated Woodpecker."

In unison, Lydia and Judy say, "Woody, the Woodpecker!"

"We are lucky to see him or her one time a year."

They spend a quiet evening at home and start looking for board games. They put the Aggravation board on the dining table.

They all go to bed early and Andy is up by 5:00 to take time with devotions.

About 10:30 a.m. a carrier comes to the front door with a special delivery for Andy. He signs it and reads the letter from the United States Congress. When he finishes reading it, he carries the letter to the great room, where Lydia and Judy are seated. He says, "Of all the foolish, McCarthy era type proceedings!"

Lydia says, "What is it, honey?"

He says, "It's a witch hunt by the Socialist Party. I just received a hand delivered letter from the U.S. House of Representatives. It's a subpoena to appear before the House on Wednesday, January 4th, 2023, at 1:15 p.m. EST. Their hearing consists of an investigation on hate speech."

Lydia says, "Hate speech! What kind of nonsense is that?"

Andy says, "Every committee member that signed the letter is a member of the New Age Socialist Party. This proceeding reminds me not only of the McCarthy era, but over ten years ago, a New Age Socialist senator tried to get a bill passed that he called the "Freedom Act". It was designed to restrict opinions of those who supported Traditional American Party views."

Judy exclaims, "What hypocrites!"

Andy replies, "I don't disagree. It reminds me of Bible passages, where the Pharisees and Sadducees were called hypocrites."

Lydia says, "Don't worry, it's nonsense; this too shall pass."

Soon after the surprise from a branch of the government, Lydia, Judy and Andy get ready for the Christmas party at Tennessee Readiness. When Gus and Gracie get in their SUV, Andy says, "Will Gladis and Tracy be surprised, when we bring their gifts late Christmas afternoon?"

Gus says, "Yes. We know they will be home, so we didn't say anything."

By 3:00 they pull into the Tennessee Readiness parking lot. Sonya and Carey greet them with hugs. Carey says, "Help yourself to the punch and food."

Andy says to Carey, "I'm thinking about getting some things I want to give as Christmas gifts. Is it okay, if I write you a check today?"

Carey says, "Are you kidding! We would sell 24/7, if we could!"

Gracie, Judy and Lydia visit with Sonya and Carey and meet other friends of theirs. Gus joins Andy as he looks over their extensive stock of prepper supplies. Andy says, "Gus, did you ever get a Christmas gift, and knew ahead of time what it was!"

Gus replies, "More than once."

Andy says, "I want to get some prepper supplies for you and Gracie that may come in handy in the near future."

Gus and Andy look for the supplies they want, then Andy says, "Let's get some punch and food before we make a final decision." They visit with Carey and Sonya for a while and talk with some of their friends.

Andy says to Gus, "I like the benefits that Sonya and Carey are providing for the public."

Gus says, "Me too. I also like all of the camping and hiking supplies,"

Andy says, "Well, brother, let's make our final decision." Andy walks over to some prepper kits and says, "I like these." I think Judy would like a kit as well.

Gus says, "I know Gracie and I would be glad to have them.'

Andy says, "The decision is made. After we get head back to your house, tell Gracie that Lydia and I wish you and her a Merry Christmas."

Andy writes a check and hands it to Sonya for the three prepper kits. Sonya says, "Thank you, Andy. It was nice visiting with your sister, Lydia and Gracie." Sonya and Carey wish them a Merry Christmas, as they say their good byes to a lot of friendly people.

By the time they take Gus and Gracie home, it's almost dark. Andy says, "I know what you're thinking. You'll be glad when its daylight savings time again."

Lydia says, "That's the truth!"

Later in the evening, Lydia, Judy and Andy are talking and drinking hot tea in the great room. Andy asks Judy, "I think I will hit the sack. Are you staying up a while?"

Judy says, "No. I'm ready to dream of the Nutcracker Prince and the Sugar Plum Fairy."

Lydia laughs and says, "Let me know how it works out with the nut and the fairy."

Judy smiles and says, "Thank you, Andy, for the prepper kit. We never know, when we may need it."

Andy says, "That's right. Tomorrow I'll open ours, and show it to Lydia. Goodnight, princess."

Thursday morning, Andy walks out to the road to see if the mail has come early. Instead, he finds a complimentary copy of one of the D.C. papers, he use to subscribe to. As he walks back to the house, he opens it and to his surprise, he finds his picture on the front page. The headline says, "Twelve Evangelical Leaders Subpoenaed by House for Hearing on Hate Speech". The article begins by saying: "Former Secretary of State, Andy McGraig, and eleven other evangelical leaders must appear before a Congressional Hearing on Hate Speech, on January 4th. The evangelical leaders include six pastors from some of the largest churches in the country. The other evangelical leaders are nationally known evangelists who appear on radio and television."

When Andy walks in the house, he says, "Look at this," and lays the newspaper on the dining table. As Lydia and Judy walk over to look at the paper, Andy says, "There are terrorist groups, gangster and drug gangs, minority racist groups, and other criminal groups, where hate is only a by-product. Yet, socialist leaders in congress go after church leaders with false allegations of hate."

As Lydia picks up the newspaper, Judy says, "The Nazis operated the same way. They went after the Jews, then the Catholics, then the Protestants." After Lydia reads the article, she hands the paper to Judy and says, "It's so sad that the government can stoop so low to go after people, who help the country."

Andy says, "The socialists continue to stir up division. Their motto should be, "Divide and Conquer".

Lydia and Andy sit down to read, while Judy looks over Andy's music collection of vinyl and CDs.

After Andy reads another article in the same D.C. paper, he says, "Lydia and Judy, listen to this. I just finished an article called, "When Will the Bubble Burst?" This is the most shocking article I've read about the national debt and inflation. I will read just the highlights: "Most any U.S. citizen would agree that the national debt is out of control. It took 217 years, from 1791 to 2008 (n/a in 1789-90) for the national debt to grow to 11 trillion dollars. Under the last three administrations, the national debt has grown another 20 trillion dollars in just the last 13 years. It is now almost 31 trillion dollars. We know there must be ramifications, but what are they? First of all, we are currently paying over 430 billion dollars in interest annually. It is our fourth largest national expenditure; just behind defense expenditures. Inflation is the measure of the trouble we're in. A year ago, inflation grew 10%, which is one of the highest increases in national history. The past year inflation increased over 14%, which is a two year increase of 24%. At the gas pump and prices on many products in grocery stores, we are riveting from 100% increases on some products. Where it will stop; nobody knows."

Andy looks up at Judy and Lydia. Judy says, "It seems like another type of a sign of the end time."

Andy says, "It actually is a sign of the end. It's found in Revelation concerning the time of the Tribulation. It talks about the measure of wheat and barley for a day's wage. The passage reflects the extreme poverty of that time. As we know, the time before the Rapture and the Rapture is immediately before the Tribulation. After the great war, Germany experienced extreme inflation, when it would take a wheel barrel full of money to buy a loaf of bread."

Lydia says, "Wow, it makes my head reel. It's almost unbelievable, but it's happening."

Thursday is not an easy day for the McGraig household, as well as for millions of households across the country. The times are unsettling. Only those who put their trust in their Creator can find peace of mind. Even though the McGraigs go to bed with a restless feeling, they wake up Friday morning with joy in the Lord. During breakfast Andy says, "If we turn on the news, we'll hear bad news, but regardless of the news and circumstances, we know God is in charge."

Judy, "It almost makes you want to flip a coin; heads is to go outside or read and tails is to watch the news."

Lydia and Andy laugh. Lydia says, "So true."

Andy says, "It's hard to believe that Christmas Eve is in two days."

Lydia says, "I need to make final plans for Christmas Eve dinner and Christmas dinner."

Judy says, "I'll help. I need to take a shower now, and then I can help whenever you're ready."

Andy says, "While you're showering, I will add windshield washer fluid to both vehicles, then I'll get in the shower."

Lydia shouts out, "I'll be the third to shower and make it unanimous!"

After Andy showers, he goes to the computer and looks at the forecast through Christmas. He tells Lydia and Judy that today will continue to be sunny with a high of 58. He says,

"Tomorrow will be partly cloudy with a high of 52 and a low of 34.

Christmas Eve is forecasted to have a high of 46 and a low of 30. Christmas is to be cloudy with a high of 44 and a low of 28."

Judy starts singing, "I'm dreaming of a white Christmas..."

Andy says you might get a white Christmas. The chance of precipitation Christmas Eve is 55%."

Lydia says, "We're going to the store to get a few more things that I need for both dinners."

Andy say, "I'm going to walk in the woods to get some fresh air. I'll take my cell phone and .38 in case I run into a coyote or something bigger."

Judy says, "What will you do, if you run into a bear?"

Andy says, "Run!"

Right after they leave the house, Andy decides to catch up on the news, then take a walk. As he reaches for the remote, he thinks, "At least Lydia and Judy won't have to listen to more bad news." He wonders if the first news stories will be about the China War; the attacks on Israel; home terrorism; inflation; earthquakes; tsunamis; famine or plagues. The news reporter is just finishing a report about global famine. He is saying, "Famine in East Africa is growing like wild fire. The past two years about 18 million people died from famine. This year one of the largest world health organization said that over 45 million people could die from famine.

Because of the plagues, six times as many people are living in hunger and dying from famine. In addition to death by famine, the China virus killed almost four million people in its first two years. This year death by plagues are much higher."

A "Breaking News" flash appears at the bottom of the screen. The reporter says, "The past few hours we have been reporting the increase of seismic readings and earthquakes around the world; especially in the Ring of Fire. Seismologists are baffled by the enormity of the global readings and by the magnitude of the quakes. One seismologist said, "It makes me wonder, if the earth has become unglued." A Yellowstone National Park seismologist said, "In my lifetime, I have never experienced the expanse of so much earthquake activity. In Yellowstone we're getting higher readings than anything on record."

A seismologist with the EPA said, "The number of the readings and quakes in the nation and the world are off the charts. We're lucky that "the big one" has not hit. We're watching San Andreas, New Madrid and Yellowstone very closely. The senior professor of seismology at M.I.T. stated today, "Not only are major epicenter sites in the Ring of Fire reading much higher than normal, but some of the underrated fault lines in our country have readings at 5.5 to 6.7 magnitude. They include the Castle Mountain Fault near Anchorage. It has been predicted for years that the fault could produce up to a 7 magnitude. It's already quaking at a 6.5 magnitude.

The Cascado Fault Line that runs through Seattle, Portland and San Francisco is already reading a 5.9 magnitude. Its neighboring and potentially destructive Hayward Fault Line is at a 6.0 magnitude, and it runs into Berkley, Oakland and San Jose. The Ramapo Fault Line runs through New Jersey, New York and Pennsylvania. It is already at 5.5 magnitude.

We are extremely concerned about the New Madrid and San Andreas faults, which could cause intense destruction. One epicenter along New Madrid is already at 5.3 magnitude, and a San Andreas epicenter between San Francisco and San Diego is up to a 5.5 magnitude. This concludes our midday news report. I very soberly wish you a good day."

Andy thinks, "Wow, that was a mind-boggling report! I really need some fresh air now. The ladies should be back from the store before I finish my walk."

When Andy returns from the woods, the ladies are busy with the early preparations for Christmas Eve and Christmas. He is still so overwhelmed by the news report that he decides to share it with Lydia and Judy later today or tomorrow.

They spend a quiet evening at home, and they all decide to retire early.

Andy is the early riser, and before he starts devotions, he thinks about tomorrow being Christmas Eve already.

After breakfast, Andy puts a few more decorations on the Christmas tree and puts up a few more lights on their front porch. After a day's work of house cleaning and making sure everything is ready for Christmas Eve and Christmas, all three of the McGraigs sit down to make the difficult decision of which movie they're going to watch. Lydia says, "It should be a Christmas movie." Judy says, "I like a family and inspirational movie." Andy says, "I like some humor." So they all agree on the Christmas classic, "It's a Wonderful Life". Andy says, "We just happen to have it on a DVD!"

After the movie, Andy puts a cap on. Judy asks, "Why the cap?"

"I'm settling down for a long winter's nap," says Andy.

Before Andy fixes breakfast on Christmas Eve morning, there's enough morning light for Andy to watch a White Breasted Nuthatch and a Tufted Tit Mouse feeding on the suet hanging above their back deck.

After breakfast, Andy says to Lydia, "I'm going to call Davina. Do you want to talk with her?"

Lydia says, "Sure. Judy and I are going to walk in the woods in about an hour. Do you want to go with us?"

Andy says, "It sounds like a good thing."

Andy goes to his quick dial to reach Davina. When she answers, he says, "Merry Christmas Eve, sweet pea!"

Davina says, "Thank you, Dad. How are the three of you doing?"

Andy says, "We're doing well, and Judy is behaving."

Davina laughs and says, "I can hear her saying something in the background"

Andy replies, "I have to admit she acts up at times."

Davina says, "Did you hear about the drop in the Dow yesterday?"

Andy says, "No. Lately, we've been trying to avoid a lot of the news."

Davina says, "The Dow dropped 1,777 points, by far the biggest drop in the history of the Dow. I wrote this down for you: on October 29, 1929, the Dow Jones dropped 18%; on September 29, 2008, it dropped 777 points and the biggest drop until yesterday was 1,175 points on February 25, 2018."

Andy says, "More bad news, but I appreciate you telling me. Well, sweet pea, I'm looking forward to seeing you and your clan tomorrow. Your mother wants to talk with you."

Davina, "We're looking forward to being with you. Bye, Dad. I love you."

Andy says, "I love you."

Lydia takes the phone. Andy goes over to Judy and acts like he's going to box with her, but as he says, "What were you saying?", he tickles her side as he shadow boxes with her. He causes her to laugh uncontrollably.

Lydia tells Davina, "Now they're both acting up!"

After they finish their walk, Judy and Lydia gradually prepare for the Christmas Eve dinner while Andy reads, "Miracles" by C.S. Lewis. Ann arrives just a few minute before nightfall. Lydia says, "You brought a lot!"

Ann smiles and says, "Most of it are gifts for you, Andy and Judy."

After Andy gives the blessing and they start passing the food. Lydia comments, "Did you notice any birds today? I didn't see them flying or hear them singing, and we walked in the woods for almost an hour."

Ann says, "Come to think of it; I didn't see them or hear them either, and I was outside several times today."

After too much Christmas ham, turkey, dressing, sweet potatoes and green beans, Andy says, "I have to get up; I ate too much!" It has only been dark for thirty minutes, when Andy turns on the outside deck lights. He exclaims, "It's snowing!"

Lydia, Judy and Ann bounce out of their chairs (as quickly as seniors can) and rush over to look outside. Judy says, "This puts me in the mood for singing Christmas carols!"

Andy says, "You play the piano and we'll help you sing."

Judy takes a seat at the polished oak, studio piano. In good spirits, they sing several carols, including "Silent Night", "Joy to the World", and "Angels We Have Heard on High". When they finish singing, Lydia says "What a perfect Christmas Eve!"

Judy says, "When do you want to do our gift exchange?"

Lydia says, "How about after breakfast in the morning? We can open them by 8:00, since Ann has to leave by 9:30."

Ann says, "It will be more to look forward to, since we have had such a pleasant Christmas Eve."

They visit until bedtime. Andy says, "I guess we'll hit the hay. Before you know it, we'll all be back, but first we'll settle down for a long winter's nap."

Judy says, "All through the house, I don't even hear a mouse."

Ann and Lydia laugh and Ann says, "We'll be snug in our beds, while sugar-plums dance in our heads!"

Lydia finishes with: "And to all a good night."

As soon as the lights go out, the four, good friends fall into a sound sleep.

Christmas morning, Andy finishes devotions by 7:00. It only takes him a couple minutes to start the coffee. He guesses that everyone is still asleep. As he thinks about what he'll fix for Christmas breakfast, he walks into the great room to look outside.

It's a few minutes after 7:00 and it's just beginning to get light. All of a sudden, he thinks he notices the house shaking, and everything changes in a blink of the eye.

15

THE MEETING

The coffee maker ran its cycle; the aroma is tantalizing. The breakfast preparations haven't begun, and the beds aren't made. The presents are under the Christmas tree and unopened. Everything in the house appears to be normal, yet the house seems empty. There is no one calling out, "breakfast is ready" or "Merry Christmas!" There are virtually no sounds in the house. Now and then one could hear a creaking sound in the wood. The furnace still kicks on and off. There is no evidence that Andy, Lydia, Judy and Ann are in the house.

They didn't go out in the yard. There are no footprints in the snow. There is no one at Ann's house nor at Davina's house. At the moment it appears there will be no Christmas dinner and gift exchange this afternoon. Andy and Lydia have neighbors in their area, who are home on Christmas morning. Some are eating breakfast and others are opening presents. Many are home in nearby Cosby, and a good number of people are not. No one is home at the Rivera house; Gus, Gracie, Gladis and Tracy are gone.

Before noon, news gets out on the internet from Gatlinburg and on television from Knoxville that there are a lot of missing person reports. The news rooms across the country can't keep up with the volume of news flooding their computers. Those who turn to national news channels hear the same reports about people missing throughout the country as well as in other countries. They report car, plane and train accidents throughout the country. In every strange or unexplainable accident, the driver is missing.

By afternoon, the news channels on radio and television are reporting that leaders in every profession, including government, business and medicine, are missing. Some analysts are concerned about the large number of people missing from disaster relief organizations, including the Red Cross and Samaritan's Purse. By late afternoon, the news reports the escalation of problems throughout the world.

A national news anchor says, "Since early this morning, earthquake epicenter readings have increased. The epicenter between Malaysia and Australia is a magnitude 8.9. It has created a tsunami that threatens

165

Malaysia, Indonesia, the Philippines and Northern Australia. The San Andreas Fault has an epicenter reading of 9.0. Since 7:30 a.m. EST, the earthquakes between San Francisco and San Diego have already caused damage in the billions. They have hit populated cities, and thousands of casualties are being reported. An epicenter in the New Madrid fault line has produced earthquakes throughout Illinois, Indiana, Missouri, Kentucky and Tennessee. The reading is already 8.8, and it's still spawning more earthquakes. These are just a few of the earthquakes in our country and in other parts or the world. Many more are being reported.

We are overwhelmed with reports of catastrophes. The biggest news item is: "Where Are the Missing"? Statisticians from the east coast to the west coast are working on an approximate number of missing from our country. They are estimating it is roughly one-fifth of the U.S. population, which is an estimated 68 million people. The effect of the losses, including to the National Revenue, will be devastating. With the increase of high inflation and the extremely high national indebtedness, economists are predicting a bleak future."

The next day, a well-known newspaper journalist writes his story for a major Atlanta paper, and the article is picked up by the AP. Thomas Dowter writes, "I have been following worldwide news reports, since 7:30 a.m. yesterday morning. I have been up all night, and it is now 2:15 in the morning, the day after Christmas. I grew up in a Christian home in Cosby, Tennessee. My parents took me to church every Sunday morning. When I was a teen, my mom took me to youth fellowship every Sunday night. When I left for college, I started living the lifestyle I wanted to live. I became self-absorbed.

After college I took a job with a Knoxville newspaper company and left eventually for a job in Nashville. Twelve years ago, I came to Atlanta and started working for my current employer. Like many college professors, media people and others in our humanistic society, I questioned everything and stood for nothing.

Of course, I have hobbies; hiking is one of them. For the Christmas holiday, I went home to be with my aging parents. An old classmate friend and fellow hiker invited me to a special activity with Smoky Mountain Extreme. It's a nature group that has activities in the Smokies like winter hiking.

On Christmas morning, the park ranger allowed the group to meet at a scenic view of the Smoky Mountains. Their plan was to welcome the

Christmas sunrise and to take early morning pictures. Instead, I got the life scared out of me for several minutes.

Before sunrise, it began to get light a few minutes after 7 a.m. What happened was virtually unbelievable. The mountains began to shake and the earth was shaking below our feet. The mountains seemed to rise from their foundation. Everyone in the party was scared to death.

Several minutes after the unusual earthquake, sunrise began to set in. It was Christmas morning, but it felt like doomsday. Needless to say, no one wanted to stay. Everyone was gone by 7:30. I went straight to my parent's house. It was odd that they weren't home. The presents under the tree were unopened. I called their cell phone, but they didn't answer. I heard their phones ringing in the house. Their car was also at the house.

I called their closest friends first, but they didn't answer. Finally, I called the local hospital and the local police station. They simply said, "All I can tell you is that a lot of people are missing, and we are swamped with calls."

By late afternoon I heard that many evangelical leaders are missing, including nationally known ministers. On the late night news, some reporters were talking about the possibility of a mass abduction by aliens; Hogwash! Jewish leaders have been writing and talking about God's kingdom and the coming Messiah for thousands of years. For two thousand years, Christians have been writing and teaching about the Rapture, Tribulation and the Second Coming. As a child I knew about it, but as an adult, I had to look up the scriptures again.

Christ and the Apostle Paul taught about the rapture (1Thessalonians 4: 16-17). Christ (Matthew 24) and the Apostle John taught about the signs of the end; the Tribulation and the Second Coming. In Revelation 6:14, I found these words yesterday, "The sky receded like a scroll, rolling up, and every mountain and island was removed from its place." (NIV)

You may say, "It's too late", but I remember a preacher years ago talking about a second chance during the Tribulation. He said, "If you don't want to miss heaven, follow Christ daily and do not take the Mark of the Beast to buy and sell. Friend, we have a second chance. Now, it is going to take serious commitment to follow Christ. I could quote the Mark of the Beast scripture from the book of Revelation, but I will let you find your Bible; look up the scripture and give your life to Christ."

Andy, Lydia, Judy, Ann, Davina, Larry, Melissa, Aaron, Angela, Anderson and Ruth; Andy's parents, Owen and Davina, Kenny and the Rivera's with millions of others, who are part of the true church, the Bride of Christ, are in the splendor of heaven with their Lord Jesus Christ. They followed Christ daily, and they were concerned more about giving and their eternal soul, than the material things on earth. One of many Biblical prophecies has already come true in their eternal lives with Christ and each other: "Now the dwelling of God is with men, and He will live with them." (Romans 21: 3 NIV)

Meanwhile, things on earth don't look good. According to Bible prophecy, the Tribulation is now under way. The end time events that Jesus prophesied are in full gear: war, famines, pestilences (plagues) and earthquakes in many places. China has stepped up its invasion in Japan. North Korea invaded South Korea. The U.S. and Japan have heavily bombed military installations and large cities in China. Russia has scourged Northern China. Iran has caused many casualties in Israel, and Israel threatens using nuclear weapons, if necessary. The total casualties of war so far in Russia, China, Japan, North Korea, South Korea, Iran, Lebanon, Israel, Egypt, Saudi Arabia and among U.S. troops are 3.2 million.

In the past year, 29 million died from famine; 26 million have died from the original China virus and 2.6 million from the new Mortem China virus. Recent earthquakes, volcanic eruptions and tsunamis have caused 3.8 million deaths. In the past year, natural disasters have caused 6.5 million casualties. It is not likely that the countries of the world will overcome the trillions of dollars loss due to property damage. Theft, murder, arson and other crimes have become rampant throughout the world.

Ten days after Christmas, Andy was summoned to D.C. with eleven other evangelical leaders to appear before Congress about a hate speech hearing. At the designated time on Wednesday afternoon, January 4th, not one evangelical leader is present. One of the committee members announces, "It has been reported to this committee that all twelve subpoenaed witnesses are shown as "missing". The socialist members in charge of the hearing are present. Congress is left to investigate their own hate and corruption.

Many people's personal lives are in havoc from the loss of relatives and friends in every community. Bread winners are missing from many families. Fathers and mothers across the globe are missing. Many talented teachers are missing. Core individuals in the labor market are gone. Medical teams have a big gap in their ability to serve the public. There are many gaps in retail, wholesale, transportation and manufacturing. Many farmers are gone.

Just in the United States, millions of people have lost loved ones. Aaron

Michaels' wife drinks herself into a stupor. She still refuses to heed the gospel and what Aaron shared. Unfortunately, millions of people like her throughout the world are suicidal.

Even though the world is in chaos, it still has the Word of God. People everywhere, including those who go to church, have a second chance. They just need to read the book of Revelation; especially chapters thirteen through twenty-two. Five hundred years ago, Martin Luther tried to get the established church to change ninety-five corrupt practices (the 95 Theses). Instead, well over a hundred denominations through the next five centuries, developed their own varied doctrines; full of good works, but building walls instead of unity. The true church, the Bride of Christ, says, "Come". Andy, his family and friends, and millions of other saints say, "Come".

Christ reminds everyone, "Behold, I am coming, soon! Blessed is the one who keeps the words of the prophecy of this book." (Revelation 22: 7 ESV)

In the tranquil wilderness of the Great Smoky Mountains, listen closely and you can hear Andy and his eternal company singing at their meeting in the heavens:

"Angels we have heard on high
Sweetly singing o'er the plains
And the mountains in reply
Echoing their joyous strains."

"the mountains in reply"

About the Author

William Clark played piano professionally for thirty years and has been in the ministry over twenty-five years. The past six years he has had five books published and a story published in a national publication. His hometown is Muncie, Indiana. He went to undergraduate and graduate school at Ball State University. He and his wife live in Jefferson County, Tennesse, and his two sons live in Virginia and North Carolina.

Printed in the United States
by Baker & Taylor Publisher Services